KEY
WITNESS

KEY WITNESS

SANDRA BOLTON

THOMAS & MERCER

ALSO BY SANDRA BOLTON

A Cipher in the Sand

Published by Thomas & Mercer, Seattle

www.apub.com

Amazon, the Amazon logo, and Thomas & Mercer are trademarks of Amazon.com, Inc., or its affiliates.

ISBN-13: 9781477828519
ISBN-10: 1477828516

Cover design by Salamander Hill Design Inc.

Library of Congress Control Number: 2014955116

For my mother,

who taught me to love books and reading

A good traveler has no fixed plans,

and is not intent on arriving.

—Lao-tzu

PROLOGUE

Abe Freeman lay on his back, staring at water-spot patterns on the gray ceiling. He had been arrested and placed in the holding tank of the Huerfano Community Police Substation. The reek of piss and vomit permeated the cell he shared with three other inmates being held on drunk and disorderly charges. His head throbbed from fatigue and confusion brought on by hours of interrogation by the Navajo policewoman and New Mexico State cop. He tried without success to block the snores and grunts of the other prisoners.

According to the law enforcement officers, two young boys playing in an arroyo at Clayton Lake State Park had stumbled across the bloodstained body of Easy Jackson. His throat had been slit from ear to ear. Abe's newly purchased switchblade was discovered a few feet from the corpse.

Abe rolled on his side, facing the wall. How could he have been so stupid as to leave his knife behind? Before Sharon's death he had been a careful man. He covered his eyes with his forearm, not wanting to think, not wanting to live.

1

Six months earlier, when Abe Freeman placed the pillow over her face Sharon didn't resist—a brief struggle at the last moment, then nothing. He pressed down tightly to be sure, pulled the pillow away, closed her eyes, and called the attending physician. Abe sat by the body until the ambulance arrived. Cause of death: respiratory failure due to advanced stages of cancer. Emergency medical techs covered the body and wheeled it out. Alone, Abe shouted his rage to God and the world and beat his fists against the wall. Spent and exhausted, he slid to the floor and wept. Sharon's dog, Patch, crept from his hiding place to lay his head across Abe's lap.

After Sharon's death, during the brutal midwinter of 1986, nothing could keep Abe in New Jersey—not the music and not his family. They had washed their hands of him long ago. He picked up his last paycheck, hocked the piano, and spent the money on a used pickup shell and camping equipment at an army surplus store. At the last moment, he bought the knife. It folded into a neat bone handle but opened quickly into a sharp five-inch blade when he pressed a small lever. *Could be useful*, Abe had thought.

As soon as the funeral ended, he threw a mattress into the bed of his truck and loaded the dog, some food for both of them, and the rest of his gear. There wasn't much. His stash of marijuana fit nicely into the battery compartment of a flashlight. Abe pushed the apartment key under the door and scraped ice off the truck's windshield. After the fifth pump on the accelerator the old Toyota grumbled to a start. It crept through the morning rush and the slushy gray streets of Atlantic City until reaching the expressway, then gained speed. If anyone had asked where he was going, his answer might have been, "Pacific Ocean and whatever's between here and there." He only knew he had to get away.

Once on his journey, Abe stuck to back roads, driving long into the day. He passed the time trying to block the memory of Sharon's death, a vision that haunted every waking moment, by singing along with the radio to the popular songs of the '80s. When cash ran low he stopped in one of the small towns, looked for a campground, park, or some cheap motel, and any kind of temporary work. Occasionally he scored a gig playing the piano at a VFW hall or local dive, but mostly he did construction or field work for low wages. He never complained on one condition: his dog could stay with him. Abe spent two or three weeks in one place, then moved on.

The meandering route took him through the heartland. Winter changed to spring, then summer. Grimy cities gave way to farms—orchards and fields of corn and wheat—the land opening up to him like a voluptuous woman, undulating and inviting. The farther west Abe went, the more freedom he felt. He still thought of Sharon every night before drifting off to sleep. They had talked of marriage, a baby somewhere in the future. Sharon could quit singing in clubs and Abe would get a full-time job, a day job, maybe teaching music in one of the local schools. They would be a family. That all ended when cancer invaded and swept through her body like a raging storm, obliterating all their hopes and dreams of a future life together. *"If you love me, don't let me suffer any more, baby. I want you to let me go. Help me, please,"* she had begged.

4

"We're not going any farther tonight, boy," Abe said to the mixed-breed dog riding shotgun. For nine hours, thunderstorms, choreographed by capricious winds, had danced around them. Hail and rain chased the man and his dog through southern Kansas and the flat, cholla-studded plains of the Texas/Oklahoma Panhandle. When they finally crossed into Clayton, New Mexico, on a tempestuous August evening, both were dog-tired. The small cattle town claimed a nearby state park where he could set up camp for the night.

Patch cocked his head. He was missing half a hind leg and, with black markings covering the right side of his face, he appeared to be missing an eye as well. The little mutt made futile motions with the stump of his right hind leg at an itch he couldn't scratch, then gave up and settled back down on the seat. Abe scratched the dog behind the ears. "Show a little enthusiasm, Patch. We're in the 'Land of Enchantment,' a thousand miles of bad roads behind us."

After cruising the main street, Abe pulled the truck into a parking space in front of the Plato Grande Diner and stepped through the threshold into a dimly lit room that smelled spicy and well used. The diners turned their heads and watched him as he self-consciously pulled on the bill of his New York Yankees ball cap and ambled to a seat at a window booth. His Pink Floyd T-shirt, dirty sneakers, and shoulder-length hair held their attention for five seconds—then, their curiosity seemingly satisfied, the patrons went back to their meals and muffled talk of weather, cattle, and the price of hay.

Abe gazed out the window. From his vantage point he could see his truck and Patch, and in the background the tallest structure in town—a grain elevator, insular and commanding, hovering by the railroad tracks.

His reverie was interrupted by a woman with the same dimensions as his apartment-size refrigerator back in Jersey. She thrust a menu and a glass of water at him with one hand and held a coffeepot in the other. Short Brillo-Pad hair framed a raisin face. She had a dirty apron tied around her ample middle. "Coffee, hon?"

"That'd be great, and bring me the chicken enchilada plate."

"It'll be right up." The woman did a little more scratching on her pad, tore off a page, and slapped it on the table, then stared straight into his face. "You know, you got the purtiest blue eyes. They remind me exactly of Jesus's," she said, turning her own pale peepers toward a large velvet painting of a crucified Jesus with eyes the color of cornflowers.

Jesus Christ, he thought, wondering what the waitress would say if she knew she was talking to a Jewish guy from New Jersey. Better yet, wouldn't his mother flip out to hear him described in such a way? It gave him a little pleasure to think so. Just the same, Abe felt out of place—a city slicker, a Jew amid all that chambray, denim, and leather. He glanced out the window and saw Patch looking mournfully back. The dog was hungry. He'd hurry and get to the campground.

While he absently stared through the dirty glass, he became dimly aware of a black sedan with tinted windows and Kansas plates. Two men stepped out and entered the restaurant. Shortly after their arrival, a motorcycle roared down the main street, made a U-turn, and rolled into an empty parking spot. A couple clad in matching black leather jackets and leggings pulled off their helmets and walked into the diner.

Abe forgot the newcomers when the waitress placed a plate the size of a hubcap, filled with something swimming in a sea of red and green, in front of him. He couldn't identify anything, but it smelled delicious. Abe dug in, savoring the rich chili-and-cheese combo. He cleaned his plate, wiping up the last of the sauce with a tortilla, and looked at the bill, surprised at how cheap it was. Watching his cash, Abe rarely ate out. He left a tip on the table, then stood in line behind a couple of cowboys at the register.

"Howdy." One of the men, tall and angular with prominent cheekbones and deep creases around his eyes, touched his hat in greeting.

"How ya doing?"

"That yer truck with the dog, Jersey plates?" the cowboy asked, rubbing his chin. "If it is, yer a helluva long ways from home."

"Yeah, that's me, my dog. I'm looking for the campground. Gonna spend the night and head on out in the morning." They both moved up to the next spot in line. "Do you know the easiest way to get to the state park?"

"Couldn't be easier. Only one way. Follow 64 till you hit 370. Take that road twelve miles north."

"Thanks. Think we'll get more rain?"

The cowboy laughed. "Hell, yes. It's monsoon season, sonny."

Finding Clayton Lake State Park proved as easy as the cowboy said. The near-empty park offered an isolated space with a covered table near the lake. The sky had partially cleared, exposing a three-quarter moon that illuminated a trail near their site. Abe followed it with Patch for a while as it hugged the lake, but feeling the tiredness in his body, he turned around as soon as it came close to another campsite. "Nearly bedtime, Patch."

Abe gathered some dry branches and made a campfire. Sitting alone, warmed by the fire's heat, he felt like smoking a bud. He fetched the flashlight with his stash and rolled a joint. He had been careful, saving his dwindling bag for special times and isolated areas like this, rationing it out, thinking he might have to give it up someday. After two hits he felt a pleasant buzz. Wanting some music, Abe pulled the harmonica out of his pack, sat on a boulder, and played an improvised blues tune.

He began to relax, when Patch let out a low growl, then a sharp series of barks. Abe snuffed the reefer right before a lone figure appeared on the path.

"Quiet, Patch."

"Hey, dude. I heard the music. D'ya mind if I hang out? Good to have someone to talk to." Without waiting for an answer he sat down on a log near the fire, rubbed his hands over the blaze, and sniffed the air. "Smells like some good skunk, man. I ain't been smoking nothing but ditch weed for so long I forget what real wacky terbacky tastes like."

The guy looked to be Abe's height, but skinny, with a four-days' growth of beard on a pinched, narrow face. He wore dirty cutoffs and boots. A backward ball cap partially covered stringy, light-brown hair. Abe noticed a tattoo encircling the right arm near the elbow, hard to make out in the dim light. The intruder appeared jumpy and kept looking over his shoulder as if he expected some-one, his eyes shifting from left to right.

"Name's Joe, Joe Jackson, but everyone calls me Easy."

"Well, Easy, I'm getting ready to turn in. Got a long day tomor-row," Abe said, without giving his name.

"Yeah, sure, I dig it," said Jackson, not showing any inclination to leave. "Look, man. I caught a whiff of your giggle weed when I came up the path. Don't let me stop you none, but I wouldn't mind getting a hit myself." He paused to scratch his chin. "Or you could sell me a nickel's worth," he added on a hopeful note. "I only got a few bucks now, but it won't be long till I hit the big time. You might say I got ahold of my 'key to my happiness.'" He chortled, spewing the stench of cheap whiskey and stale cigarettes.

"I don't sell, and I don't have much left." But he thought, *What the hell*. He was starting to feel good when this guy showed up. He reached behind the boulder until he found what he was looking for. "Guess I can afford a couple hits. Name's Abe. Hope you're not working for the law."

"Are you shitting me? I stay as far away from those assholes as I can."

When he finished relighting the joint, Abe took a toke, filled his lungs, and passed it to Jackson.

Joe Jackson inhaled deeply, closed his eyes, and held it as long as he could before exhaling two dragon puffs through his nostrils. "Hail Mary Jane. This is some kind weed you're smokin', dude." He pulled a half pint of Jim Beam from a back pocket, took a swig, and offered Abe a drink.

"No thanks, I'm strictly a beer man."

While they finished the joint the two men made small talk, touching on where they were headed and where they had been. Abe never felt at ease around people, but the weed soothed his nerves. He stood, stretched, and stirred the fire. The night air had chilled, and since they were upwind of the feedlots, the air smelled fresh, scented with unfamiliar plant life. Lake water glimmered in the moonshine, smooth as a satin sheet, broken only by an occasional fish splash. Patch hop-walked over to Abe, tail wagging, and received a pat on the head and a scratch on the belly, then curled into a hairy ball near Abe's feet.

"Now where in sweet Jesus did you get that ugly three-legged dog?" Jackson looked at Patch as if the dog had leprosy, slurring his words from the effects of the whiskey and marijuana.

"My girlfriend found him." Sharon had spotted the pup lying on the side of the street, his mangled leg attached by a single tendon. "We were coming home from a late gig when she saw him. Made me stop the car while she got out and wrapped her jacket around his bloody body. He looked dead, but she said no. We took him home, then the next morning to a vet. Sharon treated him like a baby, nursed him back to health, and now he gets around as good as any four-legged dog."

"So, where's the girlfriend? Guess you ended up with the dog and the girlfriend split. Women." He grinned.

Abe didn't respond. He'd had enough of Joe Jackson and wished the guy would leave. He took his knife out, picked up a piece of firewood, and started whittling. After a few minutes, he turned to Jackson. "Look, I'm ready to crash. It's been a long day, and like I mentioned, I have an early wake up tomorrow."

"Yeah, yeah, okay. But listen, man, since we're both headed in the same direction how 'bout a lift. I ain't got no wheels and I need to get to Bisbee, Arizona. Got a buddy out there with a place we can stay as long as you like. I'll kick in for gas. What d'ya say?"

"I don't know," Abe hemmed. He knew for sure he didn't want this guy traveling with him. Abe was a loner. "No offense, but I'm not going to Bisbee, and I like to travel alone. I don't know where I might stop along the way or for how long. I'd help you out, but . . ."

"Well, let me catch a ride with you as far as you're going tomorrow, okay. You won't even know I'm there. I'll sleep the whole way," Jackson persisted. He craned his neck, looking nervously back along the trail. "I oughta get goin'. I'll come by early."

From the glow of the fire Abe caught the outline of Jackson's tattoo—a large spiderweb covering the right elbow. He noticed the guy nearly jumped out of his skin with every night sound. Abe didn't try to stifle his yawn. "I'm hitting the sack now. See ya."

"Okay, man. Catch ya later, tomorrow morning." Before he stood to leave, Jackson tilted his head back and took a long drink of whiskey, toppled backward off the log, and banged his head on a boulder. "Son of a bitch." He rubbed his bump and stumbled to his feet. Still clutching the bottle, Easy Jackson staggered away and disappeared down the path toward the main campground.

"We'll be gone before that guy wakes up, Patch." The buzz had worn off, leaving him sleepy and feeling the full extent of the long day. He left his knife laying on the boulder where he sat, pulled his bedroll from the camper, and spread it out near the fire under the New Mexico sky. The sandstone bluffs surrounding Clayton Lake loomed darkly in the moonlight like ominous ghosts of past dinosaurs who had left their tracks embedded in the rocks around the lake millions of years ago. Lying awake, Abe brooded over those dinosaurs and their untimely demise, and other things lost forever. He drifted off to sleep thinking of Sharon and how much he wished she could see these stars. He hadn't slept long, when he was awakened by the din of a revved-up motorcycle.

2

Abe got up at four thirty the next morning, too early even for birds. The gibbous moon had dropped below the horizon, dragging the stars with it. Only Venus remained visible, a bright beacon in the west reflecting the sun's promise of dawn. He tripped over last night's pile of wood, cursing under his breath as he attempted to load his gear into the truck without making noise. Working in darkness, Abe's hand brushed against a small cloth sack on the ground by the log where Easy Jackson had sat the night before. Abe dropped it into his backpack and immediately forgot it. He hurried to his truck, barely able to see, hoping he had not left anything important behind.

Patch wanted a walk, but Abe quickly ushered the dog into the cab with a curt, "Not now, get in the truck." He would stop and give him food and water when they were safely down the road, far from any chance of running into Easy Jackson.

The truck crept over muddy potholes as it made its way through the silent campground. There appeared to be more vehicles than the night before, latecomers still bedded in their tents and pop-up campers, curled in their sleeping bags. In the dim predawn light he thought he saw a Harley parked near a picnic table, but couldn't discern the riders.

Abe didn't turn on his headlights until he reached the road to Clayton. From there, he followed Highway 64 where it intersected with I-25. The morning light revealed vast rolling plains dotted with black-faced cattle and small herds of grazing antelope. He looked for a radio station and found that with his crummy radio and broken antenna he had a choice of two, country or Spanish. He settled on Spanish, humming along with the ranchero music.

After several miles Abe saw a rest stop and pulled over. While Patch ate he retrieved his map from the glove compartment and decided where to go. He once read about Chaco Canyon, an ancient Native American cultural center located in a remote part of northwestern New Mexico. The seclusion of the site appealed to him, and the visitors' center had a campground where he could stay while he explored the area. He figured he could buy some breakfast and groceries in a town called Cuba and arrive at Chaco before lunch.

Back on the interstate, Abe drove past signs designating various Native American tribes: Cochiti, Santo Domingo, San Felipe. He hadn't been driving long when I-25 veered south toward a range of steep, craggy mountains and the city of Albuquerque. Abe turned northwest, away from Albuquerque onto Highway 44 and what he hoped would be a relatively short drive to Chaco Canyon.

He entered a flat, treeless land, a high desert plateau crisscrossed with low mesas and many-branched washes. Odd-shaped rocks of clay and sandstone in hues of pink, yellow, purple, black, and white seemed to spring up from the earth like mushrooms or flat tables balancing precariously on slender pedestals. Sparse growths of stunted juniper and silvery windswept sage dotted the landscape. He saw little sign of life, but soon realized he was in Navajo country when he spotted a few six-sided clay structures, or hogans, with their nearby sheep corrals. Abe felt an immediate camaraderie with these people. They needed their space and privacy, exactly as he did.

The sky, which had been an unruffled sea of blue in the morning, suddenly filled with ominous black clouds. "Damn monsoons, or whatever." Patch looked at him, one ear cocked, and let out a soft whine.

"We're almost there, boy. You can wait a while longer." But the farther west he drove, the more intense the storm became. A loud clap of thunder, followed by a flash of light, caused him to hunker down in his seat and grip the steering wheel. The next thing he knew, a massive thunderstorm with blinding rain pummeled the truck. Thunder crashed from all directions. Abe put the wipers on full speed but still couldn't see six feet in front of him. He had slowed to a crawl and turned on his lights, trying to follow the white line, when he heard the blast of a horn. Abe pulled sharply to the right and felt the truck slip off the road as he caught a quick glimpse of an oil tanker speeding by. He avoided a collision, but landed in a roadside ditch full of rainwater and slippery muck.

The storm passed as quickly as it appeared, leaving in its wake the cleansing, pungent smell of crushed sage and rain-drenched earth. He had been trying for over an hour to extricate the truck only to get the wheels buried more deeply. A few vehicles passed, more speeding tankers and some pickup trucks, but no one stopped. Abe threw the shovel aside and kicked a back tire. "Shit."

While he leaned against his truck and seethed, feeling dirty, sweaty, and disconsolate, a Chevy Blazer with the green-and-yellow insignia of the Navajo Nation Police drove by, made a U-turn, and stopped behind him. A woman dressed in a brown uniform with the same insignia patch on her shirt stepped out of the vehicle and approached him.

"Having a little problem?" She simultaneously looked him over and checked his license plate. "You're a long ways from home. Lost?"

"No, stuck. Oil tanker ran me off the road in the rainstorm." The brown uniform looked good on her petite body. Black hair pulled back and twisted into a tight bun accentuated a serious expression that contrasted with the laughter glinting from dark eyes. *She's enjoying my predicament*, Abe fumed silently. "Can you call someone to pull me out of here?"

"Don't know. You may not be in my jurisdiction." She shrugged her shoulders and gave him a noncommittal look.

"What do you mean, not in your jurisdiction?" He felt the heat rising in his face and gritted his teeth. "All I'm asking you to do is call for help."

"You're in the checkerboard area of New Mexico, Mr. New Jersey. Could be federal land, Bureau of Land Management, San Juan County, or Navajo. It's hard to tell. Boundaries get confusing sometimes and I don't want to step on anybody's toes."

Abe knew she was having a little fun with him, which didn't help his disposition. He bit his tongue and held back an expletive. "Look, I don't care if it's checkerboard, chess, or tiddledywinks. I need help to get my truck out, and I'll be on my way."

The officer raised her eyebrows in a show of consternation. "Ah, you *bilagáanas* are so impatient." She almost smiled, and reached down to pet Patch, who cocked his head as if listening attentively to the conversation. "I guess the Feds won't mind if I assist a poor tourist stuck out in Navajo country. You never know what some of these wild redskins might do." After walking around the truck and checking things out, she said, "We're not going to need a tow truck. Get in the driver's seat and wait until I tell you what to do. Don't try getting out on your own; you'll dig yourself a deeper hole."

Abe watched her walk back to her four-wheeled patrol vehicle as he opened the door and whistled for Patch. The way she carried herself—straight backed and regal—made her look taller than her five foot four. She looked pretty good from the back, too, he thought before getting behind the wheel of his Toyota.

He continued watching her as she sat in her vehicle talking quietly on the police radio. Abe overheard "Code eight," and she seemed to be giving directions, but he couldn't catch much more of the conversation. The young female cop studied him for a few minutes before putting the radio away and starting up her four-wheel-drive SUV. A few feet in front of his truck she stopped, stepped out, and took a chain from the back, then looped one end around the tow bar of the Chevy Blazer and hooked it on the first link of chain it could reach. Then she repeated this procedure with the other end of the chain, securing it to the hitch on the front end of Abe's truck. He watched, feeling both embarrassed and relieved as she climbed back in her vehicle and pulled forward until the chain became taut, then got out and checked the hook on both ends.

"Now put your car in neutral and be ready on the brakes."

"I know, I know. I've done this before."

"You could have fooled me," the officer shot back before starting her vehicle.

In less than two minutes, Abe's Toyota sat on firm ground. Not wanting to look as inept as he felt, he jumped out of the cab and unhooked the chain. When she came around, he handed it to her. "Thanks a lot. Sorry to have been a bother. I really appreciate your help." He gave her his best beguiling smile.

She took the tow chain from him and stowed it in the back of her SUV. But no smile crossed her lips when she returned and approached Abe. She leveled her eyes at his. "I need to see some ID—your driver's license, registration, and insurance."

"Sure. All right. What is this about? I'm not in trouble, am I? An oil truck ran me off the road," he said while reaching in his back pocket for his wallet.

16

"Standard procedure when we offer assistance," she replied while taking his license. "Now return to your truck and let me have your registration, okay."

"Okay, okay. No problem." He put up his hands in a gesture of either compliance or surrender. "You're not going to give me a ticket, are you?"

She followed him to the truck and waited while he dug through the glove compartment. Patch jumped from the driver's seat to the passenger side, looking as if he, too, were impatient to get back on the road. With a terse "Sit tight," the officer took his documents and returned to the patrol car.

"As if I could go anywhere." Abe drummed his fingers on the steering wheel, stewing over his marijuana stash in the flashlight that he had taken out of the glove compartment while searching for his papers.

Abe checked his watch and tried to control the spasmodic twitching in his left leg. He had been waiting over fifteen minutes, sweat running down his shirt back, nerves on edge, ready to get out of the truck, even though she'd told him to sit tight, when he saw flashing red-and-blue lights approaching from the west. A San Juan County Sheriff's vehicle crossed the highway with a few quick blasts of the siren and stopped in front of his truck, blocking any thought of exit. Two burly men in olive-green khaki uniforms, star patches on their shoulders and a metal one on each of their shirts, approached him.

"Is this your vehicle, sir?" a brown-skinned deputy with a pock-marked face asked.

"Yeah." Abe noticed that the Navajo policewoman had joined the two lawmen. Her hand hung loosely over her holster. "What the hell's going on?"

"And is your name Abraham Freeman?"

"Yes, it is. Why?"

The other deputy, pale skinned with a shaved head, the beginning of a beer belly stretching the buttons of his shirt, spoke up for the first time. "Get out of the vehicle, Mr. Freeman."

"Wait a minute. What did I do?" He stepped out of his truck while competing emotions, anger and confusion, surged through his mind. *Why would I be of any interest to the cops?* Twenty years ago, as a fourteen-year-old, he had been picked up for a drug violation. It was nothing, kids experimenting with pot. Something that insignificant surely wouldn't interest the law after all this time. "Are you arresting me?"

"I need to ask you a few questions, sir," the Latin-looking man said. "Are you willing to come in voluntarily for questioning?"

He considered his options. *Questioning for what? Why should I? What if I said no?* "No. I haven't done anything wrong."

"Then we'll have to take you into custody," the deputy said. "Put your hands on the hood and spread 'em."

"You can't do this. What am I being arrested for?"

"We could start with resisting arrest," said the pink-faced deputy. "We're taking you in for questioning in a murder case, Freeman."

Abe's mouth felt full of cotton; his head swarmed with bees. *Could this be about Sharon? Have they somehow found out about me?* He put both palms on the Toyota hood and tried to quell his shaking and remain calm. The deputy patted down his upper body, then both legs. "I can't leave my dog here," Abe protested. "And my truck. What about my truck?" Patch growled at the Hispanic officer who attempted to approach the truck.

"Your truck will be impounded," the bald deputy said. "You can pick it up later, if you're lucky. Dogs, they're always a problem." He looked at Patch as if he'd just as soon put a bullet in him. "I could take care of him for you."

That's when the Navajo officer spoke up for the first time. "I'll take the dog with me." She pulled out a pair of handcuffs and positioned herself behind Abe. "Hands behind your back, sir; keep your feet spread wide." She secured the cuffs around his wrists, then asked with a nonchalance, "What's the dog's name?"

"Patch. His name is Patch. Is he being arrested, too? When this is all cleared up, I want my dog back safe and sound. And my truck." Though biting his lip to hold back the words he wanted to say, Abe still couldn't resist speaking out. "You're going to owe me an apology."

The two deputies exchanged glances and snickered. "Yeah, sure. We always apologize to the perps. He's all yours, Officer Etcitty, and take the dog, too," the Hispanic deputy said. "We sure as hell don't want him, and everybody knows you have this soft spot for animals of all kinds."

She nailed him with a steely glare, but kept her lips tight.

"What would you do if we weren't around to save your ass, Etcitty?"

"You're in my jurisdiction, Valdez," said the Navajo officer, maintaining a poker face. "I can handle it now. I'll take Mr. Free-man to Huerfano. Thanks for the backup." She dismissed them without further comment, then knelt down and whistled. When Patch came over, tail wagging, she picked him up and carried him to the front seat of the SUV. Abe ducked his head and crawled into the backseat, then turned to give one last look at his truck. For the next hour he glowered through the bars of the cage, staring at the back of Officer Etcitty's head and his dog, Patch, riding shotgun beside her.

He thought they must have driven fifty miles when they passed a steeply walled semicircular mountain jutting out of the flatlands of the high plateau. It stood alone, glowing golden orange in the afternoon sun. Less than a mile farther they reached a small, isolated complex of buildings. A large sign posted in front of a sprawling blue-and-white structure identified it as the Huerfano Chapter House and Community School. Officer Etcitty drove past the school and turned into the driveway of a cement-block building covered with faux adobe. The Huerfano Community Police Sub-station, Navajo Nation parking lot overflowed with both Navajo Police vehicles and the green-and-whites of the San Juan Sheriff's Department.

"We share space with the county for now," the officer explained. "This is a big area to patrol and the jurisdiction lines keep changing."

Abe didn't care about any of that. The day that had started off like a dream had turned into a nightmare. "Look, I have a right to know. Are you charging me with a crime of some kind? Am I under arrest? What the hell is going on?"

Officer Etcitty unlocked the back door of the Chevy Blazer and led Abe to a side entrance in the building. Patch followed docilely behind. "You haven't been charged, sir. You are a person of interest. We are holding you for questioning in an ongoing investigation. The State Police will be arriving shortly to conduct the interview."

She steered him to the end of a hallway into a small, window-less room. The institutional-green walls illuminated by overhead florescent lights cast a dreary pall on everything and everyone. The Navajo officer removed the handcuffs and told him to take a seat, indicating a metal chair bolted to the floor. A long table separated him from two chairs placed on the other side. He looked at the one-way mirror and wondered who was on the other side looking in, and wished he had never come to this godforsaken part of the country. The lady cop told him to wait, then left him alone, without even his dog around to provide a little comfort.

3

Abe sat, elbows on the table, head propped in his hands, and tried to figure things out. *Have they linked me to Sharon's death? Do they think I murdered her?* He shuddered, ran a hand through his unruly hair and a tongue over dry lips. His head felt like a train wreck and his mouth a dusty well. Random thoughts flashed through his mind. *Where is Patch?* He checked his pocket for his keys and remembered he had left them in the truck, along with the stash of dope. *What is the penalty for possession of marijuana in New Mexico? How did they find out about Sharon?* He tried to swallow, found nothing there. Sitting and waiting made him even more edgy, so he stood and paced, decided to try the door and ask for water, discovered it locked, and sat down again. He could not stop drumming his fingers on the table or tapping his foot on the hard tile floor. Abe knew he was in big trouble.

A long moment passed before the door opened and the woman who'd pulled him out of the ditch reappeared. Following closely behind her strutted another lawman—black uniform, all spit and polish.

"Sit down, Mr. Freeman. This is Officer James Harrigan with the New Mexico State Police," said the female cop. "He'd like to ask

3

Abe sat, elbows on the table, head propped in his hands, and tried to figure things out. *Have they linked me to Sharon's death? Do they think I murdered her?* He shuddered, ran a hand through his unruly hair and a tongue over dry lips. His head felt like a train wreck and his mouth a dusty well. Random thoughts flashed through his mind. *Where is Patch?* He checked his pocket for his keys and remembered he had left them in the truck, along with the stash of dope. *What is the penalty for possession of marijuana in New Mexico? How did they find out about Sharon?* He tried to swallow, found nothing there. Sitting and waiting made him even more edgy, so he stood and paced, decided to try the door and ask for water, discovered it locked, and sat down again. He could not stop drumming his fingers on the table or tapping his foot on the hard tile floor. Abe knew he was in big trouble.

A long moment passed before the door opened and the woman who'd pulled him out of the ditch reappeared. Following closely behind her strutted another lawman—black uniform, all spit and polish.

"Sit down, Mr. Freeman. This is Officer James Harrigan with the New Mexico State Police," said the female cop. "He'd like to ask you a few questions." She handed him a Sprite, which he couldn't help feeling grateful for.

Abe returned to his straight-backed chair and took a long drink while the two law officers seated themselves in relative comfort across the table. He gave the Navajo cop a furtive glance and, in his nervousness, began unconsciously rapping his fingers.

Etcitty carried a tape recorder, which she placed on the table between them; a camera beamed down from a corner near the ceiling. "Do you have any objections to this interview being recorded?"

Abe forced his hands to be still. He had better keep his cool, get this cleared up, and get out of here. "No, I don't mind."

The state cop didn't look any older than Abe, probably in his early thirties. Most likely, he barely met the minimum requirement in height, but he packed the black uniform with muscle and a military-like demeanor. He didn't smile when he looked at Abe with flinty eyes and flipped on the recorder. "August nineteen, 1987, two fifteen p.m. I'm Officer James Harrigan with New Mexico State Police and this is Officer Emily Etcitty, Navajo Tribal Police. State your name for the record, sir."

"Abraham Freeman."

"Mr. Freeman, we are conducting a criminal investigation. You have the right to remain silent. Anything you say can and will be used against you in a court of law . . . Do you understand?"

"Yes." Abe nodded. He answered their questions truthfully and caught the raised eyebrows of the officers when he couldn't provide a permanent home address or destination. The state cop continued drilling him while the Navajo sat back looking relaxed.

"I'm going west, stopping along the way to see the country. Yes, that 1982 Toyota truck is my vehicle. Yes, I spent the night of August eighteen at Clayton Lake State Park. Yes, I'm traveling alone, except for my dog." This made him stop. He looked down at his muddy clothes and shoes, frustrated by the day's events. "Where is my dog?"

The lady cop gave him a conciliatory look. "Your dog is fine. He has food and water and he's outside in a large pen in back of the building. Lots of shade. Patch, right?" She picked up the empty can. "You want another Sprite, Mr. Freeman?"

He saw how it worked—good cop, bad cop, and him in the middle. *Let them play their little game*, he thought. *I haven't done anything.* But he felt a cold sweat and, despite the drink he had downed, his mouth remained desert dry. "Yeah, thanks." Abe sat up straight and expelled a gust of air. He wanted to keep it together.

The questioning continued, trying to establish his time of arrival at the campground, his departure time, and who, if anyone, he'd talked to. "I don't know for sure what time I got there—seven thirty or eight. The sun had set . . . Easy Jackson? Yeah, this guy walked into my campsite. I'm pretty sure he said his name was Joe Jackson, but to call him Easy . . . He wanted a ride to Arizona, but I like to travel alone, so I left early the next morning, the radio said four thirty to be exact, before Jackson had a chance to come around."

Officer Harrigan leaned over the table, his face close enough for Abe to catch a whiff of peppermint breath mints. "Easy Jackson is dead. Murdered—his throat slit from ear to ear. You wouldn't know anything regarding that, would you Mr. Freeman?"

"Murdered?" He felt the blood drain from his face and a knot form in the pit of his stomach. Abe swallowed hard. "Look, you don't think I . . . He was alive the last time I saw him."

"What time was that, Mr. Freeman?"

"I . . . I don't know. I don't have a watch. It must have been close to ten. We talked awhile, I told him I had to get some sleep, and he left."

Harrigan pierced him with his icy stare. "Do you own a knife, Mr. Freeman?"

"Yeah. I bought one before I left New Jersey." His mind raced. *My knife—where is it?* Then he remembered the last time he'd used it, whittling that night in the park to pass time before he went to bed. He must have left it on the boulder.

"Some campers discovered Jackson's body at Clayton Lake State Park the morning you say you left. He had been stabbed with a five-inch switchblade and his throat slit," the cop answered. "What kind of knife do you own, Freeman?"

Abe felt a sick feeling wash over him. "I own a switchblade, but I lost it. I mean I forgot it when I packed to leave the park." *So this is what it's about.* "I didn't have anything to do with a murder. Easy Jackson was alive when he left my campsite."

The pro-bono lawyer assigned to Abe arrived from Farmington the next morning. Frank Stockett had the ruddy face and slow speech of a man who drank for a living. Frank had squeezed his corpulent body into a shabby suit resplendent with polyester shine that matched the dome of his head. He took off his jacket, displaying a rumpled shirt that carried clues to last night's dinner on the front panel. He wore scuffed loafers, run down at the heels, but Abe greeted him like a returning hero. Yesterday the cops had fingerprinted him, and he'd spent last night in a cell with drunks and petty criminals, held as a possible suspect in an ongoing investigation, and Stockett would get him out. He hoped.

"They can't hold you without charging you and they don't have enough evidence. But, you need to stick around for a while. No traveling until you're cleared. Let me hear your story now."

Abe told Stockett everything he remembered about his meeting with Easy Jackson and the exact time of his departure from the park the following morning. "I didn't kill him."

"I don't think you did it either, son. I've been doing my homework. A park ranger swore he saw you leave around four thirty yesterday morning, which verifies your story. And witnesses say they saw Jackson walking toward your campsite at six a.m. Coroner hasn't determined time of death yet, but I'm willing to bet it was sometime after you were a ways down the road. Besides, they dusted that knife for prints, and someone else left their calling card on top of yours, though they're smudged and it's hard to get a good read. So get your dog, and get your ass out of here."

A tsunami of relief washed over Abe. He gulped, then grinned and shook the lawyer's hand. "Thank you, Mr. Stockett. I don't know how I can repay you."

"The county will take care of that. Just remember, don't go far. The Staters aren't ready to cut you loose completely. They still think you might have been involved somehow. I've worked out a deal with Officer Etcitty—she knows a place nearby where you can stay awhile. Talk to her."

He found Etcitty when he went to the desk to sign for his personal property. He still wasn't happy about having been held overnight in jail, but was mollified by the fact he had been released. It could have been much worse considering it was his knife that had killed Jackson. The lady cop flashed him a smile like nothing had happened and passed him a form.

He read over the inventory, relieved he didn't see any mention of a flashlight or a cache of marijuana on the list.

"Your clothes, keys, wallet, everything you had on you is here," Etcitty said, handing him a sealed plastic envelope. "Restroom is down the hall. You can freshen up there if you want and I'll meet you in a few minutes by the gate in front of the compound."

Abe took his package and headed for the men's room, but stole a quick glance over his shoulder before he went in. She had been following him with her eyes, but ducked her head when he caught her in the act.

"Don't even think about taking off, Mr. Freeman. You're still a material witness."

4

Patch, followed by Emily, bounded up to him from behind the building, looking like he had spent a far better night than his owner. The little mutt ran in circles on his three legs and periodically jumped in the air while attempting to lick Abe's face. "Come here, boy. Am I glad to see you." Abe picked up the little dog and ruffled his fur. Looking around, he noticed his Toyota inside the open compound and carried Patch to where it waited, relieved again to spot the flashlight on the seat where he had left it. He quickly returned it, along with the envelope, to the glove compartment and opened the door for Patch. When the dog jumped into his usual place beside him, Abe turned the key in the ignition. The old truck groaned, shook, and finally started on the third attempt. He drove out of the fenced enclosure into the parking lot where Officer Etcitty waited in her Blazer, and pulled alongside her.

The Navajo cop rolled down the window. "My brother, Will, has this trailer, an old Airstream, on the other side of the mountain. It's a long ways out, real isolated. Sometimes Will or our grandfather stay there to graze the sheep. It's a good place for you to hang out a few days. Follow me."

He glanced at the box containing canned beans, coffee, and bread on the seat beside her. "Why are you doing this?"

"Why not? At least I'll know where I can find you." She spoke softly with little inflection in her voice, then rewarded him with a smile that transformed her serious-looking face into a momentary burst of sunshine.

"Sometimes, when I need to get away, I go there myself. It's not fancy, no electricity, no MTV, no Oprah, but it doesn't leak, it's peaceful, and there's a spring nearby."

The peaceful part agreed with him, and if he had to stay someplace it might as well be out in the boonies, away from everyone.

"Okay. Lead the way, officer." Before he rolled up the window, he added, "And thanks for taking care of my dog. I appreciate it."

"My name is Emily Etcitty," she said. "You can skip the officer part when we are away from headquarters."

She took him onto Highway 44, backtracked awhile, then cut to a dirt road on the north side, following it as it twisted around the bottom of the majestic mountain he had seen the day before. A milieu of puffy gray clouds fringed the horizon to the southwest, but for the most part, sky as blue as a jaybird's wings stretched from end to end.

The Toyota lurched over washes, ruts, and potholes that could swallow a less determined vehicle. Abe swerved to avoid the largest of these, cussing as he bounced along, trying to keep up with the four-wheeler in front. He was concentrating on the narrow road as it traversed an arroyo bottom when the brake lights of the Blazer flashed and it came to a sudden stop. Abe slammed on his brakes and looked around—nothing but desert scrub, sand, and the steep, rocky wall of the mountain.

Officer Etcitty got out of her vehicle and walked toward him.

Abe rolled down the window. "Why'd we stop?"

"Coyote crossed my path."

"So what? A coyote crossed your path. What's that supposed to mean?"

"It means we have to turn back. If we keep on this road, something's going to happen. That coyote came from the north." She gave him a serious look. "It's a bad sign."

Abe shook his head in disbelief. He had been eating her dust for nearly twenty miles. "Look, you're kidding, aren't you? That's just some crazy superstition."

But Etcitty didn't smile, and her expression remained adamant. "Back up until you can turn around. We're not going any farther," she said, before turning to go to her vehicle.

"This is some crazy shit," Abe mumbled before putting the truck in reverse. "Where are we going then?"

Before he could get an answer he heard a rumble that he thought at first must be thunder, but the clouds were far away. The rumble became louder, then quickly transformed into an exploding roar. Abe looked up barely in time to see a wall of water rushing down the arroyo toward them. "Jesus Christ. What . . . ?"

"Flash flood," yelled Etcitty. She sprinted back toward his Toyota, pulled the door open. "Quick. Get out. Up the bank."

Abe jumped out and tried to scramble up the steep sides of the slippery arroyo. A narrow stretch of flat land, too narrow for a vehicle but wide enough to walk on, waited six feet above him. Patch had already reached the top and stood barking at the two humans, already caught in the sudden onslaught of rising water. The current pulled at Abe, dragging him back, but he struggled until he could reach a root near the top of the bank and hung on. He turned his head, looking for the woman, and saw nothing but debris—entire trees, branches, rocks, everything ferried along by the incredible force of an instantaneous raging brown river.

He scanned the surface of the murky water. "Officer Etcitty, Emily. Emily!" Abe tugged on the root and managed to crawl to the top of the arroyo, then ran along the bank and continued calling her name. Both vehicles were nearly submerged, the Blazer on its side wedged up against his truck. Only the top half of the camper remained visible, though the rising water meant it could be swallowed in a matter of minutes. His eyes searched the length of the arroyo, looking for some sign of the woman, and spotted a logjam fifty feet downstream, a blockage of brush and logs encircled by an eddy of swirling water—and maybe something else—another branch, or maybe not. Abe ran in his heavy, mud-sodden shoes until he stood parallel to the debris. "Emily. Are you out there, damn it?" Then he saw her, obscured at times, her head bobbing in and out of the water, her arm grasping the root of a tree.

"Freeman, over here," she said through gritted teeth, mud-matted hair streaming down her face.

"Don't let go," he yelled, and immediately began searching for something to use as leverage. He wanted a branch long enough to reach her from the bank—not easily found in this high-desert country. Situated near the center in a mass of tangled roots and brush that looked like it could break free any moment, Emily struggled to hang on. He knew he couldn't swim out to her and that they would both be swept downstream if he tried. He picked up a branch, but it proved to be too short, and he tossed it aside. The second one he found, actually a twisted root, showed more promise. Abe took off his shirt, glad for the long sleeves, and tied one sleeve around a knotty end. The shirt would provide the length, if she could let go long enough to grab it with one hand. "Are you hurt?"

"My leg, but I don't think anything's broken. Don't know how much longer I can hang on," she shouted over the noise of crashing debris.

Abe positioned himself on the edge of the gully, directly across from her. "Okay, Emily, I'm going to try to reach you with this branch. I want you to grab onto the shirt with one arm if you can.

Don't let go of that tree until you have hold of the shirt." He used the root as a casting rod, his arms as an extension, and the shirt as his line, and tried to land it as near as possible to the woman. The first few tries were off the mark, either short or behind her.

Emily clung to her tether with one arm and with the other reached desperately for the shirt. Finally, after several attempts, she had it in her grasp. "Got it. Now what?"

"Try to work your way up to the root. When you get a good grip with both hands I'm going to pull you in." Abe prayed the shirt would hold, and the root wouldn't snap when she had both hands on it, and that he wouldn't be pulled into the quagmire with her.

As soon as Emily released her grip on the logjam and grasped the shirt she was swept into the swift current, her body submerged under the brown water. Abe's arms jerked with a force that felt as if they were being yanked out of their sockets, his hands scraping across the rough surface of the root, but he held tight and took a slow step back, then another.

A moment later her arms and then her head emerged. Emily took a gasp of air, coughed, and sputtered. "Hurry up. I can't . . ." she croaked before the swirling water pulled her under again.

Abe spotted a large log upstream moving their way and knew he had to work quickly. He planted his feet and, hand over hand, inched his way down the root. He moved close to the bank and crouched. When she came out of the water again, he lay on his stomach and grabbed her arms. With an enormous burst of will, he pulled her halfway out, while she clung to him and pulled herself the rest of the way onto the slippery red clay. They rolled onto their backs, gasping for air.

After a few minutes, Emily coughed and caught her breath. "First time I ever felt glad to see a white man."

He didn't say anything, just gulped in the fresh, clean air. Patch raced to him, tail wagging, whimpering, and smothered him with

31

wet dog kisses. A smile passed over Abe's face as he reached a bloody hand out and stroked his dog. In that moment he considered himself lucky to be alive.

5

Though a jagged tear running down her right pant leg exposed a nasty cut, Emily Etcitty appeared intact. In fact, she looked beautiful: her dirty, scratched, and bruised face, her long black hair streaked with mud and leaves, now undone from its neat bun and hanging in rivulets around her shoulders. "How's that leg?" He caught his breath and met her eyes.

She wiggled her legs, tried to lift her right, and grimaced in pain. "Nothing's broken, a few cuts and bruises." She reflected his tight smile. "Thanks, white man."

"No problem." Abe blinked, staring at what was once a road, the silence deafening in the sudden absence of the roaring torrent, the two vehicles tucked in logs, branches, and rubble like eggs in a nest, the Blazer laying on its side. "How much farther? To your brother's I mean . . ."

"Three miles, a sheep path will take us there." She let a slow breath escape. "Coyote caused this, you know. He's up to his tricks."

Even though she smiled, he knew she believed it.

Emily pulled herself to a sitting position and stared at the arroyo. The calmness in her face belied Abe's frustration—his truck stuck in a muddy arroyo, probably totaled, and he still a prisoner.

With growing annoyance, he wished again he had never come to this part of the world.

"Both vehicles are no doubt out of commission, but maybe the radio will work." Emily turned away from the patrol car and glanced at the clear, blameless sky. "Shit. Wait till headquarters gets wind of this. I can see it all coming down now. You should have done this—you should have done that." She tried to stand, but the pain in her leg pulled her back. "No one will come looking for us because I have the weekend off, and my mom knew I wanted to spend time at the sheep camp."

Abe gave a helpless shrug. "Stay here. I'm going to see if there's anything we can salvage." His palms were raw and bleeding from his grip on the rough *piñon* root, but he knew he was in better shape than she. He clambered to his feet and worked his way down the muddy arroyo. Patch took off after him until Abe shooed him back up the bank, where he sat down beside Emily, keening softly.

"There's a first aid kit under the driver's seat," she yelled at his receding back.

The Navajo Police SUV lay on the passenger side, the driver's window down. He pulled on the door handle, but it had been banged up badly and remained jammed shut. Abe wriggled through the open window where he bumped into a log wedged into the dashboard. The cord for the radio hung limply out of the console, useless without a microphone. Everything was covered with mud. Just the same, he tried pushing a few buttons to see if he could get a signal. Nothing. The groceries he had noticed earlier were long gone. Abe reached under the seat and felt around until his hands detected a rectangular metal box, and pulled out the first aid kit, still sealed and undamaged. A shotgun hung behind the seat on a rack above the metal screen. He tried to remember if Emily had her service weapon holstered to her side. Not sure, he searched the interior, but came up empty-handed. Grasping the first aid kit and the shotgun, he squeezed out the window of the Blazer.

Because his truck remained upright and partially blocked by the SUV, it appeared to be in better shape. A glance inside the back window of the camper shell reassured him that, thanks to the weather stripping he'd installed around the tailgate and the seams of the truck, little water had seeped inside. His bedroll, backpack, and the rest of his gear were damp, but not soaked with mud. The twelve-pack of beer and recent purchases were still in plastic bags, undisturbed. Inside the cab, however, he discovered muddy water, branches, rocks, even a dead cottontail. Debris surged out with a rush of muck when he opened the door. After removing his keys from the ignition, Abe slid across the muddy seat and worked open the glove compartment. He had some cash stowed in that plastic bag along with his identification and insurance papers. These he dropped in the backpack, then looked for his knife before remembering the police were holding it as evidence. "Fucking knife." He knew that switchblade deserved the blame for his troubles, not some crazy coyote. He rummaged around and found the flashlight, his marijuana still safe and dry in its waterproof container along with a supply of matches and Zig-Zags. Without hesitating, he dropped the flashlight into his pack, made a quick survey of the truck's interior, then closed the door and hurried back to where Emily waited.

She had ripped her pants leg along the seam, exposing a jagged cut that ran vertically from an inch above the knee to midthigh. The blood flow had slowed, due to a temporary tourniquet she'd made from a strip of her pants and applied to the upper thigh. Emily sat upright, legs stretched out in front and her eyes closed. Her lips moved as she voiced syllables, the vowels rising and falling in a baffling yet rhythmic cadence. She stopped when he approached. "It's a prayer," she said, her voice soft but unselfconscious. "I was careless, didn't pay attention, I showed disrespect. That's why we had this problem."

Abe didn't know how to respond. Since arriving in New Mexico, his life had begun to spiral out of control. The strangeness he'd encountered here did not compare to the familiar aberration he'd experienced growing up in New Jersey. He had always felt different, but learned how to survive the crowded, run-down neighborhoods, the street fights between different gangs, his mother's scorn and rages, the beatings. In his teens he rebelled with a savageness and finality alien to his quiet nature, but ultimately found refuge and a certain peace in music and long, solitary walks along the Jersey shoreline. He was in his late twenties and unattached when he met Sharon, a beautiful woman with cocoa-colored skin and the voice of an angel, and he fell in love with her. *A dirty* shvartzer, *a goy no less*, his mother exhorted before she told him to leave, that he no longer belonged to her. They had been together five years, the happiest years of his life, when Sharon received her diagnosis of metastatic ovarian cancer. Abe felt as if a knife had plunged into his heart. After she died he knew he would die as well if he didn't leave everything behind, even his God.

Still, nothing in his experience had prepared him for the mystery of this place. Abe dropped to a squat beside Emily, laid the shotgun and backpack down, and sighed. "I brought the first aid kit. The radio's gone."

The policewoman regained her authority. "I'll take care of this," she said, referring to the cut on her leg. She took the medical kit from him. "Go back and get whatever is salvageable. You forgot the ammo in my Blazer. Bring it, so this shotgun won't be alone. My service revolver, too."

"Do you want me to help you with that leg?"

"I can manage. Now go. Another thunderstorm is headed this way. We need to get moving."

He glanced at the sky, tranquil as a sleeping baby. "Why do you say that?"

"Because I'm paying attention. Now hurry." She opened the metal box and rummaged through it until she found a package of antiseptic wipes and began cleaning the area around the cut. When she saw him still watching her she added, "I have this covered. Go on."

It didn't take Abe long to gather up the groceries and the rest of his gear. He made sure he had food and a container of water for the dog, then added the twelve-pack of beer. Abe didn't know if the truck would ever run again, but he locked it anyway, and went to the Blazer to see what he could find. He noticed a metal compartment on the floor behind the seat. Inside the compartment he found Emily's police-issue revolver and a carton of shells. He put the gun and ammo in the grocery sack, but could only carry so much and didn't know how she would manage the walk. Abe slipped the backpack over his shoulders and carried the rest in his arms. The open cuts on his hands burned as he made his way up the embankment with his heavy load.

When he reached the top, Emily had finished applying antiseptic cream and had wrapped her leg tightly with gauze.

Abe dropped his bundles and sat on the dirt beside her. "Neat job."

"I studied nursing before I switched to law enforcement." She tossed him a packet of antiseptic wipes. "Clean your hands up and put some of this cream on them. I can wrap them, too, if you want. They must be hurting." She searched through the first aid kit, found a bottle of ibuprofen, popped two pills in her mouth, and handed him the bottle.

"Want a beer to wash them down?" The last two days had been a nightmare, and Abe was thirsty as hell.

"Better not, but I'll take some water. We need to start walking. Give me your arm."

Abe shrugged, swallowed the pills, then took a swig from his water bottle before handing it to her. "Wait a minute." He walked around, poking through the debris left from the aftermath of the flood. After helping Emily to her feet, he handed her a sturdy juniper branch. "Here. You can use this for support."

During the first hour of their trek, they did not talk. Perhaps the aftershock of their harrowing experience had left them speechless. Wispy, white clouds formed horsetails in a now milky-blue sky. After circling to the back side of the mountain, they followed a narrow path fringed with sage and rabbitbrush. Small golden globes dotted the landscape as far as Abe could see. Broom snakeweed, Emily said, and told him to pick a bundle and put it in his backpack for her to use later. The muted brown canvas with its montage of gold and yellow, sprinkled with stunted green juniper and *piñon*, was punctuated by splashes of bright orange flowers.

Emily pointed to one of those plants with vibrant blossoms and dull green leaves. "That's globemallow. The Navajo word means 'medicine that covers.' The Diné use the roots of this plant to treat every kind of sickness you can think of."

Abe nodded in acknowledgment. His gaze encompassed the severe landscape. He had spotted only a few patches of grass and wondered how sheep survived on such meager offerings, in fact how anything survived.

"Let's stop and rest for a minute." Leaning on her stick, Emily looked back at the mountain, isolated and prominent on the high plateau. "The Spanish call it *El Huerfano*, the orphan, because it appears so alone. It is our mountain, though, one of our most sacred places, *Dzil ná oodili*, where Changing Woman gave birth to her warrior twins." She turned to look at him, her face reflecting earnestness. "You think this is all crazy superstition, I know, but I grew up with this, white man, and wouldn't live anywhere else.

When a Navajo baby is born, the umbilical cord is buried in their place of birth, tying them forever to the land."

Abe sighed. "You don't have to call me white man. Name's Abe." He felt like he had landed on some alien planet. Spiny, prehistoric-appearing horned toads scurried across the path or sat immobile as statues on sun-warmed rocks. The blazing sun on his back told him it must be early afternoon. He wanted to drink one of the beers; his body ached from the weight of the load he carried, and his hands burned. Sweat dripped into his eyes and off his nose. Patch's tongue hung out, and the dog didn't seem able to rouse the energy to chase the occasional jackrabbit they scared up. Abe poured water in a cup and sat it down for Patch, then looked at the faded sky. "No sign of rain," he commented, before pulling the tab on a Miller and holding it out to her.

Emily wrinkled her nose at his offer, so he tipped the can to his mouth and took a long draw. The beer, though warm, refreshed him.

They began walking again, her head held high, her back straight. She gave no indication she heard his remark about rain, or that she was suffering from the pain in her leg. Several minutes passed before she spoke again. "The land disarms you; sometimes it can be hostile, but if you give it a chance, approach it with respect and patience, it will embrace you. The storm that caused the flood was south of us, but it's coming our way. If we keep moving we should beat it. We're almost there."

6

By the time Abe and Emily reached their destination, the pewter sky grumbled like an old man. On a high rise surrounded on three sides by sandstone shelves, a small trailer shared space with a traditional earth-covered hogan. The diminutive Airstream squatted near a grove of twisted cottonwoods, looking as settled in its environment as a sleeping armadillo. Even though the silvery aluminum skin had lost its sheen, the little trailer appeared solid, showing only a few dents and scuffs. Windows pushed open to the outside, and the aroma of coffee wafting through an open east-facing door indicated someone was home.

A pair of mixed-breed dogs, barking raucously, ran from a sheep pen located near the hogan toward the bedraggled arrivals. They quieted and shifted to wagging and wiggling when they recognized Emily. Patch and the pair of mutts exchanged sniffs and appeared satisfied that neither presented a danger to the other, and a gaunt old man showed himself at the door.

"This is my grandfather on my father's side," Emily said before switching to Navajo and addressing the old man.

Abe hung back, conscious of how the two of them must appear, and listened while the elderly Navajo and Emily exchanged greetings in their indecipherable language.

"I told him that the river of mud found us and took our vehicles. I said you are a friend and will be staying here for a short time while repairs are made. He answered that you are welcome to stay."

If the crooked body were somehow straightened, the man at the door would be taller than Abe. A bright, multicolored bandana tied around his forehead held back flowing snow-white hair. Obsidian pinpoints peered out from deep-set, watery eyes. The old man's nutmeg face, crisscrossed by thousands of timeworn wrinkles, resembled a roadmap of a busy city. The crevices mirrored the sun-baked and eroded land he called home. Blue jeans, a plaid shirt, and a leather vest hung loosely on his frame. He glanced briefly at Abe, then extended his right hand, the long, skeletal fingers embellished with turquoise rings, and lightly touched Abe's fingertips.

"*Yá at ééh*," he said in a strong but rusty voice, before casting his eyes off to a distant point on the horizon.

Abe nodded his head, and waited, not knowing what to do next.

"Grandfather doesn't speak English," Emily said as the first drops of rain began. "Come inside."

Abe entered the small, crowded space, then hunched self-consciously on a wooden crate, sipping stale boiled coffee the elderly Navajo had proffered. Emily and her grandfather sat on folding metal chairs at a card table pushed against the wall, and conversed quietly in Navajo. The old fellow waited a long time before responding and, when he did, used few words. Abe looked out at the riveting rain, hoping Patch had enough sense to find shelter under the trailer. He jerked to attention when he realized Emily was speaking English again.

"There's a bucket under the steps and a spring out by those cottonwoods. If you want to wash up, you can heat some water on the stove. There's soap and a towel. My brother has some spare clothes in that chest; might be a little big, but they're clean and dry." She looked at his backpack, the bag of food, and the shotgun he'd leaned against the wall when he sat down. "You won't need that," Emily said, taking the gun.

"Here's the ammo and your service revolver," Abe said, pulling them out of the bag and handing them over.

"Thanks. What about that globemallow I asked you to pick?"

Abe gave her a puzzled look, then dug through his pack for the scruffy bundle of weeds. While searching, his fingers brushed another object, something unfamiliar under the beer, his harmonica, and damp clothing. He pulled his hand out and handed the herbs to Emily.

"Medicine. I'm going with Grandfather. I'll be back later to see how you're doing."

The rain ceased after its short, dramatic outburst, and broken clouds admitted bright slashes of sunshine. After Emily and her grandfather left for the hogan, Abe went out in the newly washed air and walked away from the trailer. When he found a boulder that offered privacy and a place to sit, he reached into his pack and took out a small cloth pouch. "What the . . . ?" He pulled apart the drawstring closure. At the bottom of the pouch he found a small key and a folded scrap of paper that had been ripped in half. Abe examined the key, then unfolded the paper. Some numbers, now blurred from the dampness, were scrawled across the yellow notebook page. Thinking back, Abe recalled picking up the sack and hastily dropping it in his backpack. *Jackson must have dropped this when he fell off the log.* Abe continued staring at the key, curious about its significance, then returned the items to the sack.

Abe backtracked to the trailer to clean up. Emily and her grandfather had not returned, so he quickly undressed and scrubbed his body as best he could. He then put on the faded flannel shirt and cinched the baggy jeans around his waist. Once dressed, he tossed the dirty water out the door, laid his wet clothes on a juniper bush, and took another beer from the twelve-pack. Needing to walk and think, he headed down the trail and whistled for Patch. It occurred to him that having possession of the key might further implicate him in the murder, and he considered tossing the sack into the desert, or burying it—no one would be the wiser. He hesitated, holding the key in his hand, thinking it could also be a possible clue that would clear him. In the end he placed it back in the drawstring bag and dropped it into his pack.

He walked down from the knoll where the trailer sat and headed toward the cottonwoods. The inviting, silvery-green trees near the spring contrasted with the harsh, rocky terrain. The stillness seemed overwhelming, but when he listened carefully he heard a distant shriek, and noticed a lone red-tailed hawk circling far above him. "Probably thinks I'm a meal," Abe said, sitting down on a boulder and causing Patch to give him a quizzical look. He remained there, sipping his beer, for nearly a half hour, listening, first to the receding hawk's call, then to the silence. By the time he finished his beer, he knew what he had to do.

7

Emily and Abe sat on the trailer steps after their meal of Dinty Moore beef stew and Wonder Bread, watching the cotton-candy sky change from pink to purple. As soon as the old man retreated to the sanctity of his hogan, Abe told Emily they needed to talk. She had also bathed earlier. Her hair, still damp and smelling of yucca, framed her smooth face. She wore cut-off jeans and Abe noticed a clean wrap around one of her legs. "Your grandfather, he took care of that cut? Is he a medicine man or something?" he asked, thinking of the yellow-flowered weeds he had gathered earlier in the day.

Emily nodded. "Grandfather knows all the traditional uses of plants and ways to cure the body and the spirit." She held a cup of steaming aromatic tea, probably gathered from another local plant. "I've brought something for those cuts." She took one of his hands in hers and extracted a small tin of salve from her pocket with the other.

As Emily held his hands and rubbed salve into his palms, Abe shifted nervously, aware of her closeness and her scent. "Put more on in the morning," she said, once again all business, as she withdrew her own hand.

Abe thanked her, then took a deep breath before beginning. "Look, I want to clear up this mystery about Easy Jackson. I don't understand why this happened to me. I know I left my knife behind, but . . ." He opened his backpack and pulled out the drawstring bag. "I found this in the bottom of my pack today. I picked it up off the ground when I gathered my gear before leaving Clayton Lake State Park, and forgot it until now. I think it dropped out of Easy Jackson's pocket when he fell down at my campsite."

"Fell down?"

"Yeah. He'd been drinking, and he tumbled off a log, hit his head on a rock." Abe handed the sack to Emily.

"It's hard to believe you forgot all this. What is it?" Emily peered into the bag. When she saw the key, she stood up and went into the house, returning with a clean handkerchief. "You probably left your prints all over it, no need to complicate things with mine," she said, using the handkerchief to pick up the key. After examining it from all angles, she carefully wrapped it in the cloth and laid it beside her on the step. "Looks like a locker key, maybe. What else is in there?"

"There's a piece of notebook paper. It's wet and torn, hard to read, looks like a series of numbers."

Emily unfolded the paper, studying it in silence. "Whatever it means, half is missing. When did your amnesia suddenly clear up enough that you became aware of these items, Mr. Freeman?"

"Couple of hours ago. When I gave you those medicinal plants I felt something unfamiliar in the bottom of my pack. I've been thinking about it all afternoon—something Jackson said—'I've got ahold of my key to happiness.'"

Emily wrapped both objects in the handkerchief and placed the bundle on her lap. She seemed to be appraising him so intently he didn't know if she believed him or not. "I think you better tell me everything. Let's start with why you left New Jersey and what your business is here in New Mexico."

45

"I don't have any business here. Wish I had never come." His mind drifted back to Sharon and the terrible vision of her as she lay dying. He knew he was running away from that memory and the knowledge of how he'd contributed to her death. He couldn't tell Emily about that. Knowing he was still a suspect in the death of Easy Jackson, she would surely see him as a murderer, as he often saw himself. Abe struggled, trying to figure out where to start, how to choose the right words, which ones to omit. He decided to begin with Sharon and how she'd brought him so much joy, then so much sorrow when he lost her.

Emily waited for him to respond—not prodding or rushing him—quietly anticipating his answer. "Yeah, okay. I'll tell you why I left Jersey. Mind if I get a beer first?"

He brought one for her, too, which she declined. After a long drink he started talking. Haltingly at first, Abe described his lifetime of alienation, loneliness, and rejection—until he met Sharon. He told Emily about Sharon's kindness and fragile beauty, how she shared his love for music and life, and how happy they were together. He took another drink before talking about her illness and inevitable death, the loss still too painful, and his role during her last moments too unbearable to mention. "So I had to leave. The only beautiful, genuine person I ever loved was gone. I didn't want to play my piano anymore, though it had always been the one thing that brought me peace when all else failed. Schubert, Mozart, Liszt—nothing worked. I didn't know where to go—Sharon always dreamed of seeing the Pacific Ocean. After she died I sold the piano and everything else I owned except my truck, cut all ties, and headed west."

Emily remained quiet during Abe's discourse, letting him tell it his way. "Maybe I will have that beer," she said, following a few moments of silence. She pulled the tab and took a modest swallow. "I'm sorry about your girlfriend."

During the short time he had spent around Emily Etcitty, Abe had become aware of her calm reticence. After allowing Abe several minutes of quiet reflection, she spoke. "Anything unusual happen while you were traveling? Any run-ins with the law, make any enemies?"

"No, nothing. I found jobs here and there, earned a little money, and moved on." The sky darkened, allowing the first early stars to shyly emerge. Coyotes howled in the distance, gossiping with one another. "I keep to myself, try not to make enemies or friends. Besides, once I left Jersey I didn't know anyone."

A chill settled over the evening. Emily went into the trailer, returning shortly afterward with a woven wool blanket and a notebook and pen. She draped the blanket over her shoulders and took another swallow of beer. "I want to know what happened in Clayton, New Mexico—from the time you arrived until you left. Every little detail."

"All right, but I don't know how that will help. I already told you and that state cop everything I know."

"You didn't tell me you found a drawstring sack with a key."

Abe stretched his legs and, with hands clasped behind his head, let his mind go back to the scene at the restaurant.

"I ended up in Clayton when I crossed over from Texas to New Mexico. I was hungry and tired, saw this little café on Main Street and stopped for a bite to eat."

"What was the name of the place?"

Abe closed his eyes, forming a picture in his mind of the crazy sign in the window of the restaurant. *El Plato Grande—Open Seven Days a Week and Weekends, Too.* "It was a small family place, a hangout for locals. El Plato Grande."

"Did you see anybody there who looked like they didn't belong?" Emily said.

"They were mostly locals, ranchers and old folks or families." He paused before continuing. "A couple on a motorcycle showed

47

up. They looked Hispanic and seemed a little rough around the edges. The man and the woman wore matching black leather jackets and some kind of tattoos. Then, I guess there were two other guys that didn't fit. I noticed their car had Kansas plates. One man stood about six feet, the other shorter, and heavier, with bad skin. They both had sunglasses on so I couldn't see their eyes. Seemed like they were passing through, like me."

Emily started taking notes, looking interested. "Can you give me a description of their vehicle?"

"Maybe a Buick, a Riviera, or something else long and black, with dark windows. It looked out of place in that little cow town with all the pickup trucks. So did the guys, come to think of it. But I guess a lot of people pass through Clayton." He began to feel the night chill, gave a little shudder, and crossed his arms over his chest.

She watched him closely. "There's a jacket hanging on a hook by the door. Go get it if you're cold." When he settled back down, wearing a wool-lined denim jacket, overly large, but warming him already, she remarked, "A perfect match for those innocent-looking blue eyes." Emily rewarded Abe's blush with a teasing grin. "All right, then, if you can think of anything else about the guys with the Kansas plates, let me know, but go on. What about the couple on the motorcycle?"

Abe squirmed under her intense gaze, but a connection began to form in his mind. He wondered why he hadn't thought of it sooner. "Yeah, of course—the couple on the motorcycle. They had a big Harley with some kind of vanity plates. I saw a Harley at the campground on the morning I left."

The light from the open door of the trailer formed a halo around Emily, highlighting the sheen of her hair and skin, her dark eyes counterpoints to the stars that punctuated the night sky. The trail of the Milky Way stretched across the heavens like a silver brushstroke. Abe had never experienced such silence and emptiness. He felt alone—a captive, but captivated as well. He looked at Emily, her eyes questioning, her pen ready in anticipation.

"Tell me more," she said, and brought him back to reality. "I need a description of the couple. Take your time."

Abe fell quiet before responding, letting his eyes linger on the stars as his mind re-created the appearance of the man and woman. "The woman had dark, curly hair down to her shoulders. Kind of attractive, but in a tough, brittle way. She wore a lot of makeup, tight clothes showing off her figure, and she had a teardrop tattooed below her right eye."

"You noticed a lot about her for someone not paying attention. What about the man?"

Abe looked away, resting his chin on his palm while he thought back to the restaurant scene. "He had a mustache. One of those Fu Manchu types, and his teeth caught my attention. The canines were long and pointed. He was tall and kind of thin, but muscular. Like I said, probably Hispanic. Lots of tattoos."

Emily paused in her note taking to look at him. "What kind of tattoos?"

"All kinds—a teardrop matching the woman's, Madonnas, bleeding hearts, a spiderweb, and something that looked like a black hand with the letters *EME* inked across the palm. I admit I was staring until he caught me in the act."

"What else, Abe? Keep going." Her voice, tinged now with anticipation, sounded eager.

He was trying to remember any other details about the couple, when the image of Easy Jackson came back to him. "It just hit me. They had the same tattoo—the biker and Jackson—a spiderweb on the outside of the elbow."

"It's a prison tattoo, usually indicates the person has done time," said Emily. "Sometimes jailbirds get them to show how many years they've been in prison, or even how many people they've robbed or killed. Nowadays it's often a macho thing, some guy trying to look the part." Emily stood up and began pacing in front of him. "The woman's teardrop—it used to mean the same thing, a hit, but it could also mean that a relative or friend was killed, maybe in prison." She stopped pacing. "I think we're onto something, Abe. Do you recall what the vanity plates on the motorcycle said?"

Abe wrinkled his brow, concentrating. "They were from New Mexico, I'm pretty sure. But, some kind of special issue. It seemed like Spanish, maybe—La Em, Ema, la Eme. The letters were followed by a few numerals I can't recall."

Any further discussion was interrupted by the sight of a single headlight bouncing erratically over the rough terrain, headed in their direction.

Emily watched the approaching light. "It's Will on his old Chief, probably drunk."

The man on the motorcycle slouched under a weathered, black cowboy hat adorned with a ragged feather, and held a bottle of Old Crow in one hand. He roared up to the porch, cutting into a right angle at the last second in order to make a dramatic, dirt-throwing arrival. "Hey, little sister. Saw your government-issue ride down in the arroyo. Funny place to park," he snickered, before tilting the bottle to his lips and downing the remaining contents. Will tossed the empty bottle, stumbled off the bike, put the kickstand down, and, swaying drunkenly, tried to focus bloodshot eyes on Abe. "Who's this white guy wearing my bes' jacket?" he said before sliding like melted wax to the ground.

"Goddamn it, Will. You're going to get yourself killed one of these days," Emily said. Then to Abe, "Help me get him inside."

Once they settled Will Etcitty on the small pull-down bed, removed his shoes, and left him snoring under a blanket, Emily and Abe returned to the porch stoop, and she began to talk about her brother. "Will used to be able to handle his drinking. He's smart, studied to be a geologist, wanted to work on the rez, help his people." She frowned before continuing. "He landed a job with the big Four Corners Power Plant thinking he could put all his new knowledge to good use. He went to work excited, full of new ideas, but they assigned him flunky office work. He came to realize the corporate bosses would never allow him to work as a geologist. But even more depressing to Will was having to witness the damage the power plant did to our land and how it poisoned our air. The trade-off was money, any kind of work for hard-pressed people." Emily exhaled a long, slow sigh. "The tribe sold out."

Abe shifted his weight, watched the clouds dance past the waxing moon. Patch had left his new friends by the sheep corral and lay sleeping at his feet. He reached down and scratched the dog's nape. "What happened?"

Emily stretched her hand toward the dog, her fingertips lightly brushing against Abe's, sending a current through his body, then both quickly withdrew. She looked away, her hands now folded demurely on her lap while Abe's face burned from the jolt of unintentional contact.

"The short story is they fired him. He became a troublemaker, tried to make changes, and started getting the workers riled up, so they got rid of him. Not only that, they made sure no one else would hire him in his field. So he started drinking more and more, until pretty soon that was all he did." Emily stood, stretched, and went into the trailer, returning a few minutes later with a jacket, her gun, and a set of keys. "That's a long story, too. Maybe some other time. Right now, I have to get back to work."

Emily straddled the motorcycle and jumped hard on the kick start. After three tries the Chief came to life with a rumble. She hesitated, doubt shadowing her features, before looking him in the eye and speaking in her police officer voice. "Give me your truck keys. I don't want you to mess up, Abe, like taking off or anything.

You're in my custody, and the State Police still see you as their only suspect. I'm responsible for you, and Grandpa still knows how to use that shotgun."

"Don't worry, I'm not going to run away or kill anybody. Anyway, how could I?" Just the same, he shrugged and retrieved his keys from his backpack and handed them to her. It angered him that the law still thought he was involved in Jackson's death, and he felt a surge of sadness that she did not trust him. But then, why should she?

Emily revved the engine and turned the bike around, but before she could leave, Abe called out. "Wait. There's something else I forgot."

She swerved around and switched off the ignition, waiting for him to continue.

"Jackson. He wanted me to take him somewhere in Arizona, place called Bisbee. Said he had a good friend there."

"Did he mention a name?"

"No. Just that we could stay there as long as we liked. He didn't say anything else about the guy."

Emily pursed her lips. "How come you didn't remember any of this when we questioned you at headquarters?"

"I don't know. I was nervous, scared. I answered the questions the state cop asked about."

"Think of anything else you forgot, let me know," she said, restarting the engine. Her parting words echoed in his ear. "You did save my life. I guess you're okay, for a white man."

He watched her disappear, a receding red light bouncing over the empty landscape.

8

Early the following afternoon, as Abe carried a fresh bucket of water from the spring, Emily arrived driving a Navajo Police-issue Blazer identical to the one in the arroyo.

"Where's Will and Grandpa?" She looked pressed and spiffy in her cop uniform.

"Your brother's sleeping off his hangover. Since he couldn't find any booze in the house he ranted at me for being here, and at you for taking his bike, then went back to bed. Your grandfather went off with the sheep. Patch left with him and the other two dogs. Seems like my dog has found his calling. He's a natural sheepherder. I can hardly get any time with him anymore." Abe sounded petty even to his own ears. Then he smiled, feeling foolish about complaining of his dog's lack of attention. "You look good and rested this morning."

"I slept in my own bed at Mom's house in Huerfano—hot shower and all the perks of modernity. My mother is a teacher at the community school." Emily emerged from the vehicle carrying a pair of grocery sacks and handed one to him. "Compliments of the Navajo Nation. Our vehicles were towed to a shop in Farmington. They're assessing the damage now. And the captain put me back on duty, so I can't stay long. The station issued me this loaner, but the captain is not happy." Once inside the trailer she put the bags on the counter and pulled back the blanket that sectioned off Will's sleeping area. She glanced at her brother sprawled on the twin bed. "I impounded Will's motorcycle," she whispered. "He isn't going to like it, but he won't be going anywhere now, and it's for his own good."

Abe nodded, thinking how he and Will were stuck out here together, and wondering if they would ever get along. "Any new developments on the case?"

"I'm working on that. Let's go outside. I'd rather not wake Will and deal with him right now, and I brought some photos to show you."

They sat in the front seat of the Blazer while Emily explained how she had gone through the mug shots of prisoners known to belong to a certain gang. "That license tag, 'La Eme,' stands for the Mexican Mafia, a really vicious bunch. They were responsible for a lot of the violence during the New Mexico Penitentiary riot a few years back. DMV provided a list of all individuals who have purchased motorcycle vanity plates that begin with the initials *EME*. I've narrowed the list down, and these are shots of some members who meet your description and have been released in the past three years. Take a look." She handed him a packet of pictures.

Abe spread the six mug shots on the car seat, then picked them up one by one and scrutinized each. None of the men had a drooping mustache like the biker in Clayton. In fact, most had shaved heads and wore prison garb. He riffled through the stack a second time and paused. "This one—there's something familiar in the eyes, and he's grinning like he's not afraid of anything. The guy in the café had big canines like that."

"Rico Corazón." Emily's face darkened as if a shadow had passed over. "Locked up in the state pen on a charge of manslaughter one, but his case was thrown out. The lawyer claimed evidence was gathered illegally, witnesses gave conflicting statements, and some witnesses disappeared. They released him last March. Are you sure he's the one?"

"Yeah, that's him. He had a woman with him, the one I described earlier."

"His girlfriend, Juanita de la Cruz. She swore he was watching TV with her when someone bludgeoned the victim with a tire iron behind the Bar-None stripper joint in Las Cruces. The victim belonged to a rival gang, the Aryan Brotherhood." Emily returned the pictures to the envelope and placed them on the seat between them. "As for Corazón's girlfriend, de la Cruz is her stage name and the Bar-None is her place of business. Her act consists of erotically perverse gyrations on a pole in the shape of a cross, wearing nothing but some strategically placed rosary beads. A real class act," she added with a rueful look.

Abe tried to imagine the woman in El Plato Grande without clothing, wrapped around a cross, and chuckled in spite of himself.

The policewoman looked at him with a mixture of disgust and teasing humor. "Hey, does that turn you on, Freeman? You didn't mention that she moved you in that way when you gave your original description of the so-called lady."

"No," said Abe. He hadn't felt lust for a woman since Sharon, but he wasn't thinking about Juanita de la Cruz or Sharon at the moment. He looked away from Emily's eyes, embarrassed over his stirrings of arousal. "What about the key and the note?" he asked, changing the subject.

"We're running print checks on those items, but coming up with nothing but smudges. Your prints are on top of the others. The numbers could be anything, a phone number or part of a combination. But your friend Joseph Alphonso Jackson—alias Easy, alias Spiderman—did time in the pen the same time as Corazón. Jackson was a member of the Aryan Brotherhood, so, needless to say, those two weren't the best of buddies. There's a lot of bad blood between the Aryan Brotherhood and the Mexican Mafia." She turned the key in the ignition and brought the Blazer to life. "Let's say we've had some run-ins with Corazón in the past." Without elaborating further, Emily concluded the conversation. "I have work to do, Abe. Get out and go make yourself useful."

Abe opened the passenger-side door and scooted out. "Okay, Emily. Go get the bad guys," he said before slamming the door shut. Emily pulled the vehicle around, then turned to wave before driving away. His eyes pursued her until only a dust trail remained under the flawless, cerulean sky. "Useful," he said aloud. "Useless, she means." He walked toward a small lean-to, determined to work off his frustration on the woodpile. The information Emily had shared with him buzzed in his head like a swarm of hornets, but still made no sense.

Abe picked up the axe and relentlessly drove it into the tough *piñon* wood, mumbling and cursing to himself. That's how Will found him when he stumbled out of the trailer later that afternoon, shading his eyes from the bright sun but not able to conceal his shaking hands.

"What the hell are you making so much noise for? My head is killing me, man."

"Yeah, well, too bad." Abe brought the axe down with a vicious swing.

"Hey, cool it, white man. Why are you so pissed off? You got free room and board."

Abe slammed the axe blade into another log. "Nothing much. I've been accused of killing some guy I barely met, got thrown in jail, my truck is ruined, I'm stuck out here, and I can't do a goddamn thing about it." The log split with a resounding crack, sending a piece sailing toward Will's head. "Even my dog deserted me for a couple of mongrels and some scraggly sheep. I want my name cleared and to be done with this bullshit."

Will ducked the chunk of wood. "Put that axe down, man, before you kill someone. Your dog is fine. Pinko and Shorty are the best sheep dogs on the Navajo Nation, and they'll teach that mutt of yours something, if he can keep up." He rubbed his hands together and licked his lips. "By the way, white man, you got anything to drink with you?" Will stood over six feet tall with a barrel chest, wide shoulders, and the tree-trunk legs of a linebacker. He wore his long hair pulled back in a messy club. Though Will was not much older than Abe's thirty-four years, his features looked worn and weary. Puffiness around the eyes and flab around the belly chronicled a body abused.

Abe leaned the axe against the woodpile and sighed. He felt better since burning off some of his anger. "I have a few beers left, guess we can share since we're stuck out here together." Shaking his head, he added, "I have a name, too. It's Abe Freeman, and my dog can keep up with anything on four legs, maybe run circles around them."

"All right, Abe Freeman." Will nearly grinned, but couldn't quite manage it. His eyes darted, his head twitched, and he wrung his hands. "Look, I need a drink. I don't have any more bottles stashed around here. Don't you have anything stronger?"

"Sorry. Beer's all I brought."

They sat under the cottonwood on a couple of stumps. Will chugged his first Miller and reached for another. "You say my little sister impounded the Chief and left me out here without my wheels or any liquor. She's turned into a regular Navajo Nazi since she put on that damn uniform." He scowled and took another long chug. "This beer is going to be gone in a couple more swallows, Freeman."

"Yeah, well try not to drink that last one so fast because that's the end of it." He drained his can and stood up. "I'll be back in a minute." Abe thought he might as well roll a joint and relax. He didn't think Will Etcitty would mind one bit.

They passed the joint back and forth while Will reiterated the story of how he lost his job trying to bring attention to the emissions problem at the power plant, how his friends decided they didn't want to hang around with a guy who didn't have a job or money, and eventually, how he gave up. "You look at the horizon when you wake up in the morning—over to the west. Shit, look any direction," Will said bitterly. "You can't miss that ring of yellow, scummy sulfur dioxide lying there hugging the land, passing time till it kills everything." He drew on the joint, closed his eyes, and passed it to Abe.

Abe inhaled the pungent smoke slowly, pondering the Navajo's words, and nodded. "Life has a way of screwing up your plans," he muttered, then related his story while the other man listened silently, emitting an occasional grunt or nod of agreement. When Rico Corazón's name came up, Will's face darkened, and he spit on the ground before growling something in Navajo.

"What? Do you know this guy?"

"I know him, and his kind. They're pigs, have no respect for anything."

"How do you know Corazón?"

"A bunch of bikers rode through here one day, tore up the trading post, and stole everything they could get their hands on. On the way out they knocked over an old lady and left her lying in the street, beat up some of the old-timers who hung around—used clubs and tire irons on unarmed men. Asshole made sure everyone knew his name, bragged and laughed about it. 'You want to fight me?' he says. 'Look me up anytime. Rico Corazón. I'll be waiting for you,' he says." Will scowled and kicked at the dust. "I'll never forget that name." He pulled back his hair, exposing a three-inch scar. "Yeah, I tried to stop him. He hit me with a tire iron, knocked me out cold. I've been waiting a long time to get even with that shit-head Mexican."

The tinkle of a bell on the lead goat's neck announced the return of the sheep. They crowded into the corral, the three dogs nipping at their heels, and Grandfather bringing up the rear. The old man seemed aware of what they were smoking and nodded knowingly.

"Grandpa is cool with weed. Fact is he smokes a little himself when he can. But he doesn't like the booze. Wants me to do a cleansing ceremony, sweat it out." Will stood and went to meet his grandfather. "*Yá at ééh,*" he called.

Patch ran over to Abe, tail wagging. After a quick greeting he hopped back to the sheep and his new friends. Abe filled a bucket with water and washed his face and arms.

When he returned to the trailer, he found Will assembling a stack of bologna-and-cheese sandwiches. He piled them on a plate and plopped it down in the middle of the table. They might as well have been steaks the way the men devoured them. When he had his fill, the elderly Navajo man sat back in his chair, lit a cigarette, and closed his eyes.

"Freeman," Will said after his grandfather's head dropped forward and the old man's breathing slowed, "you and I need a plan." He snubbed out the still-smoldering cigarette butt, and stood. "But first, there's something I have to do."

9

Will Etcitty returned to his bed and remained there for two days and nights, shivering and sweating as he suffered through the throes of alcohol withdrawal. Whatever plan he'd had in mind, he kept to himself. Etcitty was drying out, and the demons he experienced in the process remained private. He arose from bed on the third day, and looked like someone resurrected from the dead. Abe watched while Will removed his clothing and walked to the sweat house, a small pyramidal structure resembling a miniature hogan. It blended so completely with the landscape it had gone unnoticed by Abe.

The elder Etcitty spent most of the early morning using a round fire pit to heat large rocks, which he then shoveled into a smaller pit inside the sweat house. Abe watched as the old man emerged to fetch a ladle of water, which he poured over the heated stones. He came out briefly, indicating to Abe through sign language that he should assist by heating more stones and bringing fresh water when needed, then he also removed his clothing and reentered the sweat house to join Will in the cleansing ceremony.

Whenever he brought newly heated stones and ladles of water, Abe heard singing and chanting from inside the tent.

The sweating continued throughout the day, and when Will emerged that evening he appeared thinner, his face drained of color. He told Abe to bring a bucket of cold water, which he poured first over his grandfather's body, then over his own. Will's hands shook, but despite the tremors and weakness, he seemed calm. Abe brought each man a blanket and left them alone while he walked with his dog and contemplated the strangeness of it all.

Will didn't even make a fuss over his motorcycle when his sister returned later that night bringing coffee, potatoes, and a real treat—steaks for dinner. Emily gave her brother a bemused look but said nothing, and left soon after washing the dinner dishes without offering any news concerning Abe's truck or the case.

A routine developed over the next several days. During the morning hours, Abe and Will added to the growing stack of wood in the lean-to. They spoke little, one chainsawing log lengths from the large pile of dead *piñon* and cedar, while the other used an axe to chop branches into stove-size pieces. Abe sometimes hummed a discordant melody while Will cursed and mumbled under his breath. They labored until muscles ached and sweat ran down their bare backs, taking short breaks for copious drinks of cold springwater.

By noon, the sun made it too hot for swinging an axe, even though the late afternoon inevitably brought cooling rain, so they would stop for a lunch of more bologna sandwiches and coffee. While they ate and rested, Abe sat quietly, listening to Will converse in his mysterious language with Grandfather Etcitty, not understanding anything but mesmerized by the music of their voices.

After lunch the men returned to work. But when the afternoon sky transformed into a sea of purple bruises illuminated by slashes of iridescent lightning, they retreated to the shelter of the Airstream, all conversation obliterated by the hammering rain. Will, though stronger each day, would lie down to rest. Abe loved the storms. He thought he could smell the ozone and feel the molecules in the electrified air. The rain cleared his mind for a time, allowing a sense of peace. The tempests reminded him of music. Sometimes he took out his harmonica and played to the accompaniment of crashing thunder and the rhythm of a thousand tiny drumbeats dancing on the roof. The monsoons, though dramatic, were usually short-lived. In their wake they left the earth with a clean face and an odor of heady freshness. After the storms, he took long walks through the high desert land, always accompanied by Patch and sometimes by Will, with Shorty and Pinko tagging along. Abe began to appreciate the stark, barren landscape of northwestern New Mexico. During one of these walks, Will shared the history of the land.

"See those hills over there in the north." Will directed Abe's attention to a group of soft dark-gray bluffs. "Those crests over there are Mancos shale, and the light cliffs, picture cliffs sandstone, Cretaceous formations." He hesitated and let a self-deprecating smile curl his lips. "That's what the white man's university taught me, anyway. This land, this sacred land of the Diné, the San Juan Basin as some call it, one hundred and fifty miles across, is the bed of an ancient sea. Dead plant and animal life compressed over time. They discovered oil way back in 1896. Since then, this land that no white man wanted has been a battleground, with the government and petroleum companies fighting over who has first rights to all that coal, natural gas, and oil lying below the surface."

"Doesn't this land belong to the Navajo Nation?"

"It's complicated." Will watched a black-tailed jackrabbit zigzagging in long leaps, with the dogs in hot pursuit. "The oil was on the reservation, and the elders weren't interested in changing anything." He stopped to steady his hands as he lit another cigarette. "Nothing happened until 1924, when congress negotiated with the newly formed tribal council and set the terms for the Indian

Oil Leasing Act. A few months later they discovered a rich field on the rez in a place called Rattlesnake Dome." Will paused, and after exhaling a cloud of smoke, began speaking again. "The northwest plateau is cut up in squares, part BLM, part county, and part Navajo. Our people, the Diné, never had the desire or the money to pursue a mining or drilling operation." He whistled for the dogs, who were no match for the jackrabbit's speed, and they reluctantly gave up the chase, returning with their tongues dragging.

Three crows huddled on a twisted juniper and cawed like bickering morticians as they studied the corpse of a kangaroo rat. They took flight when the men neared, complaining loudly, but returned quickly when they passed. Abe looked up and spotted a lone turkey buzzard riding the warm currents in concentric circles. The bird's sharp eyes and keen sense of smell had also detected the rat, whose body would not go to waste. "Why did you want to become a geologist?"

"I was always interested in the land. Being young and stupid I thought I wanted the life those white men had—big truck, nice house in town, money in my pocket. I studied hard, earned a scholarship to New Mexico Tech, and came back to make my claim." He frowned, snuffed out his cigarette, and started walking again, head down, his long strides kicking up stones, hands stuffed in his pockets. "No sense bringing that up."

Abe caught up with him but said nothing as he painfully remembered his own dreams, now seemingly irredeemable. The two men were opposites in many ways—one an urban, rebellious, Jewish kid from a crowded East Coast city; the other, Native American, stubborn, proud, accustomed to the openness and freedom of the West. Yet, as they lumbered mutely over the rough terrain, their differences diminished. Perhaps it came from a shared sense of loss.

After a while, Abe broke the silence. "All I ever wanted to do," he said, eyes fixed on a point somewhere in front of him, "was make beautiful music on the piano." A sadness as profound as anything he had ever felt washed over him. He forced his fingers to stop their interminable play as they sought the silent keys of a melody forever engrained in his memory. "Anyway, that's all over. Let's get back to the trailer. And," he added after a moment's hesitation, "maybe you can explain that plan of yours."

The tense mood snapped, and Will's face took on a feverish glint. "Find Corazón and nail him."

The implausibility of that happening, however, caused Abe to laugh. "Get serious. We're at least twenty miles from a main road, we don't have any transportation, we don't know where to look, and what would we do if we found him? Besides, that's the law's job. Emily says they're working on it."

The expression on Will's face didn't change. He looked Abe squarely in the eye. "The law has its limitations."

Without further discussion they approached the trailer. The setting sun reflected brilliant hues of orange and purple on the distant bluffs, evening bats swooped through amorphous clouds of insects, and Emily, perched on the trailer step, awaited their return.

10

The dogs saw her first and raced ahead, tails wagging. She ruffled their coats, laughing as they climbed over each other competing for attention, then waved at the approaching men. "*Yá at ééh*. Mom sent mutton stew and fry bread. Come and get some. Grandpa couldn't wait any longer so he started without you."

It had been over a week since Abe arrived at the Etcitty sheep camp. The generous hospitality the family had extended, so unlike anything he had ever experienced on the East Coast, embarrassed him. He reached into his pocket for his wallet. "Emily, let me pay you, or your grandfather, someone, for the food and lodging."

"Forget it. That would be an insult." But she smiled when she said it. "I'll let you pay for that big sack of dog food I bought for Patch, and you can carry it in," she said as she entered the trailer.

Abe picked up a twenty-five-pound sack from the passenger side of her vehicle and brought it inside. "You must think we are going to be here awhile. It will take Patch six months to go through this," he said.

"You never know, but I do have good news. Your truck is up and running. The mechanics didn't find too much damage. They drained the transmission and brake fluid and changed the oil in case water got in there, replaced a few wires, and cleaned it up. If you have insurance, it should cover everything."

She dished up bowls of steaming stew and carried them to the table where Grandfather Etcitty wiped the gravy from his first serving with a piece of fry bread. He said something in Navajo and held out his bowl for seconds. A plate of flat fry bread sat in the middle of the table. Will passed him the plate and Abe took one, bit into it, and found it delicious, crispy on the outside and soft in the middle.

"It'll be great to have my truck back," Abe said. He dug into his stew of tender mutton, potatoes, and green chilies. "This is so good." Will, too busy eating to stop for conversation, nodded and shoveled in another spoonful.

Emily watched Will as he cleaned his bowl and went for more. "You're looking a lot better than the last time I saw you, big brother."

He nodded again, grunting a soft "hmm," and kept eating.

"The woodpile is looking pretty good this year, too," she added, receiving another grunt in acknowledgment.

For a while, the only sounds were metal spoons clinking against the sides of bowls and some satisfied-sounding slurps and burps. When he finished his stew, Abe reached for another piece of fry bread and broke the silence. "How soon before I can get my truck and get on my way, Emily?"

Emily brought the old percolator to the table and poured them each a cup of coffee. "Well, tomorrow is Sunday, and they're closed. So Monday, I guess. I can pick you up and give you a ride into town, but you have to come back here. We don't want you taking off yet." She held a coffee cup with both hands and brought it to her lips, only partially hiding her smile. "I'm afraid I'd have to arrest you again."

Abe noticed how Will perked up when Emily made the announcement about his truck. When she turned her back, he lifted his head and shot Abe a conspiratorial glance. Abe shook off the look, swallowed some of his scalding coffee, and wondered how the rest of them could drink this stuff without burning the lining of their throats. It burned like acid all the way to his stomach. Nevertheless, as he chewed his second piece of fry bread, he thought he might learn to like this place, bad coffee and all. That is, if his troubles were cleared up and if he didn't feel so restless, and if he had a piano—maybe.

"Anything new on the case?"

"We haven't found Corazón or the Kansas vehicle yet, if that's what you mean—still looking. And the Staties aren't convinced yet that the vehicle the park ranger saw leaving Clayton Lake at four thirty was yours. They say the headlights were off, and it was too dark to tell."

"My headlights were off," Abe protested, "because I didn't want Jackson to see me leave."

Emily shrugged. "They say you are still a suspect. It was your knife."

"You know I didn't do it." He felt mounting anger and frustration. "You told them about the motorcycle I saw in the campground, right?"

"Of course, but they aren't convinced you saw Corazón," Emily said.

They cleared the table and he helped her with the dishes while Will and his grandfather talked quietly in Navajo. Abe paid her for the dog food, glad to be paying for something.

Emily told him, as they sat on the steps after dinner listening to the coyotes' mournful call and answer from the bluffs, that his presence had been good for Will. "There's something about my brother you don't know, Abe," she said after a few moments of quiet, her voice lowered to a near whisper. "Don't tell him I told you. Will's gay. It's not something he wants to share, especially on the rez."

The news didn't surprise or shock Abe; nothing did anymore. It didn't make any difference to him whether Will Etcitty was gay or not, as long as no one tried to make moves on him. He had crossed paths with homosexuals of both genders in the music business. "Why are you telling me this?"

"Because this is a big part of the problems he has to deal with, this conflict—that he has to deny his true nature in order to be accepted—and I don't want you to judge him on that basis if you should guess."

"What would happen if he came out?"

"In our traditional culture, nothing. He would be accepted as a *nádleehí*, a two-spirit person, and he would play an important role in society. But with the coming of Christianity and the mission schools, attitudes changed. Now he would be ostracized, beaten up, or worse."

"Don't worry. It's his business, not mine."

She added that she had the weekend shift and wouldn't be back until Monday morning around ten. Then Emily reentered the trailer to get her gear. She came back carrying her set of keys, snapped on her holstered gun, and positioned her hat. After bidding her grandfather good night, she left.

As soon as the vehicle bounded out of sight, Will cornered him. "Let's go outside and smoke some of your stuff."

Abe knew his pouch of marijuana wouldn't last much longer, but pot seemed to relax Will and take his mind off drinking, so he agreed to meet him out by the sheep corral. He had just finished rolling a stick and lighting up when Will emerged from the shadows and joined him.

The Navajo waved a key in front of Abe's face. "By the time she realizes it's missing, we'll be gone."

Abe had just inhaled, and nearly choked on the acrid smoke. "You took that off Emily's key chain? Are you crazy? She's going to know."

Will held up the small key. "This goes to my Chief. I didn't know which one unlocked the compound gate, so we'll have to use bolt cutters." He slipped the key into his pocket, satisfaction lighting up his face. "She won't be looking at her keys unless she needs to get into the compound. It's a chance we'll have to take. Monday, after you get your truck back, we'll wait till dark, then drive out to the station. I'll sneak the Chief out and we'll take off. I need my bike, and once we finish with our business you can just head on out to California, or wherever the hell you're going." He crossed his arms over his huge chest, grinning broadly. "Hey, are you going to let me have some of that?"

Abe held on to the joint, transfixed. He felt dumbfounded, like he needed another hit. "Take off where? What business? What are you talking about, Will?"

"We're going after Corazón. Cops couldn't find their own ass in an outhouse, and that includes my sister. We'll find him. Are you going to share some of that or not?"

"I'm not supposed to leave here, and you want me to help you steal a motorcycle and go with you to track down a potential killer, then just take off for California? Uh-uh, no way. Besides, the cops can't find Corazón because he's hiding out somewhere, probably in Mexico. We wouldn't know where to start looking, and even if we did find him . . ." Abe shook his head in frustration. "What then?"

Will began pacing, pounding his huge fist into his palm. "We'll make him talk, kick his ass. Then we'll bring him back here."

Abe was taken aback by the other man's vehemence. "You've been drinking, right? This is nuts, Will. Here, I really think you need some of this to calm you down," he said, handing the joint to him. "Why are you so set on getting him, anyway?"

"Look, you don't know how much I want a drink, Abe. I crave it—I'm on edge all the time. I'm sick, sick of drinking, sick of not drinking. My gut hurts; I'm broken. Everything I've tried to do is screwed. And I've got my reasons," he growled. His hand trembled as he put the reefer to his mouth, but Abe saw how his eyes burned with determination when the end of the joint lit up his face.

"You said you wanted to get to the bottom of things, clear your name; well, this is your chance. Are you with me or not?"

Abe walked away, his hands clasped behind his head, turned around, and came back to face Will. "Damn right I want to clear my name, but we don't know for sure Corazón killed Jackson, and even if he did, how do we prove it, and how does this get me off the hook? Another small consideration—where are we supposed to start looking for him?"

"Think about it. You told me you saw Corazón's bike at the campground when you left. They were in the pen at the same time. They hated each other, belonged to rival gangs. Don't you think that's just a little too much of a coincidence? He's your killer, Abe. I'm willing to bet Grandpa's sheep on it." He sucked out the remnants from the roach, nearly burning his fingers, and tossed it to the ground, squashing it with the toe of his boot. "Where was Jackson going?"

"Someplace in Arizona—Bisbee, I think. Bisbee, Arizona. He said he had a buddy there."

"Then that's where we're going. Bisbee, Arizona," Will said, as if it were perfectly obvious.

"We don't have a name. We don't know anything in regard to this buddy of his. And why would Corazón go to Bisbee for Christ's sake?"

"I don't know. It's our only connection, so it's where we start."

"How the hell are we supposed to find this no-name friend of Jackson's?"

"It's not a big town, sits a little ways off Highway 80 near the border. Shouldn't be too hard to find a stinking Aryan skinhead out there." With a faraway look, Will added, "I have some buddies in Bisbee. We can ask around."

Abe walked in a circle, then threw his hands in the air. "Okay, you can look up your buddies and ask a few questions. But what are we supposed to do if we find him? Say, 'I'd like you to come with us, please?' It's police work, Will, and it will be dangerous."

"We're not going empty-handed. We'll take the shotgun and Grandpa's pistol. We'll work out the details along the way." For maybe the first time, Will looked him hard in the eye. "Listen, man, you know that woman that Corazón knocked down when his gang of bikers rode through here? That was my grandmother, Grandpa Etcitty's wife of fifty-five years. She had all kinds of complications from diabetes that made her weak and feeble. What kind of an animal would shove an old lady down in the street? Granma never recovered and died soon afterward. Emily didn't tell you that, did she?" He crossed his arms over his chest and with a resolute look demanded, "Are you coming with me, Abe, or do I go alone?"

11

Abe Freeman had always been a quiet, peace-loving man and generally abhorred violence of any kind. In fact, when driving, Abe would go out of his way to avoid running into a butterfly or hitting a snake, turtle, or even a tarantula on the road. But bullies and trouble had dogged him all his life. His mother had tormented the entire family, especially his father, until the man couldn't stand it any longer. One morning his father left for work and didn't return. Abe never heard from him again, but after his father's departure he became the target of his mother's wrath. Being small for his age and more interested in music than sports, he was bullied at school, and excluded from the groups of popular kids. He became a loner, taking long hikes in the woods and collecting insects and garter snakes that he made temporary homes for in the basement. He gathered beautiful rocks—solid, nonthreatening, inanimate objects that would never hurt him—and learned to cope with adversity by avoiding it.

As an adult he tried to reconcile his life of isolation and loneliness by immersing himself in music. He practiced classical pieces on the piano for hours each day, then played jazz at night in the clubs. Abe was convinced he would never find anyone to love, that he would always be alone, until he met Sharon. She made him laugh, accepted him for who he was, and as his love for her grew, he began to feel he couldn't live without her. But Sharon was gone as well. Abe shuddered at the memory of her emaciated body on the bed. At that point the morphine no longer had any effect on alleviating her pain. The doctor said she had a week at the most—a week of unbearable suffering—so he had given in to her pleas. It felt as if he were killing himself.

Now he had become a victim once again, a suspect in a murder he hadn't committed. At least, that's how he saw himself—a passive, hapless, impotent victim.

He had spent the last three nights tossing in sleeplessness, tortured by night demons. He could find no logical reason to do what Will wanted, except of course to prove his innocence. He felt certain Corazón had come to the park the night before Jackson was killed. If Abe and Will could show that Corazón was involved in the murder, he would clear his name. He decided to go with Will, for whatever good it would do, even though the decision went against every coping mechanism he had learned in life. And maybe that is precisely why he wanted to do it. Since Sharon's death, he had only been half-alive, anyway.

The hard part would be deceiving Emily. Lying did not come naturally to Abe. He preferred honesty, even when it hurt. Besides, he liked her. And now, right on time Monday morning, he found himself sitting next to her in the front seat of a Navajo Police Blazer, driving to Farmington to pick up his truck, and he was going to lie.

"Remember, you need to stick around," said Emily. "You aren't off the hook yet. We might need your testimony when we get these guys, and we will get them."

"Sure." *That could be a long ways off, or never,* Abe thought. *If they don't find the real killer, they may decide it was me.*

"I know you're anxious to get your truck back. Drive it around out at the ranch, or even if you need to run to town, but don't take Will if you do. It would be better if he stayed there for now, if you know what I mean."

"All right."

"Will's not a bad guy, but if he gets picked up drunk again, or gets in another fight, it's jail time." Emily gave him a quizzical look. "Why so quiet? I thought you'd be happy to get your truck back. Did you bring your insurance papers?"

"Yeah."

This continued—her asking questions, him answering in monosyllables—for the duration of the forty-mile trip to the outskirts of Farmington. The dun-colored landscape, interspersed with natural-gas pumping stations, gradually gave way to strip malls, payday loan offices, used-car lots, and pawn shops.

"Farmington still isn't too friendly with our people, but it's better than it used to be."

"That's good."

"This town's a whole lot greener than the surrounding countryside, due to the fact," she explained to Abe, "that three rivers converge here—the San Juan, the Animas, and La Plata."

They crossed the serpentine San Juan River and drove west until they were on the opposite side of town, an area of warehouses, welding shops, storage facilities, and more pawn shops.

"Here we are," she said as they turned into the A and B Auto Repair. "I'm dropping you off, but if you have a problem, here's where you can reach me." She handed him a card that read "Emily Etcitty, Navajo Tribal Police," with her number at the bottom. "Your keys are inside the shop."

Abe stepped down from the vehicle, holding his packet of papers, and walked around to the driver-side window. "Hold on a minute, Emily. Before you go, there's something I want to tell you."

She rolled the window down, a questioning look on her face. "What is it, Abe?"

He hesitated, ran his free hand through his shaggy hair, and sighed. "Oh nothing, just wanted to say thanks for everything."

"No problem. I'll see you tomorrow. We should know Corazón's whereabouts soon, though he may have hightailed it into Mexico. And when I get a day off, I'd like to make lunch, a picnic, and show you some of our beautiful country." She pulled her vehicle around, pointed back to headquarters, gave him a wave, and took off.

Abe answered with a feeble wave and a guilty conscious. "Shit." He knew he was not only a liar, but that he would never even get the chance to say good-bye.

That night Will Etcitty talked with his grandfather for a long time. The old man nodded solemnly, then beckoned Abe to join Will on the sofa. He went to his hogan, and Will told Abe what to expect.

"*Shinali*, Grandfather, knows I have to do this and that you are going with me. He understands it's a question of honor, and he wants to do a prayer ceremony for us before we leave. I didn't tell him what exactly we will do or where we are going. That way he won't have to lie to Emily when she asks."

Abe silently nodded, feeling ashamed for his part in the deceit.

"After the prayer we'll pack a few things and take off, partner."

When the elder Etcitty returned a few minutes later, he was carrying a bundle of herbs in one hand and a small pouch in the other. He lit the herbs, filling the room with pungent smoke, and began to sing in a scratchy voice. Will repeated the words of the chant, and as he did the old man scattered something from the pouch in the direction of the two men. When he finished he bowed his head in farewell and returned to his dwelling.

75

Will told Abe it had been corn pollen in the pouch, offered as a blessing. He made it clear they weren't supposed to discuss the meanings of the sacred items used in the ceremony, so Abe didn't ask questions. He felt edgy and conflicted enough as it was.

They filled a five-gallon jug with water from the spring, and packed cans of Vienna sausages, sardines, and crackers in a knapsack. Will gathered up his rain slicker, some leather gloves, and blankets and put them in the back of the truck. "I'm going to get the bolt cutters and the shotgun. Grandpa gave me this." Will pulled an ancient-looking Enfield revolver out of a holster and showed it to Abe.

Abe shook his head. "I don't need the shotgun. I'm not shooting anyone. I'm going along to clear my name and to make sure you stay out of trouble." Looking at Will's gun he added, "Do they still make ammo for those things?"

"Hell, yes. This gun has a lot of history. Go on, take the shotgun, Abe," Will insisted. He donned his scruffy old cowboy hat with the feather. "Are you ready?"

Abe picked up his backpack and a sack of dog food. "I'm taking my dog."

"What for? Your dog will be better off here."

"Where I go, my dog goes. That's the way it is." Abe went outside and whistled for Patch.

They didn't talk much on the trip to Huerfano. Abe concentrated on picking out the ruts left by Emily's tracks on the now-dry road and tried to stay on course. Patch attempted to claim his spot by the window, but Will shoved him to the middle. "How do you think that would look? You and me sitting close together and the dog on the outside like that."

Shortly after ten o'clock on a moonless night, they reached the Huerfano community and drove by the compound. Abe still didn't know how Will planned to get his motorcycle.

"Pull over there behind the school and turn off the lights."

Abe followed Will's instructions, noting the near-empty parking lot. He scanned the few vehicles, but they all looked the same and he didn't know if Emily's Blazer might be one of them. Streetlights surrounded the compound, and he spotted Will's bike near the entrance. When he turned off the engine in the shadows near the school basketball court, Will got out.

"Take off, Abe. Drive nice and slow. Head southeast on 44 till you get to Nageezi Trading Post. It's fifteen miles. Pull around to the back and wait for me. I won't be long."

Abe let Will disappear in the shadows before he started the truck. He drove slowly with his lights off until he cleared the school grounds. When he approached the intersection, he felt an urge to turn west, keep driving, and forget everything, but dismissed the idea as a hopeless gesture. Instead, he headed southeast on Highway 44 until he spotted a small wooden building on the right side of the road. The Nageezi Trading Post, sitting slightly back from the highway, looked desolate and deserted at this hour. There were no other vehicles in the back where he parked, with the nose of the truck facing the road so he could see the highway.

Abe rolled down the window and watched for approaching vehicles. While waiting, he drummed his fingers nervously on the dash, a composition from Erik Satie's *Gymnopédies* coursing through his brain. Sporadic traffic sped past on 44—oil rig trucks, tankers, Navajo families going to or from Farmington. It seemed a long wait, but ten minutes later he heard a motorcycle engine slowing down and saw the single headlight.

Will pulled alongside Abe with a big grin on his face. "The Spanish didn't name us Navajo for nothing. Guess I am a renegade, even if they meant it as an insult."

"So, it was easy?"

"Easy as finding a cop at a donut shop," Will joked. "But we need to get moving before they notice the bolt's cut. Guess Emily is going to catch hell for this one, too, soon as someone realizes my bike is missing."

"Yeah, I guess she will." Guilt gnawed at Abe's conscience. "We better get back on the highway."

"We'll only be there a little while. We're sticking to the back roads. There's a dirt road three miles from here that cuts south. It goes past Chaco Canyon and Crownpoint and ends up in Thoreau. They're less likely to look for us out there. It's kind of rough after the rains, but there's no traffic—and it's still Indian country."

Though Abe had bought in to the idea of finding Corazón and somehow proving his own innocence, he still was not convinced they were going about this in the right way. The plan seemed nefarious at best. "Will, do you have any idea of the consequences? We could both end up in prison, you know."

"Yeah, I know. I gave it a lot of thought when I sat in the sweat lodge. I know what I'm doing, Abe, but do you? You can back out if you want. This is personal for me."

Abe had been doing nothing but thinking while waiting for Will—weighing the pros and cons of continuing on this crazy quest for a killer. It seemed like a shot in the dark, but now that Sharon was gone, he didn't feel he had much more to lose. And the truth was, since meeting Emily and Will, he'd begun to feel more alive than he had in a long time. "No, I've made up my mind to see this through. When I leave I don't want Emily thinking I'm a murderer." He turned on the ignition. "Let's go. You lead the way."

The dark, moonless sky hung above Abe like an inverted colander, filled with stars. Even from the confines of his truck, he could identify the constellations: Pegasus, Draco, and, of course, Ursa Major and Minor. It was easy to see how the ancient people of Chaco Canyon relied on the heavens to help guide their way, both temporally and spiritually. He wished he could stop in this strangely haunted landscape and simply lie under those stars, but Will gave no sign of slowing down. They passed a sign that read "Entrance to Chaco Culture National Historic Park," and he recalled that this had been his destination before everything came crashing down.

Beyond Chaco the road became a washboard, and Abe struggled to keep up with Will's motorcycle as he wove his truck around the worst potholes. Occasionally Will would turn onto some side road invisible to Abe, as though the Navajo were guided by intuition or mere whim. Once on Interstate 40, Will veered off on another state road that led through the curious village of Pie Town near the entrance to the Gila National Forest. Will flashed the lights on the motorcycle, then pulled to a stop on the side of the road, with Abe following suit right behind him. The two men stepped down from their vehicles and stretched.

"What's up?" Abe said.

Will muffled a yawn. "Might as well get some rest. We'll find a place to sleep up ahead in the Gila and head on to Bisbee tomorrow."

"Damn good idea." Abe massaged the stiffness in his shoulders. "I've had enough for one night. How much farther?"

"About twenty miles more. We're gonna stay on this road till we hit Highway 12, then we'll cut into the Gila."

At two o'clock on a chilly morning, the two men pulled into an out-of-the-way spot and spread their bedrolls on the ground. Abe dropped off immediately into a dreamless sleep, only to awaken in what seemed like minutes to a bright morning sun. He stirred, feeling more aches in his back, and saw Will rustling through the box of provisions.

"Better eat something." He filled his canteen from the jerry-can in the truck and grabbed some sardines and crackers.

Abe rubbed his eyes and looked out on a dark-green world of tall Ponderosa pines, spruce, and fir. He stretched, stood up slowly, and found a tree to relieve his bladder on, then started to wash his face from the jerry-can.

Will stopped him short. "Water's for drinking. Don't waste it."

Abe turned off the spigot but used his wet hands to rub his face and wet his hair, then looked around. Two mountain ranges hugged them on either side. "Looks like we're a long ways from any desert."

"Those hills over there in the west are the Gallos, and the Mangas Range is on the east—Apache land." Will scooped up a pile of sardines with a cracker and shoveled it into his mouth. "Old Chief Mangas Coloradas was the greatest leader the Apaches ever had." He took another bite and chewed slowly before continuing. "The white men offered Mangas a treaty and he surrendered. But when the soldiers had him in custody they threw him in a makeshift cell, tortured him with red-hot bayonet points, then shot him— murdered him in cold blood. Bastards chopped off his head and boiled it so they could take back the skull." He took a long drink of water from a tin cup. "Looks can be deceiving, Abe. There's dry land ahead." Will shoved his canteen into his saddle bag and put his hat on. "Eat up. We need to get moving."

Sardines and crackers for breakfast—nothing novel to Abe, another version of lox and bagels. But Will's story of Chief Mangas left a bitterness in his mouth he couldn't wash down. He poured some food out for Patch, and a little water, then rolled up his sleeping bag and put it in the camper. He had come to see Will as a man of few words, usually quiet and circumspect. He didn't talk unless he had something to say, and that didn't bother Abe. He had grown accustomed to his own counsel as well. "I'm ready when you are."

After an hour of mountain driving, they dropped down into the semiarid lowlands of gambel oak, juniper, and cactus. Then, in the early afternoon they crossed the New Mexico/Arizona border, veered southwest, and met the desert in Douglas, Arizona, a stone's throw from the Mexican border. Bisbee was only twenty miles away.

Outside of Douglas, Abe followed Will into a truck stop where they discussed their next move over greasy hamburgers.

"There's a bar in Bisbee where we can start." Will lowered his voice, looked around to see if anyone might be listening. "It's called Dick's," he mumbled. "You go in and ask some questions."

Abe gave him a quizzical look. "You've been there before?"

"Yeah, I'd come down here now and then. I have a few friends out this way."

"Why don't you go in?"

"Don't want to go into a bar right now, okay," he said, a stubborn edge to his voice. He picked up some catsup-drenched French fries and popped them into his mouth.

Abe finished his hamburger and wiped his fingers with a napkin. "So, what kind of place is this, Will? A beer joint where motorcycle gangs hang out? I'm supposed to walk in there and say, 'Hey, any of you guys ever hear of a skinhead called Easy Jackson, alias Spiderman, who belongs to a motorcycle gang called Aryan Brotherhood'?" He threw his napkin down on his plate. "They're going to take one look at me, by the way, a Jew boy from New Jersey, and beat the shit out of me."

"I didn't know you were a Jew boy. Well, for a Jew boy you sure got Jesus Eyes."

Abe cringed at the reference. This was the second time someone in New Mexico had made that comment about his blue eyes. It didn't make any sense. "For Christ's sake, Will. I always thought Jesus was a dark-eyed Jew from the desert."

"Maybe he was before the Anglos got hold of him." Will smirked. "Doesn't matter anyway. It's not a biker bar I'm talking about." He twisted in his seat to peer out at the trucks speeding down Highway 80, dawdled with his coffee cup, and stared at his hands before meeting Abe's eyes. "It's a gay bar, and if anyone has information relating to some skinhead bikers in town, they will. It's like the old saying, Abe. Know your enemy. Know where they hang out, and keep your distance."

81

12

Tombstone Canyon shouldered both sides of Bisbee's narrow main street. The town, despite its picturesque facade, looked tired in the afternoon sun. Only six tourists walked the sidewalks, lined on both sides with art galleries, coffee bars, and souvenir shops. The once-bustling copper-mining town rode the boom-and-bust roller coaster of the mining industry until the bust became permanent. Instead of the town dying, the diehards stuck around and set up shop. Hippies, artists, and a flourishing gay community settled in. Bisbee was reborn as an arts colony and retirement center for those looking to recapture the nostalgia of the Old West, or perhaps escape their humdrum pasts. Situated in the mile-high Mule Mountains, Bisbee maintained a certain kitschy charm, but seemed an unlikely spot to find a white-supremacy-motorcycle-gang member or the Mexican Mafia.

Abe looked beyond the claustrophobic street, captivated by the sight of curtains of rain falling like bridal veils over the western slopes. They seemed to have a life of their own, moving at will, leaving contrasting shades of hazy darkness and bright amber light. He snapped back to attention when he was suddenly confronted by an imposing limestone formation that appeared smack-dab in the middle of the road. In reality, the main street veered sharply around the obstruction, causing Abe to almost miss Will as the motorcycle slid onto a crooked little side street.

Dick's Hot Licks Café and Bar sat at the lower end of the street, wedged between a tattoo parlor and an adult bookstore. Abe didn't think he could get much information on his own since he was a stranger in town. He tried reasoning with Will that his old friend would be more likely to open up if he knew the person he was talking to. After some discussion Will agreed to accompany Abe into the bar. They found a parking place and Abe left the truck windows partially open. The street lay in shadow, and the waning afternoon air carried the scent of rain and a cool breeze from the mountain storms. Abe gave Patch a conciliatory pat on the head. "Be back soon, boy, then I'll let you out." He locked the truck's door, then met up with Will on the wooden sidewalk.

As soon as he pushed open the heavy door, Abe felt a rush of cool air mixed with the aroma of cigarette smoke and stale beer. He glanced at Will, saw him close his eyes and take a deep breath as the two men entered a dimly lit rectangular room. Windows to the right of the door provided light for diners who sat at scattered tables. The windowless left side contained a long bar, a jukebox, and billiard lounge. One man racked balls at a green felt pool table, while another leaned on a cue, smoking and waiting his turn.

As his eyes adjusted to the semidarkness, Abe noticed the long, curved bar in the back of the room. Back mirrors reflected sparkling, jewel-like bottles of liquor. He heard the clink of glasses, the murmur of voices, and saw the black leather and red velvet–padded bar lined with stools, and on every stool sat a male patron. Conversation lulled as the men swiveled to check out the newcomers.

"Let's get this over with." Abe headed for the bar, but Will grabbed his elbow and directed him toward a small table in the corner of the dining section.

"Over here, out of the way." Will pulled out a chair and sat down at the table. He seemed to be studying the customers, as if he feared he might see a familiar face.

Abe slid into the other chair. A strapping, pumped-up man in a muscle shirt and tight jeans appeared at their side. His bleached-blond hair stood at attention in pointy spikes, and an array of earrings encircled each ear. The waiter beamed a toothsome smile at the pair.

"Hi. My name's Dutch. What can I do for you boys?"

Will licked his lips. "Club soda, no ice."

"Club soda," the waiter said, with a wink. The smile became teasing when he turned his attention to Abe. "And for you, baby-blue eyes?"

Abe wanted a beer, or something stronger, to quell his thirst and nerves, but thought of Will and said, "I'll take the same, lots of ice."

"You want some food to go with those drinks?" Dutch stood poised with pencil in hand, batting his eyelashes.

Abe looked around the room. Black-and-white photos of athletic young men in various stages of near nudity were backlit against the walls. Will and Abe were still being appraised by the patrons, some of whom sat at tables decorated in the same red-and-black color scheme, their heads close together. "No thanks," he said.

"How about you, big guy?" the waiter addressed Will.

Will shook his head. "Does Paco still work in the kitchen?"

"Sure does. Makes the best *chiles rellenos* in town. Simply divine, with all that melted cheese oozing out. Shall I order a plate for you?"

"No. Tell him Will Etcitty wants to talk to him."

"Righto." He turned to go but, before he reached the bar, he looked back at Abe and Will. "I can add a cherry, make those Shirley Temples for you."

"Bring the sodas and cut the crap." Abe felt the heat rising in his face and wanted to get out of there as quickly as possible. Dutch's harmless blather reminded him of childhood taunts he had endured as a youngster. He had been a target because he would rather play the piano than sports, because he was undersized as a kid, and because he abhorred violence. *Jew boy, Jew boy. Sissy, faggot, Jew boy.* Though not homophobic himself, he had remained single for a long time, and he knew many people assumed he was gay—an assumption he resented.

Dutch brought their drinks without any further fanfare and disappeared behind two swinging doors in the back. Shortly afterward a ponytailed, short, stocky man with Hispanic features emerged from the kitchen. He wiped his hands on a salsa-stained white apron, then burst into a wide grin when he saw Will.

"Guillermo. Where you been so long, *compadre?*"

"Hey, Paco. Long time no see, huh. How's it goin', buddy?" Will stood up and the two men embraced.

"*Bueno, bueno.* But what's that you're drinking? Hey, Dutch, bring a bottle of tequila over here to my friend. The best." After giving Will a second appraisal he added, "You don't look so good, *amigo.*"

"No booze, Paco." Will shrugged and took a deep breath. "I'm on the wagon," he said, looking ready to change his mind. "Can't drink," he added with a little more conviction. "I need to ask you a few questions, that's all."

"Okay, *compadre*, if you say so." Paco waved the tequila off when Dutch brought the sodas, then gave Abe the once-over. "I see you have a new buddy."

"It's not like that," Will said. "This is Abe Freeman, a friend of my sister's. We're working on something and we need your help."

Abe shook hands with Paco. "How you doing, man?"

"I'm doing great. *Oye*, did you know I bought this place, Will? Yeah, Dick finally retired and sold it to me, but I kept the name. Keeps the customers coming, if you know what I mean." Paco yelled to Dutch who stood behind the bar mixing drinks. "I'm taking a break. Give your orders to Manny." He pulled a chair over to the table and sat down. "What do you need?"

"The place looks good, Paco. I'm glad for you," Will said. Then, "We're looking for someone."

"Yeah. This someone got a name?"

Abe took a long drink before he spoke. At least it was cold. "We don't have a name—we think he's a white guy, skinhead, probably belongs to a motorcycle gang." He downed his club soda in one more gulp. "Something else—he might have a tattoo on his arm, a spiderweb around the elbow."

"Somebody like that—you know he wouldn't be hanging out here," Paco said. "I think I've seen his type riding through town, though."

"It's important we find this guy, Paco," Will cut in. "According to our source, he lives somewhere around Bisbee."

"Why didn't you ask your source the guy's name?"

"Because our source is dead," Abe said.

Paco's expression turned serious. "Hold on for a minute." Then, the proud new owner of Dick's Hot Licks left the table and disappeared into the kitchen.

Abe squirmed in his seat, saw Will breaking out in a sweat, licking his lips, and he knew they needed to get out of the bar, get moving somewhere. He didn't feel comfortable himself, especially when a big cowboy, complete with rhinestone-studded cuff links and alligator boots, sauntered over to their table and doffed his Stetson.

"You fellers looking for company?" he drawled.

"No. We want to be left alone," Abe snapped in answer.

"So, that's the way it is." The cowboy looked from Abe to Will and winked. "Well, I'll leave you two lovebirds alone then."

"Get the hell out of here," Abe growled, feeling the heat again. Luckily Paco emerged from the kitchen to rejoin them, and the cowboy ambled off to commiserate with a group in the bar who had been watching the whole scene.

"Manny thinks he knows where that *gringo* might live. Says he's heard of a guy matching the description out by Tintown. Manny's still got family there. They've seen a bunch of them riding through town wearing their dumb-ass jackets with swastikas and shit."

Will sat up straight, paying attention. "Tintown. Isn't that a little south of Bisbee?"

"Right. Go past the Lavender Pit. Take 92 at the junction and you'll run into Tintown. But that's all I know, Will." He looked from one man to the other. "It can be rough out there. Those people don't trust strangers."

Abe looked thoughtful. "Maybe we should call Emily."

"No," Will said. "We don't want the cops."

"They're going to be looking for us anyway. Probably already noticed the missing motorcycle and figured out where we're headed."

Paco furrowed his brow, but didn't ask whatever question he might have had. He rubbed his chin and looked at Will. "What are you driving?"

"I brought the old Chief, and Abe has a Toyota truck. When we find out what we need, Abe is heading to California." After a moment he added, "It's possible Emily might have called them in missing, or she will soon."

"Bring your rides around back. I'll put the motorcycle in the shed, and we'll change the plates on the truck." Paco scratched his nose, then shrugged. "Guess you two know what you're doing."

13

A person might easily miss Tintown. A faded wooden sign a few miles south of the Lavender Pit, a gaping hole in the hard rock landscape left behind by Phelps Dodge Mining, directed them down an unpaved road. It became immediately apparent how the town had earned its name—all the roofs and side walls of buildings were made of corrugated tin. Ramshackle houses, some deserted, a few with trucks or cars parked in dusty front yards, lined the street. The unpaved main street showed little indication of life, and most of the buildings were boarded up or falling down. A bakery with a faded sign, "*Panaderia*," sat next to what must have once been a church. In its place the statue of some unknown saint welcomed visitors to a homeless shelter. But judging from the sounds of barking dogs and the sight of clothes whipping on lines, some folks still lived in Tintown. The few people Abe saw appeared to be of Mexican descent. A young boy followed them with hooded eyes as they slowly cruised the main street.

Abe made a couple of loops through the neighborhoods looking for something that might give them a clue as to where they were going—a motorcycle, maybe. On his second go-around he and Will noticed the same small, dark boy he had seen earlier, peeking at them from behind a rusted Chevy truck.

"Stop over there in front of that store. Let's see if the kid knows anything."

Abe pulled up alongside the battered building, aware of curious and unfriendly stares from a few housefronts. He stepped out of the truck and walked toward the boy. "Hi there, buddy."

The boy looked at him, eyes wide, but didn't respond to Abe's greeting. He appeared ready to run.

"Wait. I just want to ask you a few questions."

The boy backed away, and Will jumped down. So did Patch, who hopped over to the youngster, his tail wagging. A shy grin spread over the kid's face as he reached out his hand and Patch began licking it. He drew it back with a jerk when the big Navajo approached, but relaxed when Will broke into Spanish as if he had been speaking it all his life. Abe watched from the sidelines as the two engaged in an animated conversation, punctuated by occasional giggles from the boy. The kid pointed toward the west, and Abe saw his face change from friendly to somber. Will reached into his pocket and drew a dollar bill from his wallet, and the youngster's eyes lit up again. Then the kid approached Abe with a smug smile, hand outstretched, and Abe dug into his wallet, wishing he didn't feel like the newly arrived on an alien planet.

"I had the impression at your place that you didn't much care for Mexicans," Abe said when they returned to the truck. "Now I hear you speaking Spanish like it's your mother tongue."

"Never said I didn't like Mexicans. I hate Corazón and his type. That's all."

Abe digested this. He figured he still had a lot to learn about Will Etcitty. "What did you find out?"

"Two miles south of town there's a cemetery, and right past it on the right is a dirt road. The road winds around the hills for a couple miles, then ends up at an old abandoned turquoise mine and shack. Some kids from Tintown snuck out there one night and saw a bunch of guys with motorcycles hanging around a fire drinking beer. The party got pretty wild and some bikers noticed the kids. They started chasing them and firing guns, scared the little shits to death. Anyway, I think maybe our man lives out there."

Driving to the shack in broad daylight sounded like a bad idea to both men, and they still didn't have a plan. "Let's wait till dark, sneak up on the place, and check it out. We'll find out how many are out there. What do you think, Will?"

"Now you're starting to sound like a Navajo—sneaky. I like it. Drive back to Bisbee. We can discuss it some more over Paco's *chiles rellenos*. I'm hungry."

14

Later that night, clouds erased any light from the moon or stars. The old graveyard, marked with a jumble of wooden crosses, hid behind an overgrowth of cactus and weeds.

Abe drove past it twice before Will finally spotted a marker and told him to slow down. When they reached the road to the mine, Abe parked the truck behind a shelf of protruding rock formations. Before getting out he told Patch to stay put and rolled the windows down a couple of inches. They were going to walk the rest of the way and couldn't take a chance on the dog barking and alerting whoever might be in the shack.

The moon, when it peeked through, was a mere slice. Abe stumbled on something hard and thought ruefully of his flashlight, useless to him with its cache of marijuana instead of batteries. Will had stuck his grandfather's cumbersome pistol in the back of his pants, but Abe rejected the idea of taking the shotgun.

"You might need it." Will kept his voice low. "Self-defense."

"I won't need it."

They had decided to do nothing that night but watch the place, figure out who and how many occupied the building. If it became apparent Jackson's buddy was alone, they'd approach him to see if he would talk. Beyond that, they had no plan.

"I'll show him the gun," Will offered, "if the guy gets belligerent."

"Do you think Emily is on our tail yet?" Abe whispered, after several minutes of silence broken only by the soft thud of their shoes on desert sand.

"Yeah, Sis is tracking us like a bloodhound. She's part coyote, part eagle, you know." Will paused and smiled, as if remembering something about his sister, before he continued. "But she's mostly a woman looking for Mr. Right. Hey, I think she likes you, though I can't say why." He chuckled quietly. "You ought to hook up with her after we settle the score with Corazón. Doesn't matter to me that you're a white guy. She hasn't had much luck with red men in the past."

Will's words caused mixed emotions in Abe—pleasure, guilt, embarrassment. He didn't know how to respond, so he laughed. "Why would you say a thing like that? Are you nuts?" Before Will could answer, Abe continued, "She sure as hell doesn't like me now. When she finds us, we're both going to jail."

Will started to say something, but stopped short and held his hand up for Abe to do the same. "Shhh. I think I hear something."

Abe listened, and heard it, too. "It's a car engine. Quick, get off the road." He ran to the side and fell flat on his stomach, with Will diving right behind him. Cactus thorns pricked his hands and legs, gouged his arms, but he stayed frozen in place. A vehicle's headlights shone briefly, then disappeared before reappearing at the top of a rise.

"Keep your head down," Will warned.

The vehicle came from the direction they were headed and, judging from the rumble of the engine and distance between headlights, it was a big car, so low to the ground it occasionally scraped bottom. Abe hugged the earth as the vehicle neared them, but glanced up when it passed. Kansas plates glowed in the taillights. He felt a sense of déjà vu, positive the car, a black Buick, was the same one he had seen in Clayton, New Mexico.

The two men stayed where they were until they could no longer see or hear the vehicle. When it seemed safely down the road, Abe stood up and brushed at his hands, trying to dislodge cactus spines embedded in his palms. He wanted to explain the Buick's significance, but decided to do it later when they could speak freely.

Will lifted an index finger to his mouth, cautioning Abe to keep quiet. They moved ahead, walking toward the house. "Either he had company, or he's leaving home," Will whispered. "Let's find out."

A parting of clouds provided enough illumination from the silver sliver of moon to allow a quick glimpse of a wooden structure built onto the side of a cliff. Light, fluttering as if from a kerosene lantern, flickered through a broken window, but no sounds emanated from the building, and except for a far-off coyote call, a pervasive quiet engulfed the scene.

Spooky, Abe thought. He surveyed as much of the surroundings as he could in the obscure darkness and felt a chill run up his spine, and the hair on the back of his neck prickle.

Will, silent as a ghost, approached a window to get a better look inside while Abe lingered behind. When Will reached the window, a sudden explosion rocked the structure, bursting it into flames and sending debris flying.

Abe called out, "Will, get back," then dove for the ground, his head crashing onto a boulder. *So this is what they mean by seeing stars*, he thought briefly as the pain nearly blinded him. He buried his head under his arms while pieces of burning wood flew around him. One landed on his leg, and he quickly rolled over, kicking it away. He shouted Will's name again, but received no answer. Then, in the glow of fire, he saw the big Navajo lying ten feet from the burning building and ran to him. "Oh shit."

Will wasn't moving and appeared unconscious. He lay on his stomach, head to the side, his hair and clothing smoldering. Abe took off his shirt and beat the still-glowing embers. Then he knelt down and put his face close to Will's nose. The Navajo man groaned, and Abe detected a faint breath. He appeared badly burned, and Abe didn't know the extent of any other wounds, but he had to move him to a safer place. The shack had turned into a raging inferno. If there had been anyone inside, that person could not have survived.

"Sorry, buddy," Abe said as he carefully removed Will's gun and rolled the man onto his back. He shuddered when he saw his burned flesh, but grasped him under the armpits and dragged him to a clearing another twenty feet from the flames. "Goddamn it, Will. Why did I listen to you? We should never have come out here, you son of a bitch." Abe gently positioned the wounded man's body on the soft sand, then covered him as best he could with his flannel shirt.

After he did what he could to make Will comfortable, he stuck the bulky gun into his pants and took off running in the direction of the truck. Along the way he tripped over a boulder and fell, bashing his head once more. Blood ran down his face from the open wound. He wiped the blood from his eyes, disoriented, not sure where to go or why, then remembered Will and pulled himself to his feet. Running blindly ahead, he didn't know if he was going toward or away from his truck. Then he heard Patch, and followed the sound of the dog's barks.

Once he reached the Toyota, he debated whether to drive into Tintown and call for help, or go back for Will and take him to the hospital. He started the engine, and decided he could not lift his friend into the vehicle without doing more harm. Abe spun the truck around, the wheels throwing sand and gravel, shifted into third, and bounced down the potholed road, hell-bent for Tintown.

As soon as he arrived at the outskirts of the village, he started looking for anyone, at least a building with a light on. He didn't have to go far. Word of a fire at the old miner's shack had spread through the community, and a throng of people stood in front of the abandoned slaughterhouse, staring at the orange glow lighting up the southwestern horizon.

Abe pulled to a stop in front of the crowd, put the truck in neutral, and jumped out. "I need help," he shouted. "My friend's hurt. Call an ambulance!"

Suspicious and uncomprehending gazes turned in his direction.

Oblivious of how he must look, drenched in blood, Abe pleaded: "Somebody, listen, please. My friend needs help. Don't you understand?"

A barrage of incomprehensible Spanish met his appeal for assistance.

"Telephone," Abe said, making the sign of a phone to his ear. "Isn't there a phone in this town?" He had never learned Spanish, but now tried desperately to remember any word that might help him get his point across. Then, he spotted the boy they had spoken to earlier that afternoon. The kid emerged from the crowd and approached him. A teenage girl, perhaps an older sister, rushed forward to join him.

"The fire department is on its way. As soon as we saw the flames, my father called them. The firemen are coming from Bisbee. They'll be here soon."

The high shrill of a siren drowned out her voice. Then, a man who might have been the father of the two children approached. "You're hurt, mister. Paramedics are coming, too. They'll take care of you."

Abe had forgotten the cut on his head. "Not for me. My friend. You have to find him. Someone else . . . in the shack . . . the Buick." He could no longer form the words he wanted to say. Abe felt his head spinning just before his knees buckled. He had to lie down, at least for a minute. Abe shook his head and fought to keep from losing consciousness. "Find Will," he said, then, in a final burst of resolve, he reached into his pocket and pulled out Emily's card. "Call this number . . . tell her . . . sorry." Before he could say more, Abe slipped into darkness.

15

His head pounded in perfect sync with the rhythmic beep-beep-beep emanating from something nearby. He opened his eyes to a washed-blue wall, and then to the matching eyes of a skinny gray-haired woman standing over him. He realized he was in bed, and lifted a hand to his throbbing head.

"Where am I?" He tried to focus on her Winnie the Pooh scrubs. "What happened?"

The woman hung a plastic drip bag on a stand and checked the tube connected by a needle to his wrist. "Copper Queen Hospital. You have a concussion and lost a lot of blood, plus you're dehydrated." She whipped out a thermometer and stuck it under his tongue while she gripped his free wrist with a sun-spotted hand. "I'm the day nurse. Sally's my name. Don't move, now."

Abe cringed as a sharp pain shot across his forehead and through his eyes. He reached for the bandages that encircled his head. Fragments drifted through his mind—running; flames everywhere; someone on the ground; Will; Patch barking. He pulled the thermometer out of his mouth and tried to sit up, but the surprisingly strong hands pushed him back while another lightning bolt cracked across his skull.

SANDRA BOLTON

"I said, be still. Now we're gonna have to do this all over again."
The nurse gave him a scolding look and put the thermometer back
under his tongue.

"What happened to my friend? And my dog? Where's my dog?"

Sally furrowed her wrinkled brow and pursed her lips into a
thin line. "I don't know nothing about a dog, but if your friend is
that big ole Indian, he's down in intensive care. Burned up pretty
bad." She finished her ministrations and jotted a few notes on a
clipboard hanging at the end of the bed. "Your vitals look good. Got
a doozy of a knot on your head, and that cut had to be stitched up.
Lost some blood, like I said, a few first-degree burns on your hands,
nothing too serious." She handed him a small cup with three pills of
different colors, and a glass of water. "Swallow these down—pain-
killer, antibiotic, and something to help you rest. You've been out
for a whole day, and there's a lady out there that seems real anxious
to talk to you, but I told her no visitors yet." The nurse moved as if
to leave, then turned back. "What were you boys doing out there,
anyway?" Shaking her head, she slipped out the door.

What were we doing out there? He realized it had to be Emily
who wanted to see him. What could he possibly tell her? Abe tried
to sit up again, but felt weak and dizzy. He slumped back on the
pillow, a shitload of worries on his mind. But even in his anguished
state, he succumbed to the sleeping pill.

In the dream, fire-throwing demons with shaved heads and tattooed arms covered with festering pustules chased him through a
maze of cacti. Each time he chose an escape route, another identical
group confronted him. He could hear Patch barking, but when he
tried to call him, no sounds came from his mouth. He awoke and
opened his eyes in a state of panic, to find a very non-dreamlike Emily
staring at him, her own eyes squeezed into narrow slits of rage.

"Why?" Her voice was as cold and sharp as a frozen yucca point.
"As soon as they dismiss you, Freeman, I'm arresting you for theft

98

of an impounded motorcycle, criminal endangerment, illegal flight, and that's only the beginning," she hissed while extracting a pair of handcuffs. "My brother almost died because of you. He's scarred for life, crippled," she said, her voice breaking. "I don't know what's stopping me from shooting you right now."

"Wait, Emily, let me . . ."

"Shut up. Your free days are over, asshole, so don't try to talk your way out of this one." Showing no sign of her former professionalism, she stood stiffly in front of him in blue jeans and a plaid shirt, tousled hair hanging in messy strands, eyes piercing him like poison darts. Without another word, Emily Etcitty clasped a handcuff around his free wrist and one to the bed frame, spun around, and left before he could say a single thing in his defense. He heard her voice in the hall, arguing with the nurse.

"I don't give a damn if he dies. He's my prisoner and I'm staying right here until he's discharged. Then he's going with me, handcuffed and shackled if necessary."

The nurse's voice barked back in outrage. "Nobody leaves this hospital without the doctor's clearance, and don't you go in there pestering that patient, young lady. There's a no-visitors rule in place. You don't look like the law to me, anyhow. Now get on out of here before I call the sheriff and have you arrested."

"I'm an officer with the Navajo Nation Police, and if you need some ID, I have it right here. I cuffed the prisoner because he's a flight risk. He ran away once before. Go ahead and call your sheriff," Emily shot back.

"You what? Now you listen here. This is a hospital. You can't go around handcuffing patients, and I do believe you are out of your jurisdiction. Ain't no Navajo Police station around these parts."

As the voices faded, Abe closed his eyes and tried to piece together the events that led to his present situation. Remnants of his dream and the sound of Patch's howling kept coming back, but gradually his thoughts coalesced into a semicoherent memory. He heard the explosion and saw the fire, saw Will's body, blackened, unmoving. He had tried to save Will . . . run for help. *Oh, Christ. Is Will going to die? Where is Patch? What happened to my dog?* Abe had to find out. He tried to get out of bed, but felt the pull of the cuffs and fell back. *Emily. If I can get through to her and explain things, I might have some answers.*

Abe maneuvered the IV tube and managed to reach the call button with his free hand. He pushed, waited a few minutes, pushed it again, and again—finally he held it down.

After what seemed like forever, Sally flew in like a hot desert wind. "What's so God-almighty important? I've got my hands full with that feisty little Indian gal, who'd just as soon string you up as look at you." She craned her turkey neck over the bed and caught sight of Abe's cuffed wrist. "Holy shit. She did cuff you. I don't know what kind of trouble you boys got yourself into, but if this don't beat all."

Abe fastened his eyes on the nurse's limpid, watery orbs. The elderly woman appeared an unlikely ally—weathered, wrinkled, wiry, years past retirement age, standing over him in her childish smock and baggy green pants. "I'll explain it, Sally, if you'll help me. Can you get these handcuffs off first?"

"Now why should I trust you? That girl said you stole a motorcycle and almost killed her brother." But he saw her eyes soften and thought she didn't believe it. Sally stiffened, as if she knew he could read her, and added in a gruff voice, "Sheriff wants to ask you some questions, but I told him, no visitors for twenty-four hours. He'll be back tomorrow, and you better have some ready answers. Tch-tch-tch," she scolded. "Don't be pushing that button while I'm gone. I have some bolt cutters out in my car trunk."

When he gave her a questioning look, she quickly explained, "Those durn combination locks on the hospital lockers are always jamming. Somebody has to be prepared around here."

"Is Will going to die?" he asked before she left the room.

Sally gave him a look of encouragement. "Is he that girl's brother? No, he's not going to die. We'll patch him up and he'll be almost good as new. Well, maybe not as pretty." She left only to return a few minutes later, lugging a heavy-duty bolt cutter. After several unsuccessful attempts to cut through the cuff attached to the bed frame, Sally said, "God durn, must be some special kind of steel. I'm going to cut the chain and you will have to wear a bracelet till that gal comes to her senses." Sally grasped the bolt cutter with two hands and squeezed until the links snapped. "Whew. That was a tough one."

"Thanks, Sally," Abe said, shaking his free hand. He rubbed his wrist. Do you know where Emily went?"

"If you mean that Indian gal, she's with her brother. She's mighty spunky, but I could tell she's real broke up. Well, I'm off duty now, so where's that story you promised?"

16

You mean to tell me that car out by the burn site was the very same one you saw in Clayton, New Mexico?" Sally had been listening for the past hour, interrupting with an occasional shake of her head, or a "well, I'll be damned." "Jesus Christ in a miniskirt," she blurted when he told her about the time Rico Corazón and his biker gang raised hell at the trading post and knocked Will's grandmother down, causing her untimely death. "Well, no wonder he set out to find him. What kind of rattlesnake would shove a helpless old woman down?"

Abe, tired from talking, closed his eyes and changed the subject. "I really need your help with Emily, Sally. I have to explain things to her. She's a good person and she trusted me. I let her down." When he reopened his eyes, he stared earnestly into hers. "I have a dog. I left him in my truck that night, the night of the explosion." He closed his eyes again, his head aching from the cut. "Patch might still be there. I left the windows cracked, but he'd be hot and thirsty, wondering where I am." Abe felt a wave of guilt as he pictured Patch waiting for him, no water or food in the cab of the truck.

"Looks like you're worn out and the duty nurse will be along any minute with your meds." Sally sighed heavily. "Oh, lordy, I'll see what I can find out." She stood up, shaking her head and mumbling, "Blown-up building, burned-up Indian, another one mad as hell, lost dog, and a dead man to boot."

"A dead man?"

"Yep. You didn't know? They found what was left of him inside that shack that burned down. Sheriff's gonna be here soon to ask you what you know about that." Sally started to say more but stopped when a portly nurse carrying a tray of pills entered the room.

"You still here, Sally? It's two hours after your quitting time. Boy if I had known you wanted to keep working, I would have come in late."

While the women chatted, Abe closed his eyes, pondering Sally's news that a body had been found in the mine shack. *The dead man must be Easy Jackson's biker friend,* he reasoned. *It's all tied in with whoever was in the black Buick. What were they doing out there, and why would they kill Jackson's friend?* It made no sense to him in his present state of mind. He rubbed his throbbing forehead and opened his eyes to see Sally preparing to leave.

"I'm on my way out, Lulu. Take good care of this boy." She paused long enough to give him a conspiratorial wink. "So long, Abe. Get some rest now. We'll talk later."

After Abe awoke from another pill-induced nap, he felt rested enough to get up and go to the bathroom. The fog in his head cleared somewhat when he washed his face and brushed his teeth, even though the bandaged bum staring back at him from the bathroom mirror looked like a stranger. When he left the bathroom, he saw Emily sitting in the chair, studying him.

"I'm still mad at you. I want you to know that."

"I know. I'm sorry." Abe sat on the bed meeting her flat-eyed gaze. "How's Will?"

"He'll live, no thanks to you. But life won't ever be the same for him." Emily paused, looked at the blank wall. "He told me everything, why the two of you came to Bisbee, everything. And then that skinny old white nurse gave me a good talking to. But that doesn't get you off the hook. You're a screwup."

"Yeah, I sure am. I'll go back with you, Emily, but I want to find Patch, and I'd like to talk to Will first."

"You're too late to talk to Will. They flew him out to the burn center in Phoenix this morning."

He regretted not being able to see Will, but knew the move was for the best. "Those specialists can do great things these days, you know." He wanted to ask her more—what her brother's prognosis was, and specifically if she had gone to the truck and rescued Patch. "Uh, Emily . . ."

She had combed her hair and cleaned up since he last saw her. She looked beautiful but beaten down with worry. Her voice softened a little when she said, "Your dog's with me. I used a slim jim through the cracked window to work the lock. Patch is okay. I came out as soon as I heard the call, so he didn't have to stay in the truck too long."

Abe closed his eyes, relieved, and almost smiled as well. "I feel better already. Do you always carry a slim jim with you, and a pair of handcuffs?" Before she could answer, he added, "They'll probably release me tomorrow, then I'll go wherever you want, but could you take this cuff off my wrist? The other half is still attached to the bed."

She gave him a rueful look, but took a small key from her pocket and unlocked the handcuff.

"Thanks. Where's Patch now?"

"He's in my car, but we're not going back," she said straight-faced. "They took me off the case. I have no jurisdiction here, anyway."

"What do you mean?"

"I said I was going to Bisbee to find you and my brother. The boss said it wasn't my case anymore. We argued, and he put me on administrative leave, said Harrigan and the State Police were handling everything, and I was out. I said, 'fuck you,' and left."

Abe straightened up, surprised that she had walked out on her post and was going rogue. "What are you going to do now?"

"I'm going to find Corazón, and you're going to help me. I want the asshole that started the fire, too. So, get out of that cute little nightgown and into some clothes. My car's out front. I'll be waiting for you."

"You look tired. Don't you want to rest, leave fresh tomorrow? The sheriff is coming to talk to me today, and if I'm not here, it won't look good."

"Every day the trail gets colder." Emily appeared to be thinking it over, though. "Okay, Abe. We don't want the sheriff of Cochise County on our tail, but as soon as you and the law have a talk, get your ass out of here. We're leaving."

"Let's do it tomorrow morning. That way Sally can get the paperwork done, and we can leave without any suspicions."

"Sally?"

"The nurse."

"So you two are old buddies now. Maybe we should invite her along." She seemed peeved, but relented. "Oh, all right. No one is after me, or knows where I am except my boss, not even Mom and Grandpa. But the New Mexico Staters are going to find you pretty quick. I need to call the hospital in Phoenix to check on Will. I'm going to have to call my mom at some point, too, and let her know what happened." Emily started to say something, then changed her mind. Instead she concluded the conversation with a terse statement. "Patch and I will stay with Paco tonight, and your truck is in his garage. You won't need it. I'll be back first thing in the morning in my Bronco. You better be ready."

105

"I will be. Uh, Emily, how'd you start the truck without the keys?"

"Trade secret."

After Emily left, Abe lay back on his bed. It looked like he wouldn't get much rest before things started up again. Though consoled by the knowledge that Emily seemed to have forgiven him, Abe knew he was still considered a suspect in Jackson's death by the authorities in New Mexico. He held the fervent hope that by helping her find the killer, he would be able to establish his innocence once and for all.

The portly nurse, Lulu, brought in a tray of food, and he sat up, determined to eat it all. *Might need the energy*, he thought.

17

The sheriff didn't show, but late that evening one of his deputies dropped by to take Abe's statement. The meaty, red-faced lawman, sweaty and disheveled, slumped in the plastic chair beside the bed. He took a pencil and small notepad out of his front pocket and began with the standard questions, jotting down Abe's responses between yawns.

"What do you know concerning the feller living in the old miner's shack?"

"Nothing, except he might have been a member of a motorcycle gang, the Aryan Brotherhood. My friend Will and I were trying to locate an acquaintance. We thought this guy could tell us where to find him. But before we could talk to him, the place exploded."

"You a member of this 'Aryan Brotherhood'?"

"No. I'm Jewish as a matter of fact. I don't think they would want me."

"Uh-huh. You didn't know that was a meth lab, then?"

"No." The news surprised him, but it made sense and helped explain the intensity of the explosion. "Like I said, we were trying to track down someone. Neither of us knew the guy that lived there, or what he did."

"So you didn't even know the man you came to visit? Well, you must know the name of that mutual acquaintance, then?"

Abe hesitated, not sure he wanted to divulge Jackson's name. "Joe Jackson, but he liked to be called Easy, Easy Jackson." He didn't mention Rico Corazón. It would complicate things.

The deputy scribbled something on his pad, and waited for Abe to continue.

"Someone arrived before us. A car, dark-colored Buick or Lincoln, passed us on its way out."

The deputy paused in his note taking and perked up a little. "You see the driver?"

"No. The windows were tinted and it was night. I couldn't make out anyone."

"What about the license plate?"

Abe tried to picture numbers and letters on those tags but came up blank. "They were Kansas plates. That's all I could see. Whoever was in that car left the shack before we arrived."

"Well, as far as I'm concerned, good riddance to another damn meth-head. The person who blew that place up ought to get a medal. Maybe the idiot blew himself up." The deputy put his notebook and pen away and lumbered to his feet. "Sorry about your Indian friend, but it's been a long day and I'm ready for a beer. You sticking around in case we have some more questions?"

"Sure," Abe said, swallowing the lie.

The doctor came by later and performed a cursory checkup. He told Abe everything looked good, but he should stay a couple of more days for observation. When Sally came on duty that night, Abe sat up in the bed and told her Emily would pick him up at seven in the morning.

"Where are my clothes and wallet?"

"They're right here in this closet, but where do you think you're going?"

"I can't say for sure. We have to find Rico Corazón and whoever was in the black Buick."

Sally looked at him as if he were a headstrong, foolish child. "Well, you need some kind of a plan, don't you?"

"Right now my only plan is to get out of here. Can you help me or not?"

"Any adult who's in his right mind can discharge himself from the hospital, Abe. You don't need me for that, but I'm not sure you are in your right mind." You could almost see the wheels turning in Sally's head as she narrowed her eyes in apparent concentration. "I'm getting an idea how I might be able to help you two." Then she broke into a devilish grin. "I haven't had this much excitement since I put superglue in my cheatin' ex's Grecian Formula hair dye."

Abe gave her an incredulous look. "This is no joking matter, Sally. I don't see how you could help. Anyway, you shouldn't get involved."

"Oh, hush up. You two are coming to my house in the morning. I'll tell you my idea then. Now get your rest. I'm going to make sure you have the meds you need when you leave here—just in case, you know."

"Sally, you sound like you've done this sort of thing before," Abe said, after swallowing his assigned pills and lying back on the bed.

"Sonny, you'd be surprised what I've done."

That night Abe's dreams were filled with high-speed chases in endless circles. At times he played the pursuer; alternately he was being chased. All the while Sharon looked on with a bemused smile. *"You really did it this time, didn't you, baby?"*

The rising sun was peeking through an array of wispy pink and orange cirrus clouds when Emily pulled to a stop in front of the hospital and rolled the window down. "We don't have time for this, Abe," she said when she saw Sally standing beside him. "Get in. Let's go." Patch sat in the backseat, wagging his hindquarters and whining with joy at seeing his owner.

Sally came up to the open window and bent her wiry body down to look Emily in the eye. "You better take time young lady, because I have something you don't have. Why, hell, you don't even know where you're going in such a hurry."

"Oh, right. And what do you have that we don't?"

Sally crossed her arms over her flat chest. "An idea."

Abe, busy reuniting with Patch, broke into the conversation. "Let's hear her out, Emily. What do we have to lose?"

"Time, that's what." But curiosity got the best of the police-woman, and she shrugged her shoulders. "What the hell. Get in, both of you."

"No. Got my own wheels," said Sally. "You follow me and Lizzie." And she strode off to a faded purple Volkswagen that looked nearly as old as her.

Emily tailed Lizzie for three miles, then ate her dust as they rumbled down yet another dirt road.

"How much have you told her, Abe? More to the point, why have you told her anything?"

"I told her everything. I needed to talk. She helped me, and I felt she could be trusted."

Bitterness tinged her response. "Well, I thought you could be trusted. First impressions can be wrong. I should have learned that by now."

"Look, I said I'm sorry. Will and I thought we were doing the right thing."

The road, and the conversation, ended in front of a tidy adobe house, resplendent in bright turquoise paint. The surrounding land looked desolate but strikingly beautiful. Purple-edged mountains fringed a desert plot accented with saguaro and organ pipe cacti. A few crimson flowers remained clustered at the end of rambling ocotillo. In the back stood a shed and fenced corral where a gray donkey and white nanny goat shared space with free-roaming chickens. Sally parked in front of the house and waited for them.

"Come on inside. There's some iced tea made, or I can put on the coffeepot."

The sun burned off the meager clouds, and heat rose like shimmering ghosts from the desert floor, but inside Sally's house was cool and inviting. Her home formed an L shape, with an open kitchen-dining-living room in the larger leg and two bedrooms and a bath in the smaller. Mexican blankets covered a worn leather sofa and two matching easy chairs. Colorful woven mats and Indian rugs lay scattered on tile floors. On a shaded side of the house, one large window offered a view of distant mountains.

"Those are the Huachucas," Sally said. "My first husband, Bill, found a little gold claim up in those hills. That's how we paid off this place."

Emily sighed. "It's a real nice place. Now what's this so-called plan of yours?"

"Sit down and hold your horses." When the coffee finished perking, Sally filled three cups and brought them to the table.

"I've been thinking," Abe began. Emily, holding the cup with both hands, rolled her eyes, but he continued. "I know it's a long shot, but I think I found something both Corazón and the men in the black Buick want. Something valuable, only they don't know I have it."

Emily frowned and gave him a speculative look. "The key you found in your backpack that Jackson must have dropped, and that offhand remark he made about possessing the key to happiness. Might be a bit of a stretch, but . . ."

"And you have that key, Abe?" Sally said. "You didn't tell me that. Hmm. That's perfect. Means this plan I'm working on makes even more sense."

111

"I don't have it anymore. I gave it to Emily."

Emily held her coffee cup in both hands. "And I turned it in as evidence in the murder investigation. What's this plan you keep bringing up, Sally?"

"Why run around all over the country, not knowing where you're going or who you're looking for, when all you need to do is trick them into coming to you?"

"You mean, throw out some bait." Abe churned the idea over in his head. *If it's the key they're after, they'll show up. Why not get it over with? Emily can arrest Corazón and I'll be free and clear.* After a few minutes of silence all around, he added, "I like it. And I'm the bait, but how do we get the word out?" He swallowed some hot coffee and looked at Emily. "What do you think?"

She hesitated, but Abe could tell she was thinking about it. "I could drop some information in the right places, maybe draw Corazón in." She shook her head. "I don't know. It could be dangerous—for you, Abe." Emily linked her hands behind her head, leaned back in her chair, and chewed on her lower lip. "There are too many unknowns." Then, turning her attention to Sally, she asked, "Where does Abe meet them, if they do swallow the bait? These aren't guys to play around with. There's more going on here than you understand—gang wars, revenge killings. On the other hand, I think you're right. Somehow, that key unlocks the puzzle." She looked back at Abe with a somber expression. "You know, they wouldn't hesitate to murder you as soon as you show yourself."

"Why come all the way out here to kill me before they get what they're after? I don't think they'd do that. Besides, I won't be alone like Jackson was. I've got you covering my ass, Emily." He finished his coffee, and Sally stood up to get the pot.

"Don't forget, you've got me, too, and I'm mighty handy with a gun," Sally said. She held onto the coffeepot while pacing the kitchen, her eyes sparkling. "Listen, Abe could stay here. Let them come out to the ranch. We could hide in the shed and wait for them."

"What's this 'we'?" Emily said. "Don't be naïve, Sally. You're not involved—that is, even if I decide this has a chance of working."

Abe started drumming his fingers on the table. "You always say 'I,' Emily. This isn't only about you. You've been taken off the case, remember?" He stopped drumming and furrowed his brow while fixating his eyes on her. "I was minding my own business, passing through, and got arrested, thrown in jail, and accused of something I had nothing to do with. Then I waited around at your place for the law to figure it out, sat on my ass and did whatever you told me until your brother convinced me I needed to do more. This is my life, too, and you're not a cop out here."

Sally stood up, put her hands on her hips, and faced Abe and Emily. "Get off your high horse, you two. I've probably been handling a gun longer than both of you put together. I can shoot the short hairs off a pig's balls blindfolded, and he won't even squeal. Never been scared of nothing, and never will be. Now I say we start working out the details and quit whining."

Sally's sudden outburst silenced Emily and Abe until they looked at each other and started smiling.

"I didn't know pig balls had short hairs," Emily said, unable to stifle a fit of giggles.

Abe cracked up. "I'd like to see that kind of shooting."

Sally grinned back at them and the tension broke. "Are you ready to figure this thing out?"

Back at the table, fresh coffee in their cups, the three discussed ways to draw Corazón and the occupants of the Buick to Bisbee.

Sally grabbed a notebook and pencil from the desk. "Tell me what you know."

"Well, there're the two gangs," Abe said.

"Right," Emily added. "Hate each other's guts—the Mexican Mafia and those skinheads that have been hanging out around here, the Aryan Brotherhood. Since Jackson was a member of that gang, maybe they know something about the key or why he was murdered."

Sally stopped scribbling and scratched her head. "So, where are you most likely to run into those characters, Emily?"

"Prison. I could call a guard I know, start a rumor going around the Aryans . . ."

"That there's a man in Bisbee who wanted to see someone about a key given to him by the recently deceased Easy Jackson," Abe finished her sentence. "But he arrived at the guy's place just in time to witness a car driving away before the house exploded, killing the person inside."

Sally paused in her note taking and looked at Abe. "That should get them riled up and curious."

"And we might find out some more information in the process," Emily said.

Abe, caught up in the growing exuberance, placed both hands on the table and completed his thought. "The man who met Jackson still has the key, and he's laying low in Bisbee."

"It might get their attention." Emily sounded dubious. "But, a quicker link to Corazón would be through his girlfriend."

"You mean the stripper from Las Cruces?" Whether caused by his early departure from the hospital or the intense concentration, Abe's head began to throb. He put a hand to his forehead, shielding his eyes, trying to hide the pain. "What was her name?"

"Juanita de la Cruz," said Emily. "What's wrong, Abe?"

Ever the observant nurse, Sally jumped to her feet and went to the kitchen for a glass of water. "His head's hurting, that's what." Passing the glass to Abe, she said, "Now swallow those pills and lie down on that sofa over there. Me and your girlfriend here can work this out."

"We're not . . ." Abe protested at the same time as Emily, but he took the pills and followed Sally's advice. "We're in this mess together, that's all." He read skepticism in her look. "Okay, after I check on Patch, I'll be on the sofa." Abe looked out the window and saw his dog sniffing the donkey while dodging a rear assault from the goat. For Patch, a onetime city dog, life appeared to be nothing short of a series of new adventures. Abe found the sofa, assured his dog could adjust to any situation.

"After I call the prison I'll drive to Cruces and drop in at the Bar-None, see if I can catch Juanita's act," said Emily.

"That's nuts," said Abe from the sofa. "They'll be suspicious of a woman coming into a strip joint. Besides they'll smell cop all over you. I'll do it."

"She'll recognize you. Remember, you gave her quite the once-over in Clayton."

"No, I didn't."

"Okay, it's settled." Sally waved her hands in the air, signaling the end of the conversation. "I'll do the talking. Who's going to be suspicious of an old broad like me? I already took a week's vacation from the hospital, and I don't plan on sitting around here on my caboose waiting for the action. My neighbor will take care of the critters and watch the place. We'll all leave in the morning after this guy gets a night's rest."

Abe listened from the sofa—the two women making decisions. He sat up. "I don't need any more rest than you two. Why don't we leave today? Feed your animals, Sally. Emily, get in touch with your prison guard buddy."

Sally cleared the table and rinsed the cups. "Your dog can stay here, Abe."

"My dog goes where I go."

18

I want to see Will first," Emily said, and they agreed to the detour, though a run up to Phoenix took them well out of their way. After all, Abe reasoned, it was her car they were traveling in, and he wanted to talk to Will as well—although he was apprehensive, not knowing what to expect, a mummified version of his friend or someone scarred beyond recognition.

When they reached the hospital in Phoenix, Sally tried to assure them that Will was getting care from one of the best burn treatment centers out West, and since the emergency technicians had reached him quickly, his prognosis looked good. "There'll be scarring for sure. You have to expect it with third-degree burns, but the docs have some new techniques that are nothing short of miraculous. Why don't you two go on in and visit with the brother? We have plenty of time. Those bad guys aren't going nowhere."

They entered the main lobby of the hospital and asked the receptionist for the room number of Will Etcitty. He was on the second floor, room 223, just down from the cafeteria. "I'll grab a snack and wait for you in there," said Sally, leaving them outside Will's room.

Abe tapped lightly on the door and heard a faint "Come in." Will Etcitty peeked out from the dressings covering his face, milky eyes amid stark whiteness, both hands swathed in bandages, a tube running from his wrist to a bag of fluid hanging from a stand by his bed.

Abe swallowed his shock and lied. "You're looking good, pal."

"The doc said I'll be even better-looking after they take some skin off my butt and graft it onto my face."

Emily blinked away tears. "Oh, Will. Always the kidder. Are you in a lot of pain? What are they giving you?"

"Whiskey with a chaser of morphine." When he elicited a grin from Emily, he added, "They're taking good care of me, Sis. Doc says I've got second- and third-degree burns on my face, hands, and chest. But thanks to Abe pulling me out of there and getting help, I'll be all right—good as new."

"You would have done the same for me," Abe said. "Now we're going after the assholes who did this." He told Will about their plan to go to Las Cruces and set a trap for Corazón and whoever caused the explosion.

"Damn." Will's voice cracked. "I wish I could go with you."

Abe gently brushed the swathing on Will's hands with his fingertips. "Your job is to get well, buddy."

"Your spirit's going with us, big brother," said Emily, smiling bravely.

After leaving Will with assurances they would keep him posted, Emily and Abe located Sally in the cafeteria, stocking up on sandwiches and extra coffee, using her wheedling skills and position to get them for free.

"This should hold us until we get to Las Cruces. We have a six-hour drive ahead." She pulled a hamburger patty out of the sack.

"I even brought something for Patch. Make sure he poops and pees before we hit the road."

Slightly less than six hours later, Abe driving, the air conditioner turned off in the coolness of the desert night, they were cruising the valley between the Organ Mountains and the Rio Grande, entering the city limits of Las Cruces, New Mexico.

"Look for a pay phone, Emily," Abe said. Sally, dozing peacefully in the backseat of the Bronco, hadn't stirred for the last two hours. "We need the address of that place the girlfriend works. What's its name—the Bar-None?"

Abe pulled into a gas station off Main Street and filled the tank while Emily checked the yellow pages of a phone book still chained to a broken pay phone.

"Bet I can tell you what kind of neighborhood this is," she said when she returned to the Bronco. "Think you can find Corona Street?"

After further discussion, they agreed Abe would be the one to make contact with Juanita de la Cruz, girlfriend of Rico Corazón. The conditions were that he hide his face under the battered brim of Sally's first husband's cowboy hat, and wear her departed spouse's old western shirt and fringed buckskin jacket in case Juanita remembered him from the Clayton diner. Abe argued that she had so many men gawking at her all the time she probably couldn't recall any of them, but he went along with the disguise.

He felt a little like Jon Voight in the movie *Midnight Cowboy* as he drove past the hookers on Corona Street. Abe circled the block a couple of times and cruised the alley behind the strip bar. Once everyone felt familiar with the layout, he looked for a parking space near the flashing nude silhouette in front of the Bar-None.

"Guess the competition from Juarez is too much for the locals," said Sally, commenting on the small red-light district and lack of visible clientele in Las Cruces. "Cheaper over there in Mexico, I bet."

"The laws in Texas are more lenient, too," added Emily. "No totally nude dancing allowed in New Mexico."

Sally, tsk-tsking, shook her head. "Hard for a working girl to make a living in this state."

Abe slipped into an empty spot and killed the lights. "Look, I sympathize with the ladies of the night as much as you two, but we didn't drive all the way out here to worry about their working conditions." He gave himself a quick glance in the mirror and pulled down the battered brim of the Stetson so that it shaded his eyes. "What do you think, Patch?" The dog answered with a yelp, which Abe took as approval.

"Let's go over it one more time," Emily said.

Abe stared at a poster in front of Bar-None that highlighted a full-color blowup of Juanita de la Cruz wearing nothing more than a couple of pasties and a G-string. Her leer clearly stated, "Come on in." "The sign says her act starts at ten. It's five till."

"This will be quick. Will you concentrate, Abe? You don't have to see the whole damn show, you know."

Sally broke in. "Okay. I get in the driver's seat, go around to the alley and park a little ways down from the back door, keep my eyes and ears open, and the motor running. Soon as you and Abe hightail it back to the car, I burn some rubber." Sally seemed even more full of vinegar after her nap. "Got my pistol loaded and ready if we need it."

Abe glanced over at Emily. "Don't worry, I can handle it," he said. "I'm doing the easy part—watch her act, slip a twenty to the lady, and tell her to meet me in the alley to discuss a missing key. Then I go out and wait by the back door. That's where you come in."

119

Emily furrowed her brow. "She'll be curious, and most likely cautious. There'll be one of Corazón's thugs nearby acting as her bodyguard. You won't see me when you come out, but I'll be nearby, close enough, in case anyone tries to get cute."

"When she arrives I tell her about the key and the meeting at Dick's with Jesus Eyes," Abe said. "And that her boyfriend, Corazón, better come alone and bring the cash. Kind of pushing it, don't you think?"

"Nah," said Emily. "That's the way these guys play. If you didn't want something out of it, they wouldn't think you were serious."

"Why don't we cut out the 'Jesus Eyes' crap? I never heard any of that until I came to New Mexico."

"What's wrong? You have a Jesus complex or something?" Emily chuckled.

Abe cringed inwardly at the reference once again. "Jesus, King of the Jews. Why should a nice Jewish guy from Jersey have a Jesus complex? I just don't get it."

Sally watched the banter in silence, her eyes switching from Abe to Emily.

"Haven't you ever been in any of those Catholic or Protestant churches and looked at that blue-eyed Jesus nailed to the cross? No, I guess not," she said, answering her own question.

"Okay. I'm ready." Abe wanted to get it over with. Had they even considered an alternative plan? He knew he'd have to think fast if Corazón showed up. Abe checked himself one more time in the rearview mirror, lowered his hat, slipped out of the car, and sauntered toward the front door. When he turned to look back, the Bronco was gone. He took a deep breath and approached the Bar-None. But, before he could step inside, he had to get past a giant in an orange suit.

The blimp glared down at Abe and stuck out a ham-size palm. "That'll be twenty bucks."

Abe hesitated, considered saying he only wanted to give a note to one of the dancers. He hadn't counted on a cover charge, but decided he had better pay up and reached into his wallet, reluctantly pulling out a twenty. This little show was costing him some cash, and—who knew?—maybe a whole lot more.

19

Abe entered the crowded club and blinked. A revolving disco ball hung from the ceiling, reflecting garish colors off scantily clad females serving drinks. Before he reached the bar, an Amazonian of a woman with a platinum beehive hairdo sidled up close enough for Abe to feel the heat of her body and get a whiff of cheap perfume.

"What can I do for you, baby?" The Latin accent didn't quite go with the blond wig. Her blouse gaped open to the navel, barely concealing bountiful breasts.

He backed up, looked around the smoky room, and saw an empty table off to the side. "I'll have a Corona," he said to the melon-size boobs at his eye level. When the waitress brought his beer, Abe stuck a five-dollar bill in the tight cleavage of her breasts. She winked, and he pulled his hat brim a little farther down.

Abe sipped his beer and scanned the room for any sign of Corazón, wondering if he would recognize him, hoping he wasn't around. He didn't see anyone with a Fu Manchu mustache and tattooed arms, so he turned his attention to the action on stage. A bunch of blurry-eyed college kids sitting near the front began whistling and shouting. Their drinks sloshed as they banged their fists on tabletops and chanted in rowdy unison: "Juanita, Juanita, Juanita." They were joined by a group of cowboys and businessmen in dark suits.

The chant turned to a roar that drowned out the voice of the emcee when Juanita de la Cruz came on stage with a slutty, slow walk. She wore a see-through black negligee that barely concealed the lacy low-cut bra. A black G-string and hip-high black boots completed the outfit. Juanita's long, dark hair curled provocatively over her breasts. Glitter on the teardrop tattoo at the corner of her right eye sparkled in the strobe lights as she began gyrating with the first number. She teased the crowd with a pole spin, then a pole flip, and the college kids started yelling, "Take it off." While Abe wondered if she had quit using the cross as a prop, a couple of guys carried a large metal one onstage and snapped it in place in front of the pole. Not your usual cross, it was bedecked with twinkly lights and feathers and utilized in a very provocative way, some would say sacrilegious. But Abe had to admit, Juanita de la Cruz was something to behold.

The third set ended and she had already discarded most of her flimsy clothes, leaving both of her pasties in discriminate places—as far as a strip act could go in New Mexico. Juanita stepped down from the stage and started mingling with the crowd, teasing customers for tips. She skipped the college kids, who were drunk and probably out of money. Abe beckoned her with a twenty.

"You want a lap dance, handsome?"

"No, just a few minutes of your time." He held out the twenty but didn't let go. "I liked the show, but I have something you'll like even more."

"Yeah, yeah. I've heard that a million times." She tugged at the bill, but Abe held on.

"I think your boyfriend might be very interested in a key that belonged to my friend Joe Jackson, better known as 'Easy.'"

Juanita narrowed her eyes and stared at him. "What do you know about this key?"

"Meet me in back of the club when you're finished here." Abe released his hold on the twenty. "I'll tell you all about it. Come alone."

She took the money and sauntered off to work the crowd, but turned her head, tossed her hair seductively, and hissed at him, "Half an hour."

Abe stood and walked outside. When he reached the sidewalk, he looked over his shoulder, but didn't see anyone following him, and made his way to the alley. He could barely make out the outline of the Bronco parked near the corner, partially hidden behind a Dumpster. Abe found the back door of the club and leaned up against the wall, wishing he hadn't given up cigarettes. He didn't see Emily. *Maybe that's good*, he thought, feeling a chill. He stuck his hands in his pockets and waited.

Fifteen minutes passed before Juanita de la Cruz stepped out the back door. She didn't come alone—the big guy who had taken Abe's first twenty followed behind her. He walked up to Abe and grabbed him by the jacket front.

"The lady says you got something belongs to her."

"I told the lady to come alone and I would talk to her. I don't have anything to say to you."

"Let him go, Chulo."

The giant released his grip on Abe and shoved him back.

"He's just doing his job, cowboy. Rico told him to look out for me. Now where is the key?"

"I'm the messenger." *Where the hell is Emily, anyway?* "Tell Rico Corazón to show up at a bar in Bisbee, Arizona, at nine p.m., next Friday night. The place is called Dick's Hot Licks. He can't miss it. Tell him to ask for Jesus Eyes."

"That's it? Jesus Eyes. You're kidding. How do you know Rico, anyway, *gringo*?"

"That's not important. Give him the message. The key will cost him ten grand. Either he brings the money and comes alone or no deal. Take it or leave it." Abe waited for her to swallow the bait then added, "Might be somebody else interested in that key."

Chulo jumped in his face again. Abe could feel the splatter of sour saliva from the guy's mouth as he pulled him close, eyeball to eyeball. "Tell this loser Jesus Eyes he can lick *my* dick."

Abe saw the fist and tried to dodge it. He landed his own bare knuckles on the goon's chin and felt like he had punched a cast-iron skillet. Chulo flinched, but only briefly, and Abe caught the full effect of the bodyguard's fist in his gut. He felt the wind whoosh out of him like air from a deflated balloon. He fell to his knees, bracing himself for the kick he saw coming. Juanita de la Cruz made no move to stop her psycho-pet this time. Abe rolled over and grabbed a leg, but couldn't escape the sharp end of the brute's pointed cowboy boot as it hit home in his left kidney. Groaning in pain, still holding on to Chulo's leg, he tried to pull him down, but it was like toppling an oak tree. Then he heard a vehicle screech to a stop and a car door open. He could barely make out the person standing next to the Bronco, but recognized the calm, even-toned voice with the slight melodic lilt.

Emily, her police-issue Glock pointed squarely at the big guy's head, threw a quick look at Juanita. "If either of you make a move, somebody will have to scrape this goon's brains off the wall." Abe crawled into the backseat and she hopped in beside him.

Sally drove like the lead car in the final stretch of the Grand Prix with someone hot on her tail. They zoomed around corners, zipped through red lights, and hit the I-10 ramp going west.

Abe felt a searing pain in his kidneys and rib cage. His head felt like it had been used as a bass drum by a rock band. He leaned back and closed his eyes, resting his head on something soft and sweet smelling, and felt Emily's strong fingers caressing his cheek.

"Abe, Abe. Come on. I came as quick as I could, and I never had you out of my sight."

Abe heard her voice, but thought he dreamed it and didn't respond. Patch whined softly and licked his hand.

Sally twisted her head around from the driver's seat. "I hope that boy didn't get another blow to the head on top of that concussion. Try to keep him sitting up and awake."

"The creep hit him in the face and there's a cut below his eye, lots of blood. The knuckles on his left hand are cut. I saw the asshole kick him in the side, too. We need to pull over, Sally. I want you to take a look. There's a first aid kit under the seat. I'll keep an eye out for anyone that might be following us." Emily took Abe's face in both hands. "Come on, Abe. Don't pass out on me."

Abe's eyes fluttered as he tried to focus on the face looking down at him. "Emily, I landed one. Scored with a left," he mumbled. "They got the message."

"I know, you were great." She bent over and kissed him gently on the forehead.

Did I imagine that?

"Stay with me, Abe," Emily said. "Keep talking."

"Did you . . . nah. I had a dream; I thought you kissed me." He closed his eyes and felt Emily shaking him. "Tell Sally I'm sorry. I think I lost her husband's cowboy hat."

Sally took an exit and turned down a side road. "It don't matter. I had three husbands and there're two more cowboy hats at home. Actually, that one never was my favorite."

The vehicle stopped and Emily took over the driving while Sally slipped in the backseat. She cleaned his cuts with something that

126

20

When the Bronco reached Sally's little ranch house, Abe stumbled from the car and collapsed on the sofa. Nothing had ever felt so welcoming or comfortable as that old, worn leather. He wrapped himself in the Mexican blanket and sank into the soft concaves left behind by the butts of Sally's cowboy husbands, swearing, as the sofa yielded to his body like a waiting lover, he could still smell the sage-scented open range and the sweat of horses. Emily disappeared in the confines of the guest bedroom and Sally to her own room. No one wanted any more talk tonight, just sleep, and in less than two minutes, with Patch curled near his feet, Abe was snoring.

At some point in the gray predawn light, he awoke to that mysterious sense that tells our sleeping minds another presence is in the room. He opened his eyes and saw Emily looking down at him, her long, black hair undone and falling past her shoulders to rest on her breasts. She wore an oversize T-shirt and shorts, and looked beautiful.

"I couldn't sleep. Want to talk?"

Abe sat up and rubbed his eyes, patted the couch, making room. "Sure. Have a seat." He waited for her to settle beside him, then wrapped the blanket around both their bodies. He wore only boxer shorts and was distinctly aware of the warmth of her body and the swelling of his erection as their bare legs touched. They sat that way for several minutes before Emily broke the silence.

"Remember when you asked me if I had ever lost someone I loved?"

"Yes," said Abe, thinking back to the pained expression in her eyes when he first asked the question. He slipped an arm around her shoulder and felt her tremble.

"In high school," Emily began, "I went with a lot of boys. I don't know—maybe I wanted to prove something, or find something—whatever. My mom tried to help, but she had to work all the time after our dad died from cancer caused by his work in the uranium mine out by Shiprock."

Abe let the silence hang between them. He didn't know if he should keep quiet and let her talk or encourage her to continue. He waited, knowing how it felt to lose your father when you're young, but made no comment.

"I hung out with a wild crowd, lots of drinking, some drugs, crazy stuff. Will warned me, tried to set me straight, but I wouldn't listen to my 'faggot' brother, you know, even if he was older and smarter than me." Emily looked down at the floor, pausing, then pushed her hair back and faced Abe. "Right before I turned sixteen I ended up pregnant. I didn't know who the father was." The sigh that followed sounded like a moan.

Abe felt her body tense and knew the telling cost her, and also that she had more to say. "Emily, it's okay. It doesn't matter what you did when you were a kid. It's over now. You don't have to tell me."

"Yes, I do."

"All right."

"I had the baby—a beautiful boy. I named him Christopher, and gave him a secret name, his Diné name. But, I still didn't change my behavior, not then. Mom tried to keep me in school, but I dropped out and moved in with another guy. His name doesn't matter—I can't even say it. Anyway, he drank, and beat me on a regular basis. He felt jealous of my baby because he knew it wasn't his. One day he beat me so badly I realized I had to get away or he would kill me, so I called Will to come and get us. My little boy had just turned two."

Silent tears streamed down her cheeks. Abe tried to brush them away, but she gripped his hand to stop him.

"It's all in the past, Emily." Not wanting to hear how this might end, he put his fingers over her lips.

"Let me finish, Abe." Emily turned her head toward the window. The breaking dawn transformed the sky into a glorious explosion of fire. "It had been raining all week, and the arroyos were full of water." The words were coming in a torrent. "I started packing and this bastard grabbed Chris and ran out the door. I chased him, and saw him trip and fall into the arroyo with my baby, my little boy, still wearing his blue Superman pajamas and crying for his mama. I screamed like a crazy woman and ran back and forth on the edge of the arroyo looking for Chris. When Will arrived he jumped in the water. Will went under time and time again, but he couldn't find my baby. My son was gone."

Abe wrapped his arms around her. "I'm so sorry, Emily." He knew the terrible feeling of losing the one thing you love most in the world, but he didn't say that, not now. "I feel your pain, sweetheart. I am so sorry."

She let him hold her for a few minutes before meeting his gaze. "They found the bodies three days later, several miles downstream. That's when Will started drinking, and I stopped. I moved back with my mom, finished high school and two years of nursing school, then switched to law enforcement. Will is the one with all the brains and he went on to get his degree in mining and geology, despite the alcohol he consumed more and more. He blamed himself for not being able to save Chris, but I know it was my fault, Abe, not Will's. And he has paid for it every day."

Emily slumped against him and closed her eyes, her body shuddering with silent sobs. After a few minutes, she dropped off to sleep.

Abe held her close, then leaned back against the sofa—two wounded souls seeking comfort in an old Mexican blanket and their shared melancholy. His heart ached for her. Exhaustion swept over him and he, too, slept. When he awoke again the bright sun of midday streamed through the window and Sally rattled pots in the kitchen. The clock on the wall said 12:30. He whispered Emily's name and her eyes popped open. She jumped up and skittered into the bedroom.

Reemerging later, freshly showered and looking as if nothing happened, Emily sat at the breakfast table with Abe and Sally. For once, Sally held her tongue.

Emily peered over the steaming coffee cup. "We have a lot to do today."

"Right," the other two agreed, nodding.

They ate ravenously without discussing what they needed to do, though, and spent the afternoon taking care of the animals and immersing themselves in small chores. Emily said she would check in with her contact at the prison, and Abe took his turn in the shower, luxuriating in the hot water while trying to sort out his conflicting feelings. He emerged from the bathroom, freshly shaven, his face still pink from the steaming water, feeling almost new—except for the black eye, the bump on his head, and pain in his kidney and ribs—and glad he had a week for his body to recuperate.

Sally flashed him a grin and wink.

Emily, busying herself at the kitchen sink, kept her back turned. "Joe, the prison guard, gave me an interesting bit of information. Got it from his stoolie."

"Oh yeah, what's that?" Abe filled a water dish for Patch.

"The rumor spread among the Aryans. According to Joe's stoolie, a Kansas City branch of the Mafia has a big interest in getting their hands on that key."

"I keep hearing talk of this 'key,'" Sally said. "It's gotta unlock the whole cockeyed mess. What's the story, and where is it?"

"It's locked in the evidence room at headquarters. We need that key."

Abe carried the water to the door, whistled for Patch, then turned back to Emily. "What else did your buddy at the pen say?"

"It gets complicated. Turns out Easy Jackson had been providing information to the Feds concerning the Aryan Brotherhood's involvement in the drug trade. That's how he managed to get a transfer and shortened sentence."

"Jackson wanted to go to Bisbee," Abe said. "And he knew someone was on his tail in Clayton. He jumped like a long-tailed cat in a room full of rocking chairs every time he heard a sound. Kept looking over his shoulder like he expected trouble. It could have been either Corazón, the Aryans, or the Kansas City Mafia who made the hit on him then. Maybe they all wanted the key, or maybe they had other motives. We'll have to wait and see who bites the bait."

"I'm calling a cousin of mine at headquarters, the other token female cop. Let's see what they've learned, and if we can get that key back."

Sally scratched her head. "Must unlock something important— a safe-deposit box, or maybe a locker with cash or drugs. Aren't many places with lockers in Bisbee—closest bus station is Tucson, and we don't have any gyms, except the high school."

Abe and Sally sat at the table while Emily picked up the phone and placed a call to the Crownpoint substation. Shortly thereafter, they listened to Emily in a one-sided conversation with her coworker cousin.

"Mabel, it's Em. I'm calling from Arizona. Will's doing better, thanks. Look, I'm calling because I need a quick lowdown on the Easy Jackson case. Any new developments? . . . Uh-huh . . . No shit . . . So the Staties are still handling it? You know the key that turned up on that guy, Abe Freeman?" She grinned at Abe. "Did they get a trace on it?" Emily held the phone to her ear and raised her eyebrows. "Yeah . . . sure . . . okay." After a few minutes she said, "I need a big favor, Mabel. I want a duplicate of that key, and I need it right away. If you can't make a copy, get the original. You can slip a dummy in its place . . . I can't explain anything right now, Cuz, but it concerns helping Will and Grandma . . . I knew I could count on you. I'll meet you tomorrow night at Mexican Springs, Uncle Jim's place, six o'clock. Thanks, Mabel."

After she hung up, Emily turned to the expectant faces of the other two. "Clans stick together. We'll have that key when Corazón or anyone else shows up."

"Well, don't stand there grinning like a mule eating briars," Sally said. "Give us the scoop."

"Yeah, Em. What's the story on the key found on that Freeman guy?" Abe raised his eyebrows.

"Let's go outside and I'll tell you about it. I'm getting stir-crazy."

"Good idea. I'll feed Patch first, and join you. I could use some exercise and fresh air."

Sally jumped up from the chair. "Well, don't think you're gonna leave me behind. I want to hear this."

The sun burned through a milky sky that did nothing to alleviate the midafternoon heat, but Sally led them behind the barn to a twisting trail shaded with ironwood and paloverde trees. Patch skip-hopped in front, pausing to check out each new smell and to make sure he left his mark in its place.

"This gets more and more complicated." Emily plucked a seed from one of the trees and began chewing it. "The state transferred

Easy Jackson to a small prison facility near Clayton, New Mexico, for his own protection. It worked for him because he was close to his girlfriend, Marilu DiMarco, who rented a little house in Dumas, Texas." She paused and studied the sky. A ridge of clouds had formed over the mountains, and the first flashes of heat lightning danced off their tops. A slight breeze ruffled the vegetation, stirring up the sweet scent of coming rain. "Here's the big news. Marilu's father is Vicente DiMarco, boss of the Kansas City Mafia. Maybe Marilu stole the key from him and hid it in a safe place for Jackson. She must know how valuable that key is and what it unlocks. The first place Jackson went after his early release was to Marilu's house."

"Jesus," Abe said. "That probably explains the Buick with Kansas plates, but how did the cops find out about the key?"

"Jackson was a talker. He couldn't help bragging about how he and his girlfriend were going to get rich once he was released and he got his hands on that key. Its existence was common knowledge among the prison population, but its whereabouts unknown."

"Why didn't the cops find this here Marilu and get her to talk?" said Sally.

"That's part of the mystery. Marilu wasn't anywhere around when the cops arrived, and the house had been ripped apart from top to bottom. They found her burned car in a ditch, but no body. Whoever had been there didn't find the key either, because Jackson had it when he approached you at Clayton Lake. He must have known whoever had been to Marilu's would be looking for him."

"Makes me want to know all the more why that doggone key is so important." Sally held out her hand as the first spattering of raindrops smacked the dry earth. "Did the cops ever find the girlfriend?"

"No trace of her. Her father claims he doesn't know her whereabouts. She is officially classified as missing."

"They must have turned up some information on the key," Abe said. "All I know is it was small and had a number on it."

"It could be the kind used to open a safe-deposit box, that's what the State Police think, anyway, but it had no identifying marks other than a serial number and no way to tell what bank it's from. The only identifiable prints were yours, Abe. Any other latent prints were too smudged to read. That scrap of paper is most likely a phone number—the first three digits are the area code for Arizona—possibly a contact number for Jackson's buddy."

"This is huge news, Emily," Abe said. "It means we have the right bait. We just aren't sure what or who we are going to catch."

A black cloud moved in from the mountains and hovered directly above them, then opened up and spilled its contents. The downpour had everyone running toward the barn for cover. Sally kept going in the direction of the house, but Abe and Emily ducked inside the small wooden structure, a space barely large enough for three stables and a storage area for feed. It smelled of sweet hay and slightly pungent manure. Two stalls were obviously in use, housing the mule and the goat. Clean hay blanketed the floor of the empty stall, and an oiled saddle hung over the railing. The nameplate on the door said "Mariah."

Abe fingered the smooth leather. "Must have been Sally's horse."

Emily let her hand glide over the saddle, pausing to trace the ingrained pattern of roses and vines. "Yes, Sally acts tough, but she is really a sentimental old girl."

When her fingertips brushed against Abe's, they both jumped as if lightning had struck inside the barn. It had happened before, that night on the front step of her grandfather's trailer, but this time they didn't pull back. Abe held her face in his hands, tilting it so he could look down into her eyes, not worried about the rain, or Sally returning, or Patch watching with cocked head, or for the moment, his own conflicted past. He kissed her long and hard while she grasped the back of his hair, pulling him closer, returning his kiss with parted lips, their tongues meeting with unrestrained passion. He unbuttoned Emily's blouse, revealing the dark areolae of her nipples on the small, firm breasts. As his hands caressed the contours of her body, he kissed her breasts and felt the wetness between her legs. Abe felt his growing hardness and moaned. He knew they both wanted, needed this, and when he entered her, Emily opened to him like a budding flower in early spring. They made love in a pile of alfalfa, with an urgent abandon neither had allowed themselves to acknowledge. The first time they both climaxed too quickly, so they made love again, more slowly, making it last. Afterward they shyly smiled and brushed the hay from their hair, straightened their clothes, avoiding each other's eyes. Abe had not made love to a woman since Sharon had become ill, and hadn't thought he could ever again. Now that he had been with Emily, his emotions ran the gamut between tenderness, relief, and guilt. *Am I falling in love with her? Have I already betrayed Sharon?*

The thundercloud moved on, drenching some other dry spot of land and leaving them with a fresh patch of blue sky.

"I'd like to ride to Mexican Springs with you," Abe said as they walked toward the house, closer together now, almost touching. "And I don't think Sally should be involved in this anymore."

For once, Emily agreed, at least regarding Sally. "I know, and she's going to be hard to shake. Thinks she's a regular Annie Oakley. But you should probably stay here and talk to Paco. I'll give him a call before I leave."

Abe considered her words and decided she was right. "Think he'll let us open the place, but stay away himself and keep the customers out?"

"I'm sure he will. By the way, when is the last time you fired a gun? You may need to when everyone shows up for the party."

"I never had a gun, Emily. Never wanted to kill anything, still don't."

"Sometimes it's kill or be killed, Abe."

"I don't want to believe that." They were almost at the back door, but Abe wanted to keep her talking, as well as extend his time alone with her, so he steered her around to the front of the house. "You're the cop, Emily. I'm dangling the bait. I don't need a gun."

She gave him a quizzical look. "Maybe if we're lucky either Easy Jackson's murderer or the ones who set off the explosion will bite our bait and be the only ones that show up. They'll incriminate themselves in some way and we'll have some answers. On the other hand, we may be dealing with the Mafia and Corazón with his band of hell-raisers, or even the Aryan Brotherhood. Emily paused to brush sprigs of hay from Abe's shirt. "There's more than one crime here and, I have a feeling, more than one criminal. A weapon would be simple self-protection. How'd you ever survive the mean streets of New Jersey without a gun?"

"I played the piano—Schubert, Mozart, Bach, Haydn, but mostly Satie. Music is my weapon of choice."

Emily stopped to study him, looking at his face in a new way. "You're full of surprises. Why did you leave your piano behind if you love music so much?"

The question caught him off guard. He felt a wave of sadness and guilt as his mind flashed back to Sharon. "We all lose something, Em. After Sharon died I lost any desire to play the piano. We were so tied together with music that I felt I was half-dead myself when she was gone."

Emily appeared to take this information stoically. She didn't ask questions, but she stopped him before they went inside. "Sometimes we don't think we can go on—we don't even want to. But life pulls us along, and we hang in there, kicking and screaming, fighting all the way. People say, 'You need to move on, get over it,' and you try. But you know in your heart that you will never get over it—everything has changed, the balance is skewed, and you are forever struggling not to go over the edge, fall into that black pit again."

Abe knew the words came from her heart, from her own suffering. He held her close and kissed her once more, a long, slow kiss, before he opened the door. "Thank you," said Abe, pulling a final sprig of hay from her hair. "Tonight you made me feel whole."

Ignoring Sally's raised eyebrows and her "What took you two so long?" Abe filled a glass of water from the kitchen faucet and sat down. "Hey there, Sally. Nice barn."

"I'm sure glad you found it comfortable," she said with a twinkle. Excitement lit up Sally's pale, washed-blue eyes. She rubbed her hands together. "Boy howdy this case is getting better and better. Mafia money, stolen loot, missing girl. What's my job gonna be?"

"You've done enough," said Abe. "You're out, Sally. I don't want you to get hurt."

"The hell I am," Sally bristled. With her hands on her hips and her reddened face puffed up, she looked like a Chihuahua with the balls to take on a pit bull. "Do you think I'm scared of those dipshit, lamebrained, drug-addled bozos? I'm ready for them."

"Sorry, Sally. Abe's right. You've been a great help, but . . ."

"No ifs, ands, or buts from you either. You dragged me into this, and I invited you into my home, where you made yourself pretty damn comfortable, I might add. Now you want to kick me out before the fun starts, like I'm some old, useless, senile senior citizen. Well, it ain't gonna happen."

"Sally . . ." Abe began.

She glared at them, looking like she knew what they had been up to and knew more than they did about life, or anything else for that matter. "I'm not out. My vacation isn't over yet."

Abe and Emily both sighed in resignation. "Okay," said Emily. "But you have to play by my rules, and no arguments."

Sally's face crinkled into a broad smile. "I knew you two love-birds would see it my way."

21

The next day Emily left for Mexican Springs, promising to make it back before midnight. "You can't have a quick visit to your clan's house," she explained. "I'll have to stay for supper, probably mutton stew and fry bread, some family gossip."

Abe remained at the ranch with Sally and, since his truck was still in Paco's garage, he relied on her to take him to Dick's Hot Licks for the meeting Emily had set up.

"No, you can't drive Lizzie," she said when he asked. "She don't run right for anybody but me."

The rattletrap car rumbled down the road like a lawn mower on steroids. Abe hunkered low in the passenger seat, expecting the engine to give out after one final gasp, while Patch bounced along in the backseat, but they made it to downtown Bisbee without incident. Sally found Lizzie a shady parking spot in front of Dick's, flanked on one side by a hot-pink motorcycle and on the other by a lavender van emblazoned with a rainbow arc and the words "Too Cute to Be Straight." They rolled down the windows and climbed out, promising Patch they would not be long.

"Have you ever been in here, Sally?"

"What? Course not. Why would I? I always have been kind of curious about this here gay place, though."

"Well, here's a chance to satisfy your curiosity." He held the door open for her and they stepped inside the cool semidarkness.

This time the patrons showed little interest in the pair entering their den, and acted as if it were routine for a young, long-haired guy to come to a bar with a salty-looking old gal. If the sight of two men holding hands and dancing together bothered her, Sally didn't show it. Abe reasoned she had been around long enough to have seen it all.

"Is Paco here?" Abe asked Dutch, the tow-headed, muscle-bound waiter. He had willed himself not to be offended by Dutch's overt gayness and wondered now why he ever was. The voices of customers blended with the smoky, alcohol-infused air in the crowded bar. Abe scanned the dark room and spotted a man in a white apron berating a waiter. At the same time, Dutch inclined his head in that direction.

"Paco's busy right now, making sure the new guy doesn't screw up again. It's the lunch rush, and it's so hard to get good help." Dutch rolled his eyes as if it were a personal burden he had to bear. "Sure you two wouldn't like a drink?"

Sally ordered a root beer and Abe a Shiner. Dutch led them to two empty stools at the end of the bar and told them he would let Paco know they were here, and strutted off, first to his boss, then to take care of customers, the toothsome smile never leaving his face.

"That boy knows his business. Good root beer, too." Sally slurped on her drink and looked around. "Interesting place."

Paco glanced up and saw Abe. He held up his open hand, indicating he would be over in five minutes. Four minutes later he approached them at the bar, greeted Abe, and shook hands with both him and Sally. "What's happening, Abe? How's my buddy Will doing?"

"Will's coming along. He'll make it. Is there someplace private we could talk?"

"Sure. I have an office by the kitchen. Lunch is winding down, so the boys ought to be able to handle things. Let's go on back."

Abe and Sally followed Paco through the well-organized, tidy kitchen. A couple of workers were busy, the chubby one chopping vegetables while the other loaded the dishwasher. Mexican music blasted from a small radio. Paco said something to them in Spanish and they nodded and kept working. Two huge pots, one of red chili, the other green, simmered on the stove, filling the room with a pungent, mouthwatering aroma. Paco led his visitors through a pantry, the shelves stacked with oversize canned goods and canisters of spices. Bins of onions, potatoes, and fresh produce sat near a large walk-in refrigerator. At the end of the pantry, he opened the door to a small but comfortable office. A fat orange cat with a proprietary look eyed them from the desktop.

Paco indicated an overstuffed sofa facing the desk. "Have a seat." He slid into his rolling desk chair and faced them. "Do you need another drink or something to eat?"

Abe shook his head and settled onto the sofa with Sally sitting beside him sipping her root beer. "No thanks, we're good."

While Paco stroked the cat, he looked directly at Abe. "Okay, what's up, my friend? Bet you came for your truck."

"That, too," Abe said. "I guess Emily called you." He then tried to explain their plan. "So, we've set up a meeting, here at your place next Friday night, and we're not sure who or how many are going to show up. Now that I'm talking about it, it sounds crazy." He ran his hand through his hair and took a deep breath when he saw Paco's eyes. "This little gathering is set to take place at nine o'clock. Look, I'm sorry, man. I know we should have gone over this with you before we set things up. If you don't want to go along, I understand. We'll do it someplace else."

Sally had kept her mouth shut till now. "It's going to be a hell of a party," she said.

Paco's eyes sparkled. "A hell of a party. I'm in. I'll shut down after lunch—keep from permanently losing my customers."

"Look, this is no party, Paco. It's a scheme to draw these thugs in so Emily can nail the assholes who set off the explosion that nearly killed Will. We are pretty sure the Kansas City Mafia had something to do with it based on a black Buick Will and I saw driving away from the fire. We're also hoping to find out why Easy Jackson was murdered and who the killer was so I can clear my name. I'm a suspect in that murder and I had nothing to do with it." Abe knew they were taking a big risk. Both Corazón and the Mafia might bring backup, and the Aryans were another thing. "Maybe we shouldn't involve you, Paco. I don't know what's going to happen when and if they show."

"Wait a minute. There's no way I'm not going to help my buddy Will. You think I can't handle trouble? I've seen worse in Nam than those pansy-asses could ever deliver. I still have an M1 Carbine, and I'll damn sure use it if the situation arises. Gotta keep an eye on my place, *amigo*, and yes, things are coming down here." He stood up and paced across the room. "I've dealt with these types before, and I can call in a few friends to help out. We'll stay out of the way. They won't even know my boys are around."

"Are you sure?" Abe said.

Paco stood with his arms crossed. "Dead sure."

Abe thought about it. It wasn't a bad idea to have someone covering their backs in case of trouble, and Emily had objected to his suggestion they call in local lawmen. It seemed to Abe she reacted more with her heart than her head sometimes. To Emily, getting Corazón had become a personal vendetta. Sally liked the idea of having backup, so the three of them hashed it over.

After the meeting Abe stood and shook hands with Paco. "It's a deal then. We'll come back with Emily tomorrow and go over the details." Abe retrieved the keys to his truck and rescued his dog from the hot confines of Lizzie's belly. He told Sally he'd see her back at the house and waited while Patch found a convenient fire hydrant to relieve himself on. Once the dog hopped back onto the seat, Abe rolled the windows down and pumped the gas pedal, waiting for the engine to kick in. The gas gauge registered near empty.

While he filled his tank at the Shell station, he heard the thunder of motorcycles, and looked up to see a line of bikers streaming by. The words "Aryan Brotherhood" embellished their sleeveless denim jackets. "Jesus Christ. That's all we need," he muttered. Abe paid for the gas and pulled onto the highway, wondering how Emily would react to this new set of events.

22

Emily returned sometime after midnight. Evidently she had enjoyed the time spent with her kin, and she triumphantly showed Abe and Sally the sought-after key.

"It's the original. Mabel substituted a look-alike in the evidence room, so no one will ever know this one is missing. Sorry, Abe, but you are their only suspect. They can't get a match on that other set of prints left on your knife, and even though there doesn't appear to be a motive, you owned the weapon that killed Jackson. There was no registration card for a motorcycle in the campground that night. Basically, they're left scratching their butts and looking at you."

"Well hell, that's great news," Abe said.

They sat at the kitchen table while Abe went over the details concerning their earlier meeting with Paco. Emily nodded as he spoke, but when he mentioned the inclusion of some of Paco's buddies, she jumped to her feet and began pacing back and forth.

"Why didn't you wait until I came back? More civilians involved? It's bad enough I have to worry about you and Sally. What if one of them is shot? Shit." She threw her hands in the air and groaned. "This is what happens when you work with amateurs."

"You should have thought of that when you came up with this cock-amamy plan for catching a gang of bad guys on your own, damn it."

Emily ignored his retort. They glared at each other for a long minute, until Sally slapped her hand on the table.

"Shut up, both of you. What's done is done. We could'a waited, but I can see Abe's point on this one. You were planning to go into Paco's place to conduct your business, with nothing but a greenhorn city slicker and a crotchety old nurse for backup. What did you expect Paco to say? 'Great idea. Go ahead and shoot up my place, and I'll go in the back room and take a nap—wake me when it's over.' Course he's gonna want to be there, and with his friends, too, to protect his business. But his reason for getting involved is not strictly business—he's doing it because he wants to get the jerk who hurt Will." She walked to the kitchen cabinet and stretched on her tiptoes to reach into the top shelf, pulling out a bottle of bourbon. "I'm having a drink. Anybody want to join me?"

"I'll have one," Abe said, leaning against the kitchen counter while staring at Emily's retreating backside. She disappeared into the spare bedroom, slamming the door behind her.

"She'll get over it." Sally handed Abe a half-filled tumbler. "Drink up, and then let's get some sleep." She didn't try to muffle the loud yawn that followed.

Abe tossed and turned, trying to shut down his brain. Nothing worked. The night demons kept bringing him back to Emily and Sharon, and the whole damn mess he was in. When he heard Sally's rhythmic snores, he stood, called Patch, and went outside. He followed the same tree-lined path they'd walked the previous afternoon and let the sharp, clean desert air clear his mind. The rain clouds had been replaced by a sea of stars, bisected by a quarter moon. Its pallid reflection transformed drops of moisture clinging to the paloverde leaves into shimmering pearls.

When he neared the barn, the memory of Emily's supple but firm body swept over him once again. He wanted her, but at the same time felt conflicted. He wasn't ready to commit to a relationship, not so soon after Sharon's death, even though she had told him near the end to find someone else. Her words rang in his head. *"I'm not going to be here much longer, baby. I don't want you to be alone. There's someone out there who will make you happy. Find that person. Promise me."* Abe sat down on a boulder beside the path and relived that moment. He had held her close and told her he could never love anyone else, and at the time he meant every word of it.

He heard the crunch of gravel, saw Patch's ears perk up, and looked down the path toward the house. In the pale moonlight, wearing a long white T-shirt, her black hair undone, Emily appeared like a specter, a spirit from another world.

The next day they paid another visit to Dick's. Emily wanted to hear what Paco had to say and make her own suggestions. They arrived an hour before the eleven a.m. opening so they wouldn't be disturbed. The cooks and the waitstaff kept busy in the kitchen preparing for the lunch crowd. At the far end of the bar, Dutch polished glasses and checked the liquor stock while the foursome huddled at a distant table, their heads bent in quiet conversation.

"Abe can sit over there so he can look out the window and see who's coming." Paco indicated a table that put Abe's back against a wall but gave him a clear view of the street and front door. "I'll stay out of the way, behind the bar. My homies will remain unseen unless they need to show themselves. No one will know they're around."

"Abe and I will both sit there, nursing a beer. I'll play the girl-friend and dress the part, but have my Glock within easy reach." A slight smile passed over Emily's features before she turned business-like again. She had reluctantly agreed to backup from Paco's friends. "How many of your buddies will be here?"

"Four for sure—Speedy, Gordo, Jose, and El Rubio. Maybe Mingo. Don't laugh, chica, they know their stuff, you can count on it. We were all in Nam together."

Sally sat back in her chair with arms crossed over her chest, tak-ing it all in. "What about me?" she said. "Where will I be posted?" She took a slurp of root beer and looked at each face.

Abe and Emily had discussed Sally's role and decided on the best way to keep her away from trouble. "You'll be in the Bronco, Sally, in case we need to make a quick getaway, or follow someone."

Her smiling face dissolved into frown lines. "I'd be more help inside with you, maybe a cleaning lady or something, but right there close in case you need an extra gun."

"We need a good driver. It's settled."

"Humph." Sally slumped, pouting, but didn't argue.

"We'll be here an hour before anyone else is due to arrive. It will give us time to run through everything again." Abe paused when he heard the roar of motorcycles and realized he had forgotten to men-tion his sighting of the Aryan Brotherhood to Emily.

Emily stood, surveying the long, rectangular room. She looked at the swinging doors. "That leads to the kitchen, I guess, and there must be a back door. We need a man posted there."

"Right," Paco agreed. "I'll station Gordo there." Someone rat-tled the front door and he looked at his watch. "Time to open up. *Están listos, muchachos?*" he yelled to the kitchen, then, turning his attention back to the table, added, "Stick around and have some-thing to eat—on the house." He took out a ring of keys and walked over to unlock the front door.

There were five skinheads standing outside. A swastika with three sixes superimposed over a clover leaf adorned their riding jackets.

"About fucking time," a beefy, bearded brute, evidently the leader, said as he pushed his way in.

Abe watched as he bellied up to the bar, followed by his gang. The bikers had more tattoos than bare skin. Abe studied their faces reflected in the bar mirror and concluded they would kill just for the hell of it.

The bearded leader glanced into the mirror and caught Abe's eyes. He swiveled on his stool. "What're you staring at, punk?"

"Who, me? Nothing, I'm chilling over here."

Luckily, Dutch diverted the creep's attention when he pranced up to the bar, smiling coquettishly. "Well, hello, handsome. What can I do for you and your boys?"

An ominous grumbling ensued from the group. They were on their feet, fists balled. Their leader waved them back. "Bring me and my boys Buds, princess. Make it quick. We're in a hurry." His wink and sneer brought a round of harsh laughter from his gang.

"Looks like Shredder got himself a girlfriend," the guy sitting on the next stool said with a loud guffaw.

Dutch sat five bottles of Budweiser on the bar.

The one called Shredder turned around and punched his buddy in the face, then downed his beer. "We're looking for someone. Calls himself Jesus Eyes. D'ya know anything about that?" He flexed his muscle revealing a swastika inside a shield with the word "Texas" inked below.

"Never heard of him," said Dutch.

"How about the rest of you queers?" said Shredder.

Abe and Paco shook their heads.

"Fuck it. Let's get out of here," said the gang leader. They finished their beers, stood up, and headed for the door.

"Hold it," said Paco. "You pay first, then leave."

"Oh yeah, sez who?" Shredder said.

"Twenty-five bucks. Special price for you and the boys," said Paco, the outline of a revolver showing under his apron.

Abe tensed, then saw the rest of Paco's workers emerge from the kitchen. The cook swung a meat cleaver from his right hand. Following behind him came the two mess cooks and the dish-washer, each wielding a butcher knife the size of a machete.

While the skinheads gaped at Paco and the kitchen crew, Dutch pulled a shotgun from under the bar. "Sorry you boys have to leave so soon. We were just getting acquainted, and I was so looking forward to serving you. Some other time, maybe?"

Abe, Emily, and Sally watched as the fat brute turned beet red from his bald head down to his thick neck bulging with purple veins. The Aryan leader tried to give Paco the mad-dog stare-down as he mumbled something under his breath and threw twenty-five dollars down on the bar. "Let's get out of this dump," he said, knocking over a barstool and kicking the door open. His band of merry men trailed behind. "You haven't seen the end of this, motherfucker."

Dutch, still holding the shotgun, followed the motorcycle gang to the door. "Good-bye boys. Oh, do come back soon. It's been such fun."

Abe saw the bikers flip Dutch off and roar away, their tires burning rubber on the hot pavement. Feeling leery and somewhat astounded, he looked at the owner of Dick's. "What the hell, Paco? Aren't you worried about them coming back and causing trouble?"

Paco sat back down and smirked, with a self-satisfied look on his face. "We don't put up with any kind of shit around here. See what I mean? My crew is always ready for troublemakers, and believe me, we get our share. Okay, *muchachos*, back to the kitchen. Business as usual."

Sally looked at Dutch with unabashed admiration. "You sure as hell have big balls for a queer fellow," she said, which caused everyone to crack up.

23

To Abe, the following five days moved slower than a snail in peanut butter. He and Emily passed the time hiking in the Huachucas and reminiscing about their childhoods, but apprehension concerning the upcoming showdown at Paco's dominated his thoughts and, he felt sure, Emily's as well. There were no stolen kisses or clandestine rendezvous in the barn. At nights they played poker with Sally, betting with beans and waiting.

Friday morning finally arrived, accompanied by strong winds out of the southwest. Sally filled the coffeepot and looked out her kitchen window. "There'll be a big dust storm rolling our way by late afternoon."

The sky was enveloped in a beige haze, and Abe could barely see the outline of the nearby Huachuca Mountains. Dust devils danced across the desert like twirling dervishes, then disappeared as quickly as they formed.

As the winds increased in speed, so did the anxiety that had been building since daybreak. An atmosphere of apprehension settled over the house. Even Patch appeared to know something was in the air besides dust. He followed Abe's every move and became nervous whenever his master left his sight. Abe patted his dog. "Easy, boy, it's only the wind."

"My people believe dust devils are evil winds that blow no one any good," said Emily. But then, looking sheepish, she added, "The winds should stop by nightfall."

"Maybe not, though," said Sally. "We've had some fierce night-time sandstorms in the past. Don't matter one way or the other. I know my way around these roads and could drive them blindfolded."

Abe had his doubts and gave her a skeptical look, but didn't say anything. Sally's talk was often full of bravado. Maybe she dealt with her fears by acting and talking tough. Waiting for things to happen drove him crazy—that and uncertainty. All the rehearsing reminded Abe of playing chess with yourself—you could always anticipate the next move. They had gone over each person's role a dozen times, but no amount of planning prepared you for the unknown. Tonight at nine o'clock, both sides would show their faces, and the real match would begin. *If forced into it, could I shoot another man? And am I ready to die myself?* Abe wondered. For some reason, now more than ever, he realized how much he wanted to live. While Sally aired her exaggerated bluster, and Emily assumed a professional coolness, Abe agonized. He hoped it didn't come down to pulling a trigger, but in the end, he would do what he had to do.

Sally startled him out of his trance. "It'll help us make a clean getaway if we have to run."

"What will, Sally?"

"The dust storm. None of them know their way around like I do. They'll get lost, go in circles." She chuckled. "I guess old mother earth is on the good guys' side, even after all the mean things we've done to her."

Emily paused from cleaning her gun and smiled. "That sounds like Indian talk. I didn't know you *bilagáanas* regarded our mother that way.

"What'd you call me?"

"It's not a bad thing, Sally. Means 'white person,' and thanks for giving credit to mother earth. You're a pretty good old gal, you know, for a *bilagáana*, that is. Even though you put on a tough face."

Sally looked pleased and even blushed a little. "You aren't so terrible yourself, I guess." Abe passed Emily a secret smile and said he wanted to go out and move around a little, even if the wind was howling like a banshee, and Emily said she would join him. Sally looked even more pleased, grinning like an opossum eating persimmons. "Don't get lost, you two."

The day seemed stuck in claustrophobic slow motion. Without seeing the sun's movement, it became impossible to gauge time. As soon as Abe stepped outside, the wind and blowing sand stung his eyes and felt like a million pinpoints attacking his face. "Let's lock the animals in the barn and head back in," he said, cupping his mouth so Emily could hear.

She nodded in agreement, and they located the old donkey and nanny goat huddled together, their heads turned toward each other against the blasting sand. Abe led the animals into the barn, where the chickens had already entered through an open window. Emily shuttered the windows while the hens peered at them from their nest boxes, clucking softly at the disturbance.

The howling winds diminished any thoughts of a romantic rendezvous Abe and Emily might have had. "This sandstorm complicates things," Abe yelled, as they rushed for the house.

At seven o'clock Abe called Paco. "We're leaving shortly, should be there in under an hour. Did you close the bar?"

"I locked the doors after the lunch crowd left. Told my regulars I had maintenance work to do. All my guys are here, except Mingo.

His asthma won't let him go out in this sandstorm. He was pissed that he couldn't help, but the poor guy could hardly breathe. I've filled them in on what might come down. How're you doing on your end?"

"We'll be all right."

A nervous silence followed, until Paco changed the subject. "I have a new uniform for Emily. One reserved for the small guys that work for me. Basically, it's black pants and a red T-shirt with Dick's logo across the front. Tell her to doll up a little, put on some makeup. She's a good-looking woman, but you gotta play the part, if you know what I mean."

"You tell her. She's right here. I'll see you soon." He handed the phone to Emily, who gave him a quizzical look, then a frown, as she listened to Paco.

"Screw that," she said, and hung up the phone.

Emily, dressed in jeans and a T-shirt, looked absolutely beautiful to Abe. She tucked her Glock in the back of her waistband and carried a small tote bag on her shoulder. Sally, all in black and resembling a septuagenarian ninja, had her shotgun and ammo in hand, but Abe refused the offer of a pistol that once belonged to one of her exes, explaining he still had Will's shotgun and Grandfather Etcitty's pistol in the truck. They tied handkerchiefs over their faces as protection from the dust, and pulled skullcaps down over their heads, giving the impression of a mismatched gang of bank robbers ready to pull off a heist. Before they left, Abe retrieved the shotgun and a box of cartridges from behind his truck's seat.

Sally took her position at the wheel, low beams turned on to aid visibility in the swirling sand. She carefully steered the Bronco down the dirt road through a thick soup of dust. Once they hit the highway, they could barely make out the white divider line that Sally tried to follow. Occasionally other vehicles crept by from the opposite direction, and Abe could see the dim orbs of their headlights. Otherwise, he felt completely closed in—as if he and the other occupants of the Bronco were the only living things left on the planet. "I doubt anyone will show up with this mess," he said.

Forty-five minutes later they arrived at Dick's, and Sally pulled the Bronco around to the back, close to the exit. They had come early because they didn't want to run into anyone prematurely, and had decided the back exit would provide an easier escape if they had to leave in a hurry. Abe rapped on the door and Paco let them in.

Paco burst into laughter as soon as they stepped inside. "What do you think this is, a costume party? Close the door and take off that shit. You can't drink a beer with a mask covering your mouth. Everybody needs to relax a little. We got time." Paco took charge and seemed at ease.

"I think I'm ready for a beer," Abe said.

Paco glanced at Emily. "Your new uniform is hanging in the bathroom."

"I could use a beer myself," she said before leaving to change.

Sally opted for her usual, root beer. "And have a double shot of whiskey ready for after the shooting."

Emily disappeared into the bathroom while Abe, Sally, and Paco sat at a table sipping drinks, Abe in his assigned seat with his back against the wall and a clear view of the street. While he waited, four armed men emerged from the kitchen area. They surveyed the room, caught Paco's eye, and moved silently toward the bar.

"Your friends, I hope," Abe said.

"Yep." Paco stood up. "I've got to go hash over a few things with them before our guests arrive. Are you doin' okay, man?"

Abe nodded, took a swallow of beer, and watched Paco join his buddies.

When Emily reappeared, Abe hardly recognized her. She wore tight black pants that flared at the bottom. A skimpy red T-shirt that hugged her torso like a second skin said "Dick's—Get Your

Licks While You Can." Her hair hung in a seductive frame around her face, lips glistened with bright red lipstick, and her flashing dark eyes were outlined in black. Blue eye shadow highlighted her lids, and red high-heeled shoes completed the attire. She placed her tote bag under the table. "Don't laugh."

"Whoa," Abe said, and whistled. "The real Emily comes out. How'd you manage to hide your gun in that outfit?" *She looks sexy*, he thought, though he liked the other Emily better.

"Ankle holster." Before anyone knew what happened, Emily whipped the gun from its hiding place. "Pretty smooth, huh?"

Sally's eyes rounded and her mouth hung open. "Do that again, Emily."

Abe shook his head silently and let out a sigh. He began drumming his fingers on the tabletop, and let his mind go somewhere else, lost momentarily in the music of Mozart's *Requiem*.

Emily put her hand over his and stopped the rhythmic tapping. "Are you nervous? You can leave," she said.

He looked into the dark pools of her eyes and shook his head. "I'm sticking with you, sweetheart. It's already been decided."

The howling wind subsided to an occasional gust. Paco checked his watch—eight forty-five. "Anytime now. Who do you think's gonna show first?"

The few dim lights left burning gave the bar a ghostly appearance. Paco's friends lounged on barstools, silently watching, their faint reflections making ominous shadows that danced along the wall as they tipped their drinks.

At a nod from Paco, the men rose to their feet and disappeared behind the kitchen door. "Don't worry, they'll have you covered."

"Get in the Bronco," Abe said to Sally. "You know what to do."

Something in his tone and the atmosphere inside Dick's let Sally know this was no time for a smart comeback. She stood, her mouth a determined line, and silently nodded to everyone, then slipped out through the rear exit.

Emily began clearing the table of beer bottles, her face a mask except for her eyes, which flashed hard and bright. Abe leaned his chair against the wall and watched the street while Paco pretended to be busy behind the bar. The dust had settled somewhat so headlights of cars were visible. Abe watched them as they crept by.

"Nine o'clock." Paco polished already clean glasses and lined them on a shelf. "The dust storm probably held them up."

They could only sit and wait, deal with the tension that crackled through the room like static electricity. Abe commenced drumming his fingers again, caught himself, and chewed a nail. A strong gust of wind swirled the dust and he saw a car approach, the headlights barely penetrating the haze. The vehicle turned into a parking space in front of Dick's, and Abe recognized the shape of a large, dark-colored sedan. He couldn't detect through the tinted windows how many were inside besides the driver, but he had no trouble making out the Kansas plates attached to the front bumper. Emily shot him a quick look and he responded with a barely perceptible nod. She took two Coronas out of the cooler and brought them to his table, pulled a chair up close, and sat down. Abe wrapped his fingers around the cold beer bottle, trying to assume a nonchalant attitude.

24

The driver, tall and muscular, with slicked-back hair, stepped out of the car and stood under the light of the neon sign outside Dick's. He slowly looked up and down the street, turned his back to the wind, and shielded his lighter with a cupped hand while he lit a cigarette. The flash of the lighter illuminated the man's face, his hawk-like nose and swarthy complexion, giving Abe no doubts as to his identity. He remembered that face from the Clayton restaurant. Tonight the man was dressed in light slacks, a Hawaiian shirt unbuttoned halfway down, gold chains glittering on bare chest. After a final scan of the street, he opened the back door of the sedan.

A squat, penguin-shaped man in a Western suit and cowboy hat stepped onto the sidewalk, followed closely by a tall blond in high heels and tight red dress that didn't give much wiggle room. She pulled at her hemline, straightening clothing as best she could, while the heavy guy stood by and surveyed his surroundings. He adjusted his hat and waited for the driver to precede him through the entrance into Dick's.

"The short guy's gotta be DiMarco." Abe tilted the beer to his mouth. "The tall one is his bodyguard, I'm guessing. Plenty of room to hide a gun under that loose shirt."

"And it looks like there's no one except DiMarco, his floozy, and chauffeur–hatchet man for now. I've seen that bodyguard's face somewhere." Emily took a sip of her Corona. "Wonder where Corazón is?"

Abe realized how quiet it had become outside—no wind, no roar of motorcycle engines. "I'm pretty sure I heard some Harleys earlier. Might have lost their way in the dust storm."

"It's just as well. We'll deal with them one at a time." She put her arm around Abe's neck, tickled his ear. "Relax. This will be over soon. I didn't tell you before, but I have a police-issue microrecorder tucked in my waistband. I'll turn it on when they come to our table." Emily smiled, kissed him on the cheek, easily slipping into the girlfriend role.

Abe digested this new information. How she managed to hide anything in that outfit was a mystery. Emily never failed to surprise him. But he had to admit, he enjoyed the girlfriend part.

The two men stepped inside the near-empty establishment, gave Abe and Emily a long, scrutinizing stare, then approached the bar. The blond tottered behind them on six-inch heels, knees close together. "You got a little-girls' room? Oh geez, I gotta pee."

Paco pointed her in the direction of the bathroom, and turned his attention to the men. "What'll it be, gentlemen?"

"Give me a Dewar's, neat," said DiMarco in a bullfrog voice. "Make it a double, and some champagne for the lady—preferably pink. She likes that shit. Vito, here, on the other hand, never touches alcohol. Get him whatever the hell he wants."

"Kind of dead in here." Vito twisted his neck, looking from side to side, taking in the layout of the room. His roaming eyes returned to Paco's face. "Cream soda, tall glass, lots of ice."

"We're closed to the public tonight. Special guests only." Paco poured amber scotch into a glass, pushed it across the bar to DiMarco, and filled a glass with ice.

"Vito Benavutti," Emily whispered to Abe. "I recognize that vulture face. Used to be a hired gun for the Pannini syndicate in New York. I heard he came out West when the cops turned the heat on, and now it looks like he's DiMarco's trigger man. I'm turning on the tape."

Abe nodded and hoped his rattled nerves didn't show. He could hear everything DiMarco said in his booming basso voice.

DiMarco wrapped stubby fingers around his glass. "Jesus Eyes. That's a helluva name, don't you think? Ever hear of anyone with a name like that, bartender?"

Paco opened a bottle of cream soda and tilted his head in the direction of Abe's table. The other two men followed with their eyes, locking them momentarily on Abe's. He returned their look with his own steady gaze.

DiMarco took a long drink. "Let's go get acquainted." Before they headed toward Abe's table, he pulled a couple of bills out of his wallet and laid them on the bar. "Another round for everybody, whatever they're drinking, and give the lady a bottle of the pink stuff. Make sure you keep her glass full."

The woman came out of the bathroom patting her platinum hair, fresh cherry-colored lipstick smeared on her lips. "Oh, sugar. How'd ya know that's the very thing I was dying for?" She picked up the champagne glass and downed the contents, then closed her eyes as if in bliss. When DiMarco moved away, she grabbed her glass and the bottle, intending to follow him.

The mafia boss brushed her aside. "Sit over there in that booth. Tell the bartender to bring you another bottle if you run out. I got business to take care of." DiMarco walked toward Abe's table with a slow swagger that seemed to say he had all the time in the world.

The girl pretended to pout, shrugged, and headed toward a back booth with her bottle of champagne. She tried to talk Paco into playing some music and dancing with her, but when that failed

,she slipped into the booth and began guzzling champagne while singing an off-key rendition of Muddy Waters's "I Just Want to Make Love to You."

DiMarco stood in front of Abe. "You Jesus Eyes?"

"Who wants to know?" Abe looked at DiMarco through narrowed eyes.

"Tell the broad to get lost," said DiMarco. "And you'll find out." He snapped his fingers and Benavutti giggled with a high-pitched sound that whistled through his nose.

"Uh-uh. Not unless you tell your flunky the same. My lady stays. We don't have any secrets, do we, baby?" Abe draped an arm over Emily's shoulder. She snuggled up closer and tipped her beer to her lips, smiling seductively.

Benavutti bristled like a wet cat on a hot wire and reached behind his back.

DiMarco lifted his palm. "Easy, Vito. Not now." Benavutti relaxed his trigger finger and crossed his arms, but continued to give Abe a menacing look.

"What the hell?" DiMarco glowered at Abe. "You want the broad around, don't matter to me long as I get what I came for. Vito here gets kind of testy, though, so don't try nothin' cute." He pulled out a chair and sat down, his bodyguard standing directly behind him.

"I don't think you introduced yourself." Abe grabbed another Corona from the tray of drinks Paco had placed on the table.

The mafia boss picked up his scotch and took a long pull. "Name's Vicente DiMarco. Maybe you heard of me. I'm a businessman out of KC. A little bird told me about a missing key, something essential to my line of business. Somehow it fell into your hands, I hear. You wanna tell me how that happened, Jesus Eyes?"

"Stumbled on a little key, you could say, me and my girlfriend, and heard it might be worth something—to more than one party."

"Where's my key, now?" DiMarco had an edge to his voice, and Vito looked itchy again, like he wanted to pull out that gun of his, or bash Abe's face in.

"It's in a safe place. It'll cost you to find out where. Did you bring the money?" Emily had remained quiet so far, letting Abe take the lead while her recorder continued to run.

"How do I know you aren't lying? That you won't send me on a wild-goose chase out in this stinking desert once you get your hands on the cash?"

"Give the ten grand to my lady friend, and I'll take you there myself." Abe felt Emily's kick from under the table but gave no indication. The key burned in his pocket, but he wanted to fish for more incriminating evidence from DiMarco. And even if he had to take them out to the site of the fire, Abe thought he could lose them in the dark. "You get your key, go back to KC or wherever. My girlfriend will wait an hour, then come out and pick me up."

DiMarco let out a sound halfway between a snort and a laugh. "If the key isn't where you say, you're a dead man. You know that?" Then he shrugged. "Give the chick the cash, Vito. You, Jesus Eyes, get over here. How far we gotta go?"

"Not far. A little ways out of town."

Emily opened the envelope stuffed with ten bundles of hundreds and started counting. "It's all here." She dropped it in her bag. "Let me come with you."

"No, babe. You'll need to pick me up when this is over. Wait till 10:30. You know the place, the old burned-out miner's shack where they found the body of that gangbanger." Abe listened to the wind. Between gusts he thought he heard motorcycles.

"Fuckin' A, boss," said Vito, snickering. He pulled out a .22 pistol with a silencer and pointed it at Emily. "Hand over the ten grand, bitch. We don't need you two—know the place myself—been there before. Who do you think toasted that skinhead punk? We might have another weenie roast . . ."

"Shut up, Vito. You talk too much." DiMarco turned back to Abe. "You're not too smart, Jesus Eyes. What's to stop us from taking the money back and going out there alone?"

"You don't know where the key is hidden. Hard to find anything out there, and I don't think you want to dig around in ashes all night."

"And why shouldn't we kill you once we get what we want, like we wasted that other punk?"

"Yeah, the weenie roast," Vito snickered. He still had his gun pointed at Abe. "Get in the car, asshole, and your girlfriend, too." Abe stood up as if to leave with them, moving away from Emily.

Emily looked at Paco. "I have everything I need."

Paco nodded briefly to alert his men and reached under the bar for his shotgun. At the same time, Emily made a move for her ankle holster and stood with her gun in hand. The blond had slid down in the booth, completely oblivious of the action taking place around her.

But Vito wasn't DiMarco's hit man for nothing. He quickly reached out and grabbed Abe around the neck and, holding the pistol to his head, demanded that Emily put her piece down. For a moment everyone froze—a chaotic scene with Paco's men materializing from the kitchen, their guns pulled, but no one daring to fire a shot.

This is it, Abe thought when he felt the press of cold steel. Sweat beaded his forehead, and prickly hairs stood at attention on the back of his neck. Then he heard the roar of motorcycles announcing the arrival of more visitors.

25

The front door flew open and four riders barged in, guys in muscle shirts and leather vests. The sudden commotion caused Vito to turn his head, enough time for Emily to get off a shot. The bullet caught him in the shoulder and he yelled in pain, losing his grip on Abe and dropping the pistol. Abe made a dive for the weapon and scooted over to Emily's side, Vito's gun in hand.

DiMarco looked at Vito with disgust. "Didn't you learn nothin' in New York?" he said to his whimpering bodyguard. "Get up off the floor and stop sniveling. We got company."

The bikers stood four abreast, surveying the scene with cool composure. One stepped forward. He had Rico Corazón's drooping mustache and prominent canine teeth. A tattoo of a black hand with the letters "EME" across the palm covered his left shoulder. Abe remembered the first time those letters had caught his attention, on the vanity plates of the motorcycle in Clayton. Each of Rico Corazón's companions wore an identical tattoo. It stood for the Mexican Mafia. Ironically it was also very similar to a motif from his Jewish upbringing, and he didn't know why he hadn't made the connection before. It resembled the Hamsa Hand, a popular design of a hand with the thumb and pinky pointed outward. It often depicted an eye or Hebrew letters in the middle, thought to represent protection against evil. Abe hoped it would protect him now. Emily and Abe kept their guns trained on DiMarco and his man while Paco and his men shifted their attention to the biker gang.

"I can't believe this shit." DiMarco sat down, leaned back in his chair, and emptied his scotch.

"Hope we didn't miss the fiesta," said Corazón. "We got held up by a little dust storm and some pussy *gringo* skinheads. They wanted to come to the party, but we had to send them on their way. Told 'em they needed a special invitation, like you gave me."

"Yeah, we sent them to the nearest hospital." A heavyset newcomer sniggered. "A couple of broken bones and a little carving practice. Maybe they'll live, but they'll never look the same." The rest of the gang joined in harsh laughter.

Corazón sauntered up to Abe. "You must be the one I'm looking for. Came all the way to Las Cruces to invite me to your party, and look at the scum you brought along. Now tell your friends to put those guns, very slowly, on the floor. That's not a nice way to treat guests, *amigo*."

"You son of a bitch," said DiMarco.

Blood trickled down Benavutti's arm, and he whimpered. To Abe it appeared to be no more than a superficial wound, but Vito continued whining. "I need a doctor. I'm bleeding."

"Shut up, Vito," DiMarco said.

Corazón laughed, exposing yellow teeth, then looked at Abe. "So you're the famous Jesus Eyes," he said. "You don't look like no Jesus to me, but if I wuz you, *pendejo*, I'd lay that gun on the table— very carefully. And you, too, squaw." There was malice in his voice, any pretext of friendliness gone.

Paco walked from behind the bar and pumped the shotgun. "Okay, *payaso*, the game is over. Who the hell you think you are, Superman? You're outnumbered."

"All of you, put your hands in the air," said Emily to the four bikers.

There were six guns aimed in Corazón's direction. He briefly glanced at Emily, brushing her off like a fly. He locked his eyes on Paco, shook his head. "I wouldn't be stupid enough to try anything, *maricón*. You better tell those *perras* of yours to back off." Corazón laughed and turned his attention back to Abe. "Hey, Jesus Eyes, guess who we found in the alley? *Oye*, Flaco, bring the old lady in here so her friends can see her."

Nausea rose from the pit of Abe's stomach when he saw Sally being led into the bar by a skinny, rough-looking biker. The little creep reminded Abe of a weasel, one that had gone without a good meal for a long time. His arms and chest were covered with black hair, and long, greasy strands encircled a face marked by scars. There was a mean, hungry look in his bloodshot eyes. The biker's mouth hung open, then he shaped it into a sneer-like grin.

"Here she is, *jefe*," he said, pushing Sally in front. He had a hammerlock grip on her neck and a switchblade held at her throat. Duct tape covered her mouth. Her hands were tightly bound behind her back with more tape. Sally's eyes flashed, in spite of the fear she must have felt. Though used as a human shield, she appeared stubborn as ever. "Some shitty little mutt tried to bite me when I grabbed the old lady, but I gave him a kick and sent him flying," said the brute.

Patch. The realization pierced Abe like a knife to his heart. *How did he get in the Bronco? Where is he now?*

Paco raised a palm, cautioning his men to hold their fire. "Easy, *compadres*," he said. The men lowered their weapons.

"Let her go. Take me, instead," said Abe. "I'll lead you to that key. That's what you came for, right? If you hurt her, you'll never get it." In the quiet that followed, Abe found himself silently repeating a long forgotten Jewish prayer for protection: *"HaShem is my light and my salvation; whom shall I fear? HaShem is the stronghold of my life; of whom shall I be afraid?"*

Sally shook her head—still determined to bluff her braveness to the world.

"All right. If we lay down our weapons and give you what you want, will you agree to let the lady go?" Emily said in a measured voice.

Corazón laughed. "You're in no position to make deals, *mujer*."

Flaco tightened his grip on Sally's neck. "Why don't we beat the shit outta these scumbags, and if this *pinche maricón* don't give us what we want, I'll start slicing off little pieces of granny till he changes his mind." He took the knife away from Sally's throat and made slicing motions toward Abe. "Huh-huh-huh."

"You might want to give that some thought," Corazón said to Abe, showing his canines again. "Flaco loves to play with his knife."

Taking the knife away from Sally turned out to be a careless move on the biker's part. She seized the opportunity to make a run for it, but Corazón yanked her back by the hair and held her in front of him. No one fired a shot, probably fearing, as Abe did, that a stray bullet would land on Sally. Corazón gave Sally's hair another hard pull, causing her to flinch in pain. "Don't try being cute again, *vieja*, or you're coyote bait."

"What do you want from her?" Emily said. "I know you killed Easy Jackson, but what's so important that you'd kill a harmless old woman, too?"

"Jackson got what he had coming. He was a rat."

Abe felt vindicated when the biker said those words. He hoped Emily still had the tape running because he felt they now had confirmation Corazón killed Jackson. *A lot of good it's going to do us if we can't get out of this mess, though*, he thought.

Corazón took Emily's weapon and the .22 pistol Abe had taken from Vito Benavutti, who had slipped into unconsciousness with his head resting on the table. "Now no more talking and there won't be any killing, unless I say so. Huero, Chino, Largo, take these guns and go get the rest. Frisk them all, get their money, then tie 'em up tight. Flaco, keep an eye on *la abuela*, and don't screw up this time."

Paco remained grim faced, looking like he wanted to blow Corazón away, but relinquished the shotgun when he saw the knife back at Sally's throat.

"You don't know who you're dealing with," DiMarco said. "You're a dead man, Corazón."

Rico Corazón chortled and hit him on the side of the head with Emily's Glock. DiMarco toppled to the floor. Benavutti raised his head, opened his eyes, and was sent tumbling beside his boss when Corazón rewarded him with a vicious blow.

Paco and his Vietnam buddies were stripped of their weapons and left hog-tied and gagged with duct tape. Paco's eyes burned with hot hate as he and his friends were kicked and dragged behind the bar.

"I won't show you where the key is if anyone gets hurt," Abe said. "Leave the little lady here and I'll take you to where it's hidden. If you do anything to these people, you'll never see it. You can go ahead and kill me."

Corazón appeared to be considering his options. A few minutes later he told one of his men to bind and gag Emily. She tried to say something, give Abe some kind of message, before her lips were sealed shut, but he silenced her with his eyes.

Then, having evidently made up his mind, Corazón turned the Glock on Abe. "Okay, *amigo*. You're coming with us. We didn't plan on killing anyone tonight, but if you're lying, you're a dead man, and we'll come back here. *Comprende? Muerto.*" With a long-nailed index finger he made the sign of a knife across his throat. "Flaco, take the old lady and the Indian over there behind the bar with the rest of those *hijos de putas*. Get the cash from the register and grab some bottles of tequila. Might as well celebrate after we get our prize." He cackled, exposing pointed teeth.

Corazón held the gun on Abe while another member of the Mexican Mafia, the one called Huero, bound his hands behind his back. "Lights out," said Corazón, and someone hit the switch, throwing the bar into darkness. Abe was shoved outside and ordered onto the gang leader's bike. There wasn't much room behind Corazón, and he could barely move his fingers enough to grip the back of the seat for stability.

The streets remained dark and empty. Seemed like nobody wanted to venture out in the midst of a full-blown dust storm. There were no sounds except for the sudden gusts of wind and the frantic barking of a dog.

Corazón revved his engine. "Which way, *cabrón*? And you better not lead us wrong."

Abe hoped his trip out west wouldn't end with him lying dead somewhere in the Arizona desert. "When you hit the highway, go southeast."

26

Abe squeezed his eyes into narrow slits, trying to protect them from the stinging dust that swirled in the bike's path. The highway was nearly obliterated by freshly formed dunes, and the night loomed pitch-black. With Abe pinioned to the biker's back, they rode as one, leaning together in the twists and turns, and close enough for Abe to be enveloped in the rank smell of Corazón's body. Several miles south of Bisbee, they passed through Tintown. "Slow down," he yelled over the roar of engines. "There should be a graveyard someplace around here. The road is right past it."

"Better be," snapped Corazón. "I've had enough of you stuck to my back like a goddamned leech."

"Turn your headlight over there on the left."

Corazón swung the motorcycle around. The other bikers pulled alongside and pointed their lights in the direction Abe indicated. The dim outlines of crosses, barely discernible among windblown mounds of sand, beckoned them with erratic arms.

"There's the road." Abe exhaled a deep breath, no longer feeling fear, only a dogged resignation.

The five motorcycles turned onto the dirt trail and quickly became bogged in dunes. Their tires spun, threw sand, and left them half-buried, with nowhere to go.

Corazón turned off the ignition and put the kickstand down before giving Abe a shove. "Get off my back, asshole. The bikes can't handle this shit. How much farther we gotta go?"

"A mile, maybe two." Abe staggered to his feet. "We'll have to walk the rest of the way. We need a flashlight." His hands were still trussed tightly behind his back; his head pounded from the reopened cut. He brushed that aside and concentrated on the task at hand, spurred on by the belief Emily would get free.

They were forced to abandon the motorcycles near the turn-off, and Corazón remained in a foul mood. The five members of the Mexican Mafia stumbled through the choking sand, drinking tequila from the bottle, and cursing each step while the beam of a flashlight bounced ahead of them. Corazón pushed Abe in front, pulled out a gun, and snarled, "I have half a mind to waste you right now, *gringo*, or let Flaco cut you till you tell us where the key is. You've been playing games, bringing that wop piece of shit and his dickhead hit man out here, trying to cash in on both of us." He jabbed the gun into Abe's back. "I'll leave your head on a fencepost for the buzzards if you mess with me anymore." He grabbed the bottle from Flaco and tilted it up to his mouth, guzzling tequila as it dribbled down his chin.

The windstorm subsided, leaving a sky mottled with cumulus clouds. A crescent moon peeked through the clouds, exposing its narrow face, and illuminated the skeleton of the burned-out shack.

"There it is." Abe stared at the charred hulk, the image of Will's scorched body flashing through his mind. He had made a mistake in going along with the crazy scheme. If he had stopped Will, none of this would have happened. Will would not be lying in a hospital bed, burned beyond recognition. He heard his mother's oft-repeated admonition as she held the leather strap above her head: *Abraham, you're too damn smart for your own good. Let's see you talk your way out of this.* And, to himself, he said, *Okay, smart guy, what are you going to do now?*

The one they called Huero, the pale-skinned goon with icy eyes, ran the beam of the flashlight over the burned timbers. "Don't look like a good place to hide something, *jefe*. This guy's stalling. Want me to take him out? We can go back, get the girlfriend—make her talk."

Something caught Abe's eye when the flashlight beam skimmed over the ruined building. The shack had been erected so that the back was built into the cliff, and he saw what appeared to be an opening to a mine shaft. "The key's back in there." He indicated the four-foot-tall hole in the rocky cliff. "Let me have the light; I'll go in and get it."

"Chino," Corazón yelled. The heavyset, bald Latino with slanted Indian eyes looked up but didn't say anything. "Get the flashlight and go in there with the *gringo*. Make sure he don't come out without the key. And hurry up, *andele*."

"Uh, *jefe*, why don't you send Huero in there? He's already got the light. You know, man, I don't, uh, like them closed-in places."

"What's the matter, Chino? You scared of the dark? You chickenshit or something?"

"No, man. I ain't scared of nothing. Caves and things make me nervous is all. I ain't scared."

"Then don't give me that shit. Take the flashlight and that piece with the silencer you picked up in the bar, and don't let this pussy come out without the key." Corazón took a long pull of tequila, then grabbed Abe's shirt collar, pulling him up close, his rancid spit splattering Abe's face. "You understand what I'm saying, punk? Produce, or you're not leaving this place alive, then we go back for your girlfriend and the old lady." He pushed Abe away, but the sour stench of his breath lingered, even as Abe bent down to enter the mine adit. Chino, looking reluctant, followed.

The tunnel roof did not provide room for a man to stand upright, and in some places the beams had collapsed, making it hard to maneuver. A jumble of rocks and litter cluttered the path in front of them. Shortly after they entered the cave, the two men were swallowed in total darkness with only a narrow beam from the flashlight to guide them. Abe felt spiderwebs brushing his face, but instead of loathing, he felt a certain comfort from the arachnids. As a child, whenever he found a spider in the house he would carefully whisk it outside, out of reach of his mother's swatting newspaper. The habit of rescuing spiders continued into adulthood, so that now he moved carefully through the webs, silently apologizing for destroying their labors.

Not so Chino. He batted at the sticky structures, groaned and cursed. "Get that fuckin' key so I can get out of here, goddamn it." His high-pitched voice, betraying panic, reverberated through the mine shaft.

"It's up here, on a ledge," Abe lied while he considered his odds if he made a run for it. "Cut my hands loose, so I can reach it."

Chino hesitated, but Abe insisted. "I can't get it unless my hands are free. It's behind a big nest of black widows," he said, sensing the arachnophobic biker would never put his own hand into a nest of spiders.

"Fuck this. Make it fast." The biker took out his pocketknife and cut through the duct tape that bound Abe's hands behind his back.

Once his arms were free, Abe flexed them and clenched his fists to get the circulation going. He positioned himself in front of Chino, moved faster, feeling his way along the wall, putting distance between him and the biker. When he felt sufficiently ahead, he wedged himself behind a slab of rock and waited.

175

"Hey, *gringo*. Where the hell are you? Get back here."

He heard footsteps, the clunk of metal against rock, saw a flash of light, heard the sound of gunshots, bullets pinging off the rock sides of the cave. Abe held his breath and counted—one, two, three, four, five, six—then silence. He remained in his hiding place and listened. A minute later Chino's voice echoed through the cave.

"*Jefe*, I can't find the damn flashlight. Rico . . . *jefe* . . . I can't see nothin' . . . there's spiders everywhere. *Ayee, ayúdame, por favor!*"

Abe knew it would only be minutes before the others came into the mine and started looking for him. His head felt like someone had hammered it with a sledge, and the blackness of the cave disoriented him, but he had to move forward and find a better hiding place. He eased his way out of the rocks and felt for the wall of the tunnel, then hurried along in the direction he hoped would take him away from Corazón and his men.

Loud voices and thudding feet resounded through the mine. Abe looked back and saw a faint light bobbing. Then he heard Corazón's angry voice when he came upon Chino.

"You stupid *pendejo* . . . you let him get away."

Abe heard the sounds of thuds and groans, as if someone was kicking or pummeling Chino.

"*Aye, jefe, por favor . . . no mas.* Let me get out of this cave. I swear I do anything you want. Anything, I kill him for you. *Por el amor de dios, jefe*, no, no, don't shoot."

Abe heard a scream, two gunshots, and then nothing from Chino. Shortly after, the enraged voice of Corazón bellowed through the cave. "See what you made me do, Jesus Eyes. You gonna die now. I will tear you apart, piece by piece!"

He flattened himself against the wall of the mine shaft, shaking uncontrollably, cold sweat drenching his body, his throat as dry as the Arizona desert. He couldn't think, only react to adrenaline and instinct. The voices and footsteps came closer, the light brighter.

Someone fired in his direction, the shots sounding like cannons. Abe had to move on and stumbled forward. Trying to shake off his dizziness, he groped the wall, searching with his fingers for anything to grasp, but felt instead a slimy wetness. His feet slipped from under him and he began to slide downward, plummeting through space as if there were no bottom to wherever his body headed. He thought this must be what death feels like—until the jolt of landing in a frigid, underground pool brought him to a sudden wakefulness.

As soon as he hit the water, Abe's eyes flew open and he gasped. He thrashed around in the icy darkness, not able to touch bottom, near panic. He forced himself to stop, realizing he had to conserve energy. Thinking there might be a spring or aquifer nearby, he swam until his hand touched the sides, then worked his way around the circumference of the pool. The steep, slime-covered cavity offered nothing. His body shuddered from the cold, but he kept moving, even though he wanted to surrender to the frigid water, believing this to be another sign of impending death, like one of Dante's levels of hell. *Next will be fire, if I live that long.* Shivering and no longer able to feel anything more than a dull ache in his limbs and the downward pull of water, Abe nearly surrendered to the icy lake, allowing it to swallow him. But when he heard gunshots and the approaching sounds of men, he fought back. Thoughts of Sharon, her love of life, her courage and desperate will to live, until she acknowledged and accepted the inevitability of death, compelled him to keep fighting. She would not want him to quit. He dog-paddled in small concentric circles until he felt a current moving under his legs.

Abe dove under water, groping the bottom. It was as slick as the sides, but he felt something different, movement, and a split in the rocky depths where water seemed to be flowing into the pool. His hands searched for anything to grasp and finally clutched a jagged protuberance. Using a final reserve of strength, Abe pulled himself through the fissure and up onto a narrow streambed where he collapsed, gasping for breath, in its shallow depths.

He could hear voices, but their flashlight beam couldn't reach him. One of Corazón's men said, "He must have fallen in that hole, probably dead."

Corazón answered back, his voice seething with rage. "We're never going to find the bastard, or the key."

"We gotta get out of here, *jefe*," another said.

And Corazón answered in a maddened screech. "I'll kill you, *jodido* Jesus Eyes."

27

Abe crawled on his stomach along the shallow stream, clambering upward, toward its source, scraping his body against jagged rocks and strands of slippery moss, driven to continue in the hope of finding a way out. Pain racked his body, fatigue his mind, but he pushed on, inch by inch. He stopped frequently—to breathe, to rest, but never for long. Freezing water numbed his arms and legs, and things he could not see swept across his face, wriggling past him—salamanders, fish, snakes, or perhaps large aquatic insects. They didn't bother him, and a deadness began to dull the pain in his limbs. It would have been good to lie down and sleep, but he continued moving forward, upward, letting Beethoven's *Moonlight Sonata* fill his mind, drowning all thoughts of Corazón and his men, obliterating his fear. He didn't know how long he followed the watery path, but at last his body gave out and he could move no farther.

Unsure how much time had elapsed, Abe suddenly awoke to high-pitched squeaking sounds and the thunder of fluttering wings. He opened his eyes to a weak light, and saw thousands of bats swooping above him. Rubbing his eyes and peering ahead, he discerned an opening near the top of the cave, and the source of light. In the breaking dawn, myriad bats were swarming into the cave by way of the small aperture.

He was in a grotto with a high dome, and could stand upright. Wading through the stream toward the light, Abe found the gap in the rocks and, stretching, explored it with his hands. Finding it too small for his body but large enough to poke his head through, Abe searched for something to stand on and spotted a pile of boulders against the wall. Using his remaining reserve of strength, he rolled a large boulder under the opening, climbed on top, and grasped the sides of the hole, letting his bruised and bloodied hands sink into a thick crust of guano. When Abe squeezed his head through and looked around, he realized he was on the edge of a rocky bluff. An endless desert, speckled with mesquite, saguaro, and prickly pear stretched in all directions. Buzzards circled overhead. *Are they waiting for me?* Other than those harbingers of death, there were no signs of life.

He shouted for help until his voice became a harsh whisper, but his cries were lost in the vast, empty land. Abe climbed down from the boulder and stood in a thick layer of guano. He retraced his steps to the stream in the hope it would lead to an alternative exit. That proved to be another dead end, as the stream dissipated into nothing more than a puddle formed from seepage through cracks in the limestone wall. Feeling hopeless, like a rat in a trap, running out of options, he returned to the boulder to look once again. That was when he heard the sounds, faint at first, then louder, of a barking dog. *Oh, God, could it be? Could Patch have found me?*

It seemed impossible, but there on a rise a short distance from the opening stood his scruffy, beautiful three-legged pooch, wagging his tail and barking in excited recognition. Right behind Patch, scrambling up the rocks, came Emily. Abe broke into a huge grin and let out a whoop of joy.

"It really is you. I can't believe it. You look like shit, and I bet you smell like it, too. Bat shit all over your face," she said, but her smile matched the radiance of his.

"Goddamn, Emily," Abe croaked. "What took you so long?" He heaved a huge sigh of relief. "How'd you find me, sweetheart?"

"It's a long story. But don't be sweet-talking me right now. First things first—we need to get you out of there. Are you hurt?"

"No, I'm okay, a few bruises and scratches. This is the only way out. Do you have a pickax or anything you can use to make the hole bigger?"

"It so happens I think we do. Hold tight, I'm going back to get the rest of the group. We're not that far from the road. Sally is with Paco and two of his pals, checking the mine, and Paco brought his truck. There's a big toolbox in the bed."

"Wait. First I need to know, did anyone get hurt? Is Sally okay?"

"Everyone is fine, Abe. I'll tell you all about it after we get you out."

Emily disappeared from view, but Patch remained close, barking animatedly, as if encouraging his master to climb out of the hole. Alone with his dog, Abe let the tears stream down his face as he rubbed Patch's head and marveled at the miracle that Emily and the others had managed to free themselves and find him.

Ten minutes later Emily returned with Sally, Paco, and two of his buddies. The men carried a pickax, a sledgehammer, and a mattock. When they saw Abe's head poking out of the opening in the rocks, they all let out a whoop.

Paco hefted the pickax in the air. *"Cuidado, hombre,"* he said as Abe withdrew his head and Paco brought the pick down near the opening. After two hours' work, the men pulled him free.

Sally clapped her hands and ran to greet him when Abe emerged, but backed off when she got a whiff of guano. "I sure am glad to see you, but, phewee, you stink. I wanted to give you a big hug, but I think I'll wait till you've had a bath."

Abe picked up his dog and held him close, grinning at everyone. "Not half as glad as I am to see you." When they reached the Bronco he climbed in the backseat beside Emily. Exhausted, ragged, and filthy, he closed his eyes, leaned back, and exhaled a long sigh. "Okay, Em. How the hell did you find me?" Patch laid his head across Abe's lap.

"We knew you were going to the burned shack, so we came out here and looked in the mine. When we heard someone moaning, everyone thought it was you, but it turned out to be one of Corazón's men, wounded but still alive. The rest of the gang was nowhere in sight. This guy, Chino, had been shot and left to die, so he didn't hesitate to rat on Corazón. But we'll get into that later. One of Paco's pals dropped Chino off at the hospital in Bisbee." Emily took a breath and scratched the dog's ears. "Patch is actually the one who found you. We wanted to search the mine, but Patch kept barking outside of the entrance and running in this direction. I finally followed him, and you know the rest."

"I didn't know my dog had jumped into the Bronco when we started out for Paco's. But now I'm sure glad he did."

"He must have climbed into the back when we weren't looking," Sally broke in. "Then he laid low till we reached Paco's. Once you two went inside, he jumped up in the front seat with me. Tricky little son of a gun."

Abe rubbed the dog's head. "You saved my life, boy."

"You know what they say—what goes around comes around. You saved him once, and now he's repaying the deed," Emily said.

Abe remained quiet. *Sharon saved Patch. Maybe Sharon saved me as well.*

"What are you thinking?"

"Nothing, just that . . . I wouldn't be alive if you hadn't followed Patch, Emily."

"Karma," she said, her eyes shining like polished obsidian.

No one spoke during the ride to Sally's. Abe let his head drop onto his chest, and, within minutes, he began to snore.

28

Following a long, hot soak in the tub, Abe succumbed to Sally's insistence that she examine his wounds. Finally satisfied he wasn't suffering from anything a hot meal and rest couldn't cure, she left him sitting in the living room and went in the kitchen to "put together some breakfast fixings." Abe patted the sofa cushion and beckoned Emily to sit beside him.

Emily snuggled up close. "You do smell much nicer." She also had showered and emanated a clean scent he had come to associate with her—that of rain falling on mountain sage.

"Now don't you try sweet-talking me. I want to hear how everything came down at Dick's after I left with Corazón." He draped his arm around her and nuzzled her damp hair.

"I tried, we all tried, wiggling free from the duct tape, or looking for something sharp to rub up against that might cut through, but we couldn't move, and we couldn't talk."

Abe nodded, picturing the sight of everyone hog-tied and helpless.

"Then, sometime after midnight, the blond woke up."

"The floozy that came with DiMarco. I forgot about her. She must have passed out in the booth."

"Right. She didn't have a clue as to what had been going on. She heard banging noises coming from behind the bar and staggered over to see who was making all the commotion. She was still pretty drunk."

"And probably looking for more champagne."

Emily smiled, but seemed sympathetic when she described the girl. "DiMarco picked her up in Las Vegas and promised her a good time if she came along for the ride. She's just a lost girl trying to make it in a tough world, so she obliged. Didn't really have any attachment to DiMarco or the Mafia."

Nothing stirred in the silent stillness left by the previous night's winds, and midmorning sun flooded the room. The dust storm had rearranged the landscape and settled on the surfaces of Sally's household, giving everything a muted look. "So, what did she do when she saw you?"

"First she screamed. Then she looked back and forth from me to DiMarco, her eyes round as saucers. He grunted and squirmed, trying to get her attention, his face purple with rage, but in the end she came over and pulled the tape off my mouth." Emily tentatively touched her lips. "It hurt like hell, but I started talking fast, telling her she did the right thing, that the men she came with were gangsters, they had tried to kill us, and that she should get as far away from them as possible."

"She believed you?"

"Of course. Once my hands were free, the girl and I, her name is Desiree, cut Sally and Paco and his buddies loose. Then I grabbed DiMarco's keys from Vito's pocket, gave them to Desiree, and told her to take off, go somewhere besides Vegas, then ditch the car. I took a few big bills from DiMarco's wallet to sweeten her getaway and advised her to lay low, get a new line of business, and never mention to anyone what happened."

Abe chuckled, and Emily started giggling. Pretty soon they were both laughing, whether from exhaustion, giddiness, relief, or the unlikely turn of events—it didn't matter. Cathartic laughter filled the room.

Sally appeared at the kitchen door with the coffeepot in hand. "What's going on in here that's so durn funny?"

"Who would have thought"—Abe gasped for breath—"that we would be saved by a scruffy little three-legged mutt and a bleached-blond floozy in a tight red dress and six-inch heels?"

"Huh." Sally shrugged. "Well, why not? It's another one of life's little mysteries. You know, that gal would have made a good nurse, if she hadn't taken up that other trade. Her heart's in the right place." She dismissed them with a shake of her head, as if the unexpected in life should be expected. "Who wants bacon and biscuits and coffee? You better come and get it while it's hot."

No one could mistake Sally's heart, Abe thought, while he slathered butter and honey on his sixth biscuit. His hunger satisfied, he wanted to hear the rest of Emily's account. "What did you do with DiMarco and Benavutti?" he asked between bites and slurps of coffee.

"Paco and his boys made sure their knots were tight, then they took off for the burned shack. I called Bisbee Police and identified myself. I said I was working undercover on a case involving Vicente DiMarco and Vito Benavutti. I added that while making an arrest, Rico Corazón and some of his Mexican Mafia biker gang came into Dick's, robbed the place, and left everyone bound and gagged—that I managed to escape and went after Corazón."

"You gave them your name? Isn't that going to get you in hot water?"

Emily laughed. "I gave them a false name and said I worked with Zuni Nation Police. We're always in hot water with the Zuni, anyway. Before I hung up, I told them I left a microrecorder on the bar with a taped confession of the Tintown murder and explosion."

Abe chewed on that. "That lie about the false name is going to catch up with you, Em."

"By the time they get through a big runaround from the Zuni and figure out who I really am, Corazón will be behind bars and this case wrapped up. They won't have any reason to bother with me."

Sally seemed anxious to relate her part in the story, and broke into the conversation. "I heard Patch raising hell at the back door. So, soon as I got loose, I let him in." She sliced open a biscuit and filled it with bacon. "He started sniffing all over the place, looking for some trace of you."

"And then he found me. I always knew this little fella was smart, but . . ." Abe reached down to where Patch lay curled at his feet and stroked his head. "Don't worry, boy, we won't be separated again." The warm bath and full stomach compounded his sleepiness. He fought the desire to close his eyes, and covered his mouth to hide a yawn.

When Sally caught him in the act, she ordered him back on the sofa. "We've been up all night and everyone could use some rest," she said, bossy and taking charge. Abe gladly obliged.

Abe awoke to the sound of women's voices. The lingering remnants of a disturbing but forgotten dream left him disoriented and dry mouthed. He licked his lips. Purple shadows graced the walls where there had been bright sunshine. Had he really slept the entire day? He stretched his arms, felt the soreness in his muscles, the stiffness in his back. His body ached, but he was alive, and looking down he saw that Patch had not left his side. He closed his eyes and tried to listen to the conversation taking place in the kitchen. Emily was speaking in an earnest way to Sally, as if trying to convince her of something.

"I've been thinking about it all day. I have to go. I need to see my brother first, then I'm heading back to headquarters, tell them what I found out and see if they will let me continue working on the case. You and Abe are staying behind, Sally. There's no need for you two to be involved in this any longer."

"It's my life," Sally protested. "I can durn sure decide if I want to be involved or not."

"Not anymore, Sally. I want to get Corazón and bring him in, but it has to be done within the law if it's going to stick. I've been going rogue, acting on emotion, but I know there are procedures that need to be followed. I'm going to nail that bastard and make sure he spends the rest of his life in jail. I can't tell you how much I appreciate everything you've done, but it's time I started using my brain."

Abe sat up, tried to clear his head, not sure he heard correctly, and if Emily would really leave without him.

"There's a note in here explaining things to Abe. You two split the ten thousand dollars we took off DiMarco. Tell Abe to head on out to California. That taped confession I got from Corazón should clear Abe's name. Maybe the Staties will focus their investigation on the real killer now. Good-bye, Sally. *Hágoóneé*. Whenever I pass through this way again, I'll come out and see you."

Abe thought he must have been dreaming, then he heard footsteps, the closing of a door. *This can't be happening*, he thought. *I have to stop her.* "Emily," he yelled, as he jumped to his feet and rushed into the kitchen. He opened the door and called out again as he ran down the driveway. "Emily, wait." But it was too late. The Bronco roared down the dirt road leaving nothing for his words to fall on but a cloud of dust. He felt confused, desolate, angry. As he turned toward the house, he saw Sally standing in the doorway. She held out a manila envelope and met his eyes, her face screwed into a dejected frown.

"She didn't want our help anymore," Sally said, handing the envelope to Abe. "She left the money, and a letter for you."

29

Abe stepped onto the porch and reached for the envelope. He felt stunned, betrayed, after what they had been through together. She had saved his life—he had saved hers. Why would she leave without a word? He took the envelope from Sally and looked inside. It was bulky, fat with hundred-dollar bills, but he ignored them and reached for the slip of yellow notebook paper, the sheet folded sloppily as if she had hurriedly crammed it in before changing her mind. The brief, scribbled message offered little. He read in silence, his back turned to Sally who still lingered in the doorway as if she, too, awaited more explanation.

Abe,

I'm sorry, but this is the way it has to be. I have to leave before the cops come, and so do you, but in the opposite direction. Continue your journey—see the ocean like you planned. I've caused both you and Sally too much trouble, and now I need to get back to legitimate police work. What we had . . . well, it was good. I can only say sorry again, for everything. Take your half of the money and leave. Your job is done, your record clean.

Emily

It felt like a slap in the face. Abe crumbled the note into a tight ball and tossed it on the ground. When he turned to face Sally, he couldn't hide his anger. He handed the envelope back to her. "Keep the damn money, Sally. I don't want it."

"Abe . . ." Sally began, but he cut her short.

"I mean it. You earned it. I'll get my gear together. Patch and I will clear out." He stomped into the house, then swung around and came back out to face Sally again. "Do you have someplace you can go for a while? Before the cops come sniffing around asking questions? I don't think Paco will give us away, but just in case. There's no reason for you to get involved."

Before she could answer, he reentered the house and gathered his few belongings.

Sally stood at the door, blocking his exit, arms crossed over her chest.

"I don't get it. Why would that hardheaded Indian gal take off like that? And why did she leave us all this money? I don't need it, neither. Got everything I want right here. You earned it." She held out the envelope. Abe shook his head. "I'm not moving till you take it." She didn't budge until he took the envelope from her and stuffed it in his backpack. A wistful look softened her features. "You know, I liked that spunky gal, and you two made a mighty handsome couple."

Abe put his arms around the old nurse, holding her bony body in a tight embrace. "Forget it, Sally. Some things aren't meant to be. Who knows? Maybe I'll pass back through here someday. Right now, there's an ocean I need to find." He kissed her lightly on the forehead. "Thanks for everything." Before he drove away he turned and waved good-bye to Sally's wooden figure.

Abe wanted to see Will before he left, even though a swing through Phoenix took him out of his way. He followed the two-lane highway to the small town of Benson where he topped off his gas tank at a Texaco station. His anger had drained away, leaving in its place the same cold emptiness and desolation he had been living with since Sharon's death. He reached into his pocket to pay the old man behind the counter, relieved that Sally had forced the money on him. Otherwise, he would have been left with nothing but a few dollars and change. *You're too stubborn—too much pride, Freeman*, he lamented. He would have to find a job and pay Sally back after he reached California. And how long would he stay there? And where would he go when that didn't work for him? Abe didn't have an answer.

"How much farther to Phoenix?" Abe asked the attendant.

"'Bout a hunnerd sixty miles due west." The grisly old-timer counted out change from a twenty. "Jest stay on I-10 and head straight through Tucson on to Phoenix. You got family there, mister?"

"Nah, passing through. Give me a pack of Camels, filtered, while you're at it." He quit smoking years ago, but the idea appealed to him now—might help him relax. "That'll be it," he said, accepting change and cigarettes from the old man's grease-stained hand.

The sun dropped in the western sky, setting the streaked clouds ablaze and highlighting the strange red-rock formations lining the highway. Abe sped on, chain smoking, unmoved by the spectacular scenery.

On the outskirts of Phoenix he found a place he could pull off the highway. The city spread ahead of him, an aberration of identical houses and strip malls sucking the life out of the thirsty desert. The endless urban sprawl depressed Abe. He left the rest stop and eased into heavy traffic. "Who could live here, Patch?" Then he thought of Will, held hostage in a hospital room somewhere in this unwelcoming city, and pulled into a convenience store to ask directions to the Phoenix Burn Center.

After several wrong turns and dead ends, Abe located the hospital. He parked the truck close to the main entrance and entered the lobby. A large semicircular desk with a sign stating "Information" sat in the center of the room. Abe stood in line behind an elderly couple talking to the receptionist and waited for the pair to leave.

"Yes, what can I do for you?" The attractive young woman behind the desk looked up and caught his eye.

"I'm looking for a friend. Could you tell me if Will Etcitty is still in room two twenty-three?"

The pert blond smiled sweetly. "One moment, please," she said as she scrolled through her computer monitor. "Oh yes, Mr. Etcitty. He has been moved to the third floor, room three sixteen." She batted mascaraed lashes that rimmed her sea-green eyes. "You know, you're the second person in the last hour to ask for him. I remember because the pretty Indian lady seemed in such a hurry, and she looked upset."

Abe bolted toward the distant stairwell.

"The elevator is right around the corner at the end of the hall," the receptionist chirped to his back. "Visiting hours end at eight."

He turned around, found the elevator, and punched number three, drumming his fingers on the wall while it groaned and swished upward. A stop on the second floor had him waiting impatiently in the corner as a couple of interns dressed in green scrubs struggled with a gurney. When the bell rang announcing the third floor, Abe hurried out, saw the arrow and sign that read "Rooms 301–328," and headed in that direction.

The closer he got to Will's room, the more hesitant he felt. If he encountered Emily, what would he say to her? He could give her the money, tell her to save it for Will. What if she told him to leave—that she didn't want to see him? He stood in the hall near the open door, waiting for courage. Finally he entered.

"Who's there?" The male voice sounded wheezy and unfamiliar. "What do you want?" The eyes of the gaunt figure lying in the bed were shaded by a bony hand. The right hand, swaddled in some kind of skin-colored elastic wrap, rested limply on the sheet. The same type of bandaging covered most of his face. A bag of fluids slowly dripped through a tube attached intravenously to the man's left arm. There was no one else in the room.

Abe dropped his head, felt a trembling in his lips. *Why couldn't she have waited a little longer?* Overcome by sadness and a feeling of defeat, he stared at the inert figure lying on the bed, hoping in desperation that he might have stumbled into the wrong room. Though he had visited a week before, there was nothing familiar about the person who gaped blankly with milky eyes in his direction. "Is that you, Will?"

The man in the bed smiled faintly and let his head fall back on the pillow. A whistling sigh escaped through half-closed lips. "Abe. I dreamt you'd come for me."

Abe looked at the broken body and tried to reconcile it with the robust man he had known. "Yeah, it's me, Abe, that freeloading white man. I decided to leave, head on out West, so I wanted to come by and see you first and say good-bye." Abe exhaled a long, slow breath, then rushed on. "Paco's taking care of your old Chief until you're ready for it." When Will didn't say anything, Abe continued. "And you have some money coming. It's a long story, but half of ten grand is yours, hell, all of it, if you want." Will remained silent. "I'm headed out to California. Emily doesn't need me anymore, and I'm free to go—as far as the law's concerned, I mean." He realized he was blabbering. He couldn't believe the bigger-than-life Indian had become so ravaged in such a short time. "Christ, Will. I thought you were getting better. Are they treating you all right here?"

"Okay, I guess . . . I don't need the money, Abe, but maybe Mom can use it. Don't need my old Chief either. I won't come out of this hospital alive." He took several gasping breaths. "Emily left a while ago. You missed her by fifteen minutes. I asked her to take me home, but she said she couldn't." Another pause. "Said I had to wait, continue my treatment. She told me Mom was on her way and would stay till they released me. Emily doesn't understand . . ." The effort of speaking so many words had left him panting. "Abe," he wheezed, "I'll be gone before my mother gets here. I have to go home—to Grandfather. If I'm gonna die, I want to die the Navajo way, on my land."

Abe swallowed hard. He would not see Emily. He couldn't go chasing after her, and Will wanted the impossible from him. "You're not going to die, Will. This is the best burn center in the Southwest. You'll get good care here and be home soon." But looking at the emaciated body, he didn't believe his own words.

Will slowly shook his head back and forth. "No. If I stay here, away from my land and people, I will die."

Abe waited while Will caught his breath.

"I'm almost blind, I can hardly breathe, but I know what I feel inside. I want to go home," he gasped. "A blessing from Grandfather before . . ." His words were lost in a coughing fit as tears filled his eyes.

"But, Emily . . ." Abe began.

Will drew in a deep, rasping breath before he spoke. "Emily is hardened by things that have happened to her. She's afraid to face the truth, so she closes her heart as well." He stopped, waiting for his breath to return. "Take me home, Abe. I beg this of you. Don't let me die in this place."

Abe shook his head vigorously. "Uh-uh, no, Will. I can't do it. If I take you out of here you might die before you reach your grandfather's. You need to have those fluids, the antibiotics, skin grafts, all the medicine they're giving you. And what about the pain? Hang in there, buddy. You're going to make it."

"Damn it, Abe." Will made a sudden movement and jerked the IV tube from his arm. "I'm goin' home, if I have to walk." He struggled to sit up and move his legs to the side of the bed, but the effort became too much, and he fell back, his breathing ragged and gurgling. "Help me," came out in a hoarse whisper.

Abe rushed to the bedside, panic causing his heart to pound. He raised the head of the bed so Will reclined in a more comfortable position and could breathe easier, and reached for the bell to ring the nurses' station.

Will pushed his hand away. "Don't call anyone."

"You're not going to die, Will." Even when he said the words out loud Abe didn't know if he believed them or not. He had been a conflicted man for a long time. He hated to kill anything, yet he had killed Sharon, the person he loved most. Did he run away from New Jersey to escape that memory or to somehow seek redemption? And if Will died at his hands, he would have another death on his conscience. He looked at his Navajo friend, saw the pleading in his eyes, and understood the connection Will had with his land. He believed him. As long as he remained in this sterile hospital, his friend would not heal, and Abe would never find peace by running away.

He scanned the room and saw a wheelchair against the wall. Could he possibly get Will past the nurses' station and out the door? He gently wrapped Will's body in sheets and tried to lift him into the wheelchair. Will stood a good six inches taller than Abe, and though he was much thinner now, it was like lifting a deadweight. "Sorry, pal. Let me know if this hurts." Abe carefully positioned the man's feet and arms on the rests.

A semblance of a smile took shape on Will's cracked lips. "*Ahéhee'. Baa ahééh nisin, díidí,*" he whispered.

Abe didn't understand the words, but he knew they had something to do with thanking him. He pulled the sheet partially over Will's head, concealing his face, and after checking the hallway in both directions, wheeled him out the door.

Ten feet from the elevator he ran into a heavyset red-headed nurse with a name tag reading: "Hilda Sorenson, ICU Supervisor."

"Excuse me. Where are you going with that patient?"

"Oh, just taking him back to his room. My uncle wanted to get some fresh air. Then he fell asleep."

The nurse frowned, started to respond, but was interrupted by a flashing red light and beeping sounds. "You aren't supposed to take patients out of their rooms without permission. Make sure you ring for the nurse to help get him back into bed," she said over her shoulder as she hurried down the hall.

Abe took the opportunity to duck into an elevator.

Once the door closed, Will lifted his head, pulled himself up straighter, and managed a feeble grin.

He's trying to put up a good front, but he's in terrible shape. I hope he can handle this. Will, you better hang on until I get you home, buddy. I can't deal with another death on my conscience. Abe shook his head. "I should take you back for trying to pull one over on me," he said kiddingly.

"No. Keep going. I meant it when I said I'd die if I had to stay. Food's terrible," he rasped. "I'll starve to death."

Although he said it in jest, Abe knew he was serious. "Shit. If you die on me, I'll be back in jail, you know."

"I want to go home, that's all. Grandpa will understand."

"That's where we're going. Hang on."

By the time the door of the elevator opened on the main floor, Will had dropped his head down again. Abe paused in the open doorway, looking both directions. When he saw the receptionist distracted by a group of visitors, he made his move. Pushing the wheelchair as quickly as he could, Abe dashed for the exit. In less than a minute they were beside the Toyota.

Abe opened the passenger door, mumbling to himself. "I don't know why I'm doing this, damn it. Here, let me help you."

Will pushed himself to a standing position. He wavered, his hands shook, but his voice remained resolute. "I can manage."

They left the wheelchair in the parking lot. Abe drove back to the highway and headed north, away from the flat desert of Phoenix and toward the mountains of Flagstaff.

30

Abe sensed more than saw the change in landscape as they climbed toward Flagstaff. Clouds obliterated the moon, but he felt the closeness of towering rock formations and tall pines. Will drifted off to sleep almost immediately. To Abe, each rattled breath from the dozing man sounded like a gasp for life, and further convinced him that Will's recent show of bravado had taken a toll. Fortunately, Abe still had the pain pills from his stay in the hospital in case Will needed them.

They were outside of Flagstaff and Abe had pulled over to check the map when Will's head jerked up.

"We're close to Navajo country," he said.

"How do you know? You've been sleeping the whole time."

"I can smell the mutton stew," he rasped. "Take the exit for I-40 east." Will paused, breathing heavily before resuming. "It'll be a little ways further. You'll see a turnoff for Winona. Follow it. Less chance of someone finding us on that highway."

The effort to speak brought on a coughing spell. Abe glanced at his friend to make sure he was all right. He had planned on following the route to Tuba City and then on to Farmington, and started to tell Will that it would be quicker that way. But when he looked at him, the Navajo repeated his wish to take the slightly longer route.

Abe followed the sign for the Winona exit.

As the two-lane highway stretched away from Flagstaff, traffic thinned until there was nothing to be seen but an occasional distant twinkle of lights. Somewhere between Leupp and Dilkon, Will stirred and opened his eyes.

"Head toward that light."

"What light?"

"Doesn't matter. Any one of them. The first one you see."

Abe spotted a dim glow a mile or so off the road on the right. "Do you know someone out there?"

"I know everyone out here," Will whispered. "This is the home of my father's clan. Slow down so you don't miss the road."

Abe had not encountered a single vehicle on this deserted stretch of highway. He brought the truck to a crawl and scanned the side of the road for any sign of a turnoff. Slowing at a break in the tumbleweed, he discerned rutted tire tracks that appeared to lead in the direction of the distant light. Overcome with doubts concerning the wisdom of following this path, he told Will, "I don't think we should stop anywhere until we get to your grandpa's place."

Will caught his breath after a spasm of coughing. "We have to stop here, Abe. I mean it. My people, they'll help me make it the rest of the way."

Abe glanced at his passenger and pulled onto the dirt road. "Okay, but I don't get it," he said, shaking his head. "I hope this won't take long. We should keep moving."

"When you get in front of the hogan, honk your horn. That's the Navajo way to announce yourself. Somebody will come out to see what's up." Seemingly exhausted from the strain of so much talking, Will closed his eyes and, breathing heavily from his mouth, let his head fall forward.

Abe thought Will had passed out. He drove slowly over the bumpy road, trying to avoid the numerous potholes, not wanting to jostle Will's injured body, wishing he had remembered to give him pain pills earlier.

As soon as they neared the single light, a skinny brown dog materialized out of nowhere, barking and snarling at the tires. Abe slowed so as not to hit the feisty mutt, who ferociously defended his territory. Once in front of the small hexagonal house with conical roof, he stopped behind an old Ford pickup, gave the horn three sharp blasts, and waited while the dog continued to leap at the window. Patch stood up, growling and baring his teeth in defense.

Someone pulled a blanket away from a window and Abe spotted a woman and three children peering back at him. Next, a man holding a lantern pushed open a door and stepped out. He shouted something in Navajo and Will lifted his head, responding in same. The man and woman came over to the truck to welcome their visitors, the children scampering after them. One boy, a toddler, and the girl shyly hid behind their mother's long skirt, stealing peeks when they thought no one was looking, while the older boy stood at his father's side. When the man held the lantern up to Will's face, the boy jumped back, his eyes wide. The father said something to him in Navajo, and the boy nodded solemnly, then returned to flank his father, his eyes cast downward.

No wonder they're scared. Will must look like a spirit from the dead to these people. He had no clothing except for the hospital gown and his swaddling of white sheets. His face, wrapped in bandages, had a ghostly sheen when the light from the lantern illuminated it.

Abe felt like the character in a science fiction novel he had read as a kid, *Stranger in a Strange Land*. He didn't know how the Navajo would react to his presence, and especially to his having taken Will from the hospital. He didn't have to think long, because when Will introduced him to his cousin on his father's side, Charlie Tsosie, and

Charlie's wife, Betty, she beckoned for him to follow her into the hogan. He protested that he would rather stay in the truck with his dog, but she would have none of that. So Abe and Patch traipsed behind the round-faced woman, into the stick-and-mud house. Charlie helped Will out of the truck, and the boy fetched a rope to tie the brown dog in the sheep pen.

The night loomed, cold and cloudless, but inside the hogan was warm and inviting. A cooking fire blazed in the center of the structure, and Abe could smell mutton simmering in the cast-iron pot set atop a grill. Despite his discomfiture, his stomach reminded him he hadn't eaten since the morning and growled in protest. He still didn't understand why Will remained outside, lying on a pallet of wool blankets while Charlie built a nearby fire.

Betty stood over the cooking pit, heating a kettle of water as smoke rose through an opening in the roof. Surprising him, she asked, "Do you think our cousin will die?"

She spoke in halting English, but with the same melodic cadence as Emily. "I don't know," Abe said. "We need to reach his grandfather's place near Huerfano. Do you know where that is?"

Her placid face showed no emotion as she handed him coffee poured from a blackened percolator and answered with a nod and simple, "*Aoo*, yes."

Abe's eyes skimmed the one-room interior of the hogan. There were few furnishings: a couple of trunks, a loom with a three-legged stool, a table and chairs, pallets for sleeping. But the space had a roomy, comfortable atmosphere. The young girl and toddler sat on a mattress covered by wool blankets near the mud-plastered wall. They were as silent as shadows, busy giving Patch bites of food that he appeared to relish. The woman ladled stew into a bowl and handed it, along with a shy smile and piece of sturdy bread, to Abe. He thanked her and watched as she returned to the fire to drop herbs into a steaming kettle.

The man, Charlie, entered the room and took a bundle of sage from a cache hanging on the wall.

"How's Will?" Abe asked. "When is he coming in?"

"He will sleep under the stars tonight," Charlie said. He then turned his attention to his wife. "Is the tea ready?"

She answered again with a barely audible *aoo* and poured pungent-smelling liquid into a mug. After she handed it to him, along with a bowl of stew broth, the man went back outside. A short time later, Abe heard the sound of a soft rhythmic drum, and caught the whiff of burning sage intermixed with fragrant *piñon* smoke from the campfire.

The older boy entered the hogan and served himself stew and bread. He sat on the floor a short distance from Abe and began eating. Abe caught the boy casting furtive glances his way. "Hi. My name's Abe Freeman. What's yours?"

"Joey Tsosie." The boy kept his voice low and his head bent over the bowl while wiping his mouth with one hand.

He looked to be around ten years old and had the same somber eyes as his mother and rangy limbs as his father, with long raven-black hair tied in a ponytail. His command of English seemed more assured than that of his parents.

"Joey, why doesn't your dad bring Will inside? It's getting cold."

"He has blankets and a warm fire. It's better to be outside if he must die. His *chindi*, his spirit, will be free. If he dies inside, we will have to move from our home and burn the hogan." The words tumbled out, probably more than he intended to say, so he ducked his head and turned away, eating in silence while Abe pondered the boy's words.

If Will died, how would he explain things? Emily would demand to know why he took him from the hospital. Abe felt the old familiar sense of inadequacy, of never doing the right thing, a feeling he had fought against all his life. He rushed outside with

SANDRA BOLTON

every intention of loading Will into the truck and taking him back
to the hospital, but when Charlie Tsosie saw him and raised a warn-
ing hand, he stopped. Will lay on his pallet draped in a colorful
woven blanket, his upper body propped against a bundle of wool.
Will's eyes were lifted to the stars as he chanted softly. *"Hózhó
náhásdlíí, hózhó náhásdlíí' . . ."* He looked so much at peace that
Abe turned back.

He returned to the hogan and sat by Joey. Betty Tsosie had
washed the dishes in a bucket near the fire and was busy tucking
the smaller children into bed. She hummed softly, and occasionally
joined the men in their song. "What is it they are singing?" Abe
asked the boy.

"It is the Navajo Beauty Way prayer for someone who is ill or
lost their way. It will help him be in harmony with all things and
to be well with everything in his life. There is much more to this
ceremony. My father is studying to be a *hataali*, a singer."

Abe's curiosity and knowledge of music's healing powers goaded
him on to question the boy. "Can you tell me what the words mean,
Joey?"

"Now they are saying, 'with beauty before me may I walk, with
beauty behind me may I walk. It is finished in beauty, it is finished
in beauty.'" Joey stood and went to the bucket to wash his dish,
then joined his siblings on the pallet. "Good night, Abe Freeman."

Outside again, accompanied by Patch, Abe went to the truck
and fed his dog. He smoked a cigarette, then sighed deeply and
pulled out his bedroll. After hollowing out a space in the sand and
making a mound for his head, he spread the tarp and sleeping bag
and lay down. The sky hovered above like a velvet pincushion stud-
ded with diamonds. Abe fell asleep, listening to the mesmerizing
chant, inhaling the sharp sage and smoke, wondering what it would
be like to know that you were where you belonged and a part of
everything around you.

31

Abe awoke as the sun broke over the eastern horizon. A hint of fall lingered in the brisk morning air. He stretched his stiff limbs and glanced at Will's pallet. The man was gone. *Oh, Jesus, did he die?* His heart pounded as he looked for any sign of his friend. Then he heard male voices in quiet conversation, and saw both Will and Charlie coming from the direction of the outhouse. He breathed a sigh of relief as he watched their approach. Will, still wrapped in a white hospital sheet, and supported by Charlie Tsosie, walked upright. "You can't go home looking like that," Abe said to the ghostly figure. "You need some clothes."

Charlie laughed. "My boy thought he was a skin walker when he showed up last night."

Between the two of them, Charlie Tsosie and Abe scrounged up a well-worn pair of jeans and a soft flannel shirt. The pants were too short and the shirt hung on Will's limbs like a scarecrow's garb, but it was better than nothing. Since no one had shoes large enough for his feet, Betty supplied a pair of wool socks. After a breakfast of coffee and cornmeal mush, the entire Tsosie family lined up beside the truck to say good-bye. Betty handed Abe a quart jar of herbal tea and told him to make sure Will drank plenty of it. Abe, in turn, handed her a twenty-dollar bill and thanked the Tsosies for their hospitality.

An hour later they cruised past the red-rock mesas outside of Gallup, New Mexico, and then through the outer edge of the surreal Bisti Badlands. Convoluted rock formations dotted the Martian-like landscape. Eerie hoodoos stood like sentinels along the highway's edge. *Premonitions of things to come*, Abe thought, as he pressed on.

After five hours driving, they left Farmington behind and arrived at Will's grandfather's trailer near Huerfano. Emily, her grandfather, and another woman stood outside with their arms crossed, as if they had been awaiting his arrival.

That must be Will's mother, Abe thought, seeing the stout, no-nonsense lady in blue jeans and a purple shirt. Her steel-gray hair was twisted into a tight bun held in place with an ornate silver-and-turquoise pin. The woman rushed to the passenger side of the truck and carefully embraced Will, crooning in her native tongue and completely ignoring Abe.

Will's grandfather followed behind her while Emily stood, lingering back, staring at Abe, no emotion showing on her face. Then everyone came to life, helping Will out of the truck and into the trailer, talking softly in Navajo, leaving Abe alone in the driver's seat. He let out a heavy sigh and looked at Patch. He wanted to take off, but first he took the money he had stuffed in his backpack and split it in half—they would need it, he figured, to take care of Will—and he put five thousand dollars in the envelope. He walked to the front of the trailer and left the envelope on the porch, anchored in place by a heavy rock, then turned to leave. But when he switched on the ignition and backed the truck up to swing around, he heard his name.

"Abe, wait."

As he watched her walk toward the truck, Abe shifted into neutral, but left the engine running. "I guess the hospital called and you figured I would bring Will here. Look, Emily, I know I took a big chance by taking him out of the hospital, and I know you're pissed at me. But, it's what he wanted—needed. You would have seen that if you weren't so hardheaded. Don't get on my case right now. I'm out of here, out of your life." He revved the engine as if to give emphasis to his words.

"Give me a minute, Abe, please. I'm not angry. I should have brought Will home, myself." There were blue circles under her eyes, her face a tight mask. She looked tired and vulnerable. He wanted to reach out and take her in his arms, tell her he understood and forgave her, but resisted.

He turned away and gazed at the commanding mountain, the one she had described to him as sacred, and that now cast a long shadow over the trailer and sheep camp. "I think Will understands why you did what you did." He paused and looked at her. "I hope he pulls through." Abe broke the uncomfortable silence that followed. "I better get going. Patch and I have a long haul ahead of us." He put the truck in gear, but Emily didn't move.

"Come into the house, Abe. Mother and Grandfather want to see you."

Abe let out a long sigh. "Your mother probably wants to kill me. I'm tired and I don't need the drama, Em. Tell your folks I had to go. And tell Will to hang on. I'll be rooting for him." He started to pull away, but she still hadn't moved. Abe shifted back into neutral. "What is it?"

Emily reached through the open window to the steering wheel and grasped Abe's wrist. "You have the key, Abe."

That stopped him. He had forgotten the key.

"Get out of the truck. We need to talk."

He felt anger swelling inside. "So, that's what you want from me. Are you speaking in an official capacity now? Why didn't you come out and say it, Emily? You can have the damn key. The sooner I get rid of that piece of shit, the better." He turned off the engine, jumped down from the truck, and found his backpack in the back. Patch took the opportunity to run off and join the grandfather's two sheep dogs. Abe began rummaging through the contents of his pack, throwing clothes right and left.

Emily placed her hand on his arm again. "Abe, calm down. Let me have my say."

He stopped, not wanting to lose control, and crossed his arms over his chest in a protective gesture. His voice, when he replied, was edged with frustration. "What is there left to say, Emily?"

She picked up his scattered clothes and handed them to him. "Walk with me a ways."

He pushed tousled hair back from his eyes, looked around, and realized his dog had deserted him. "Okay. I guess I can spare a couple of minutes while Patch takes a pee." He crammed shirts and socks back in his pack, lit a cigarette, and followed her along a wash until they reached a cluster of smooth sandstone boulders. Emily sat on one and Abe on another, facing her. His heart pounded in his chest.

"I knew I had to get back to work and tell my boss everything, but I shouldn't have left without talking to you."

Abe inhaled and let out a stream of smoke, saying nothing.

"Okay. I was scared. And when I'm scared, I try to avoid dealing with the issue."

"Scared of what, Emily? What issue?"

"Of staying with you—of maybe falling in love with you, damn it, that's what."

"Would that have been so bad?" Abe stood. Agitated, he began walking in a circle. He threw the cigarette into the sand and stubbed it with the toe of his shoe. "You could have told me."

"I know. It's not your fault; it's me. I can't deal with falling in love right now. I need time to work things out, Abe."

"Fine, Emily. Take all the time you need. I'll give you the key and get going." Abe turned and started walking away, but Emily's voice stopped him again.

"Rico Corazón is dead," Emily said in a broken voice. "I didn't get the pleasure of putting him away. The stupid ass did it to himself."

Her words caught him by surprise, and despite his anger, he wanted to know what happened. He faced her and waited while she caught up. "How?"

They began walking back to the trailer. Though side by side, they kept a safe distance from each other. "Corazón was messed up on drugs and booze, riding that hog like a maniac while drinking tequila out of the bottle. He tried to beat a train outside of Roswell—thought he was invincible, I guess." A humorless laugh passed through her lips. "The only identifiable mark left on his face was that tattoo of a teardrop, but some of his gang were still wandering around in a drunken daze when the state cops arrived, and they told them what happened."

"Then it's over. Why are you upset? He caused your grandmother's death, tried to kill us. He even shot one of his own gang members. The bastard had no soul."

Emily's face darkened. "I know. But I wanted him. I wanted to bring him down. Now I feel cheated."

"How did you know where to find him?" Abe said.

"I heard it on the radio just before I stopped at the hospital to see Will. There was a report of a freight train slamming into a motorcyclist. It described the deceased as being a member of the Mexican Mafia. I knew it had to be him." Emily had somehow drifted closer to Abe as they walked along the rocky dry wash. She gave him a sideways glance. "That's why I couldn't take my brother home. I drove all night to get to Roswell to help with the investigation and, after a couple hours of sleep, I drove back home." Her shoulders slumped and she bit her lip. "I promised Will I would be back for him, but he looked so broken when I left. I don't think he believed me."

Emily turned her head away, but not before Abe saw her eyes well with tears that threatened to run down her cheeks. "I took statements from the gang members who hadn't managed to escape the scene," she said, her voice sounding composed once more. "They spilled their guts, pointed their fingers at Corazón for the shooting of their buddy—the one who went in the cave with you—Chino, I think he's called. They're gonna tell all, turn state's evidence, and opt for a plea bargain."

Abe put his hands in his pockets, resisting the urge again to reach out to Emily and hold her. "I guess that's the end of the story then."

"Not quite, Abe. There's still the key, and the mystery behind it. Why were they all ready to commit murder to get their hands on that key, anyway? Don't you have a little curiosity?"

"The Arizona cops have DiMarco and his dickhead bodyguard in custody, don't they? They can get to the bottom of it."

"He won't be in custody much longer. His high-priced lawyer from Kansas City is coming to Bisbee tomorrow to bail him and Benavutti out." Emily put her hands on Abe's shoulders so she could look directly into his eyes. Her voice rang strong now, tinged with excitement. "We've located DiMarco's daughter, Abe. Her father and some of his henchmen had kidnapped her. They tried to silence her by keeping her locked in his house in Kansas City. She escaped when her guard fell asleep and contacted the police. KCPD handed her over to the FBI, and they have her in protective custody."

"What are you planning?"

"I've been assigned to go to Datil, New Mexico, where she is being held, and assist the agent on the case. She's not giving anything to the Feds. Maybe she needs a woman she can talk to, maybe she doesn't know anything, or maybe she's scared. But I intend to find out. I'm asking you to go with me."

"Why?"

"You have the key, Abe, but it's more than that. I want you there. You've been involved from the start." Emily flashed him a tentative smile. "It will be strictly business if you're worried, then you can leave whenever you're ready." Her eyes bored into his. "Let's finish the job."

All he had to do was give her the key and be done with it. The music that usually filled Abe's head in times of stress abandoned him at this point, leaving nothing but dissonant notes, as random and disconnected as his life. He, like Emily, had chosen to run rather than deal with the past.

"Think about it, Abe. Let's go inside to see Will, and I'll introduce you to my mother."

He had to admit, the idea piqued his curiosity, but he shook it off. "I'll say good-bye to Will, Emily. Then I'll go. I don't think this will work."

32

Not eager to confront Will's austere-appearing mother, Abe reluctantly followed Emily into the trailer. He knew the woman should be furious, and rightfully so, and he hoped the money might assuage some of her anger.

The envelope still lay on the steps, under the rock where he'd left it. The older woman gazed out the open doorway, her hands on her hips. No smile brightened her stern brown face. She stood a head shorter than Emily, but solid and sturdy as a slab of granite.

"Abe, this is my mother, Bertha Etcitty," Emily said. "Mom, Abe Freeman."

"So this is the Abe Freeman that kidnapped my son and hauled his poor ass back here," she said. Her commanding voice must have been put to good use in a classroom of recalcitrant adolescents.

Abe squirmed, trapped under the stare of Mrs. Etcitty's smoldering coal eyes. Hadn't he learned the Navajo thought it impolite to stare? Why hadn't he left when he had the chance?

"The man that has been cavorting all over the country with my only daughter."

"Mom . . . ," Emily started, but Mrs. Etcitty held up a hand to silence her.

"I wouldn't call it cavorting. But yes, I took Will from the hospital. I realize it was wrong, but it's what he wanted. He thought he was going to . . ."

Bertha Etcitty stopped Abe in midsentence. "Die? My son is not going to die, Abe Freeman." She put her hands on her hips and gazed at the step. "It is so like a white man to think he can take care of any problem by throwing money at it," she added, picking up the envelope from under the rock.

Abe felt a flush of anger. What did these people want from him? "The money isn't mine. It belongs to Will. If he doesn't want it, if nobody wants it, you can give it to someone who does, for all I care." He felt tired, discouraged, and angry. "Nice meeting you, Mrs. Etcitty. I'll say good-bye to Will and be on my way."

She continued to block the doorway with her stout body. Abe saw Emily roll her eyes, then a smile lit up Mrs. Etcitty's features. "Glad to see you have some backbone. Do you really think I'm crazy enough to give away good money? Will might need this."

"I should have warned you, Abe. My mom's a big tease. She's very happy that you brought Will home. Come on, Mom. Move out of the way so we can go inside."

Emily's mother chuckled and extended her hand to Abe, barely brushing his fingers in a light touch. "Had you going, didn't I?"

Abe sighed. "Yes, you sure as hell did."

The grandfather sat on a stool beside the cot where Will lay on a clean sheet. The old man nodded at Abe and flashed him a toothless smile. Abe noticed the bandages had been removed from Will's face, exposing the extent of his burns. His eyes remained covered with a wet compress. The room smelled of pungent herbs, medicinal cures the elderly Navajo had brewed. Although Will's face looked raw and scarred, he appeared relaxed.

"Hey, Abe. Is that you? I heard my ma giving you the third degree out there. Come over here so we can talk."

Abe acknowledged the grandfather, then pulled a straight-backed wooden chair close to the bed. "How are you feelin', Will?"

He answered in a calm voice. "I'm gonna be okay now that I'm home. Maybe not so pretty on the outside, but my spirit is happy, 'walkin' in beauty.'" He paused to catch his breath. "Ma knows you saved my life. She's grateful to you. She has funny ways of showing things sometimes, that's all. Thanks, buddy."

"Forget it."

"You're not in a hurry to leave, are you? Why don't you stick around for a while—for Emily's sake, and mine, too. Can you do that, Abe?"

Abe shook his head. "I don't think so, Will. I need to take off. I can't figure out where I fit in, and I guess I don't." Their conversation was interrupted by the grandfather, who held a bowl containing a white, pasty substance. He shooed Abe away and began applying it, with the lightest touch, to Will's burned face. Abe stepped back and accepted a coffee cup offered to him by Bertha Etcitty.

"Everyone calls me Bee." When she saw Emily assisting her grandfather with Will's medicinal treatments, she beckoned Abe to join her at the table. Emily's mother sipped her coffee and gazed at a spot over his left shoulder. "You have proven yourself to be a good man, Abe Freeman. I am going to ask one more favor of you. I would like for you to make this trip with my girl. She is an excellent police officer, very competent, but headstrong and foolish at times. She needs someone to look after her."

"I'm no good at that. Emily does whatever she wants, any-way."

"What else do you have to do?"

He didn't have an answer for that, and shrugged. "I'll think it over," he said after a minute of lip chewing. Abe admitted to himself it was difficult to say no to Emily, especially since she'd asked for his help, and even more so since seeing her made him want to steal a little more time with her. *Or I could leave, run away again. To what? My life has no meaning.*

He was still thinking when Emily joined them at the card table.

"Well?" said Bee Etcitty.

Abe looked directly into the dark pools of Emily's eyes. "Strictly business."

"Agreed. We leave in the morning."

Abe grabbed his backpack, checking to make sure the key remained in the inside pocket. Emily loaded a suitcase, shotgun, two-way radio, and tape recorder into the Bronco. She tucked her Glock into a shoulder holster and hung it by the door, where it would be easy to grab the next morning. Abe packed what he needed for him and Patch and spent a restless night in his camper. Sleep eluded him and, when he finally dozed off, recurring dreams of being chased through a fiery cave by Corazón and his men haunted him.

They left early the following morning, driving due south. Emily radioed her superior, Captain Benally, to report she was on her way to Datil—leaving out a minor detail: namely that a certain drifter from New Jersey who had once been a suspect in the murder of the DiMarco woman's boyfriend accompanied her. They took the Bronco rather than the Navajo Police vehicle so as to appear less conspicuous.

Abe felt relieved they didn't have to drive all the way to Kansas City to confer with Marilu DiMarco, daughter of mob boss Vicente DiMarco. The FBI had chosen Datil, New Mexico, as a safe place to stash their witness; her father's connections in Kansas were widespread, which made anywhere near that state, or Marilu's home in Dumas, Texas, an unwise choice.

True to her word, Emily made sure the trip was strictly business. Emily told Abe she would figure out how to explain his presence to the Feds—maybe as an undercover cop—and that he should keep his mouth shut; she would do the talking. *Fine by me*, Abe thought, and fell asleep shortly after they left the San Juan Basin. He didn't awaken until four hours later when they passed through the spot on the road called Pie Town, twenty miles from their destination.

When they reached the village of Datil, Emily pulled into the parking lot of the Eagle Guest Ranch. "Let's grab a bite to eat, and I'll make a call to the Feds to let them know we're on our way."

A gum-chewing waitress took their order, and when the meals arrived, Abe dug into his taco-tamale-enchiladas special while Emily picked at her burger and fries. She scanned the room until she spotted a pay phone near the door and excused herself. A few minutes later she returned with a sketch of a map on the back of a napkin.

"The agent's name is Robert Bowman, but he let me know everyone calls him Bo. Mentioned that Marilu is a real piece of work, and he's glad someone is taking her off his hands for a while." Emily sat by Abe and put the map on the table between them. "We follow Highway 12 west until we come to a sign for Frolicking Deer Lavender Farm."

"Then what?"

"Take that road and follow the curve. After five miles we'll run into a dirt road on the left. At the end there's a log cabin. That's where they're holed up."

"Are you expecting any flak from Bowman?"

"No reason, I guess, but we need to be ready for anything. Let's get moving."

Abe drove while Emily provided directions. Right before the road dwindled out, he spotted a hunter's cabin partially hidden in an overgrowth of fir and juniper. It looked like it hadn't been used in years and there were no vehicles parked in front to indicate occupancy now. But when the Bronco drew near, a man stepped out from behind the brush and flagged them down.

The FBI agent looked to be six-four and 270 pounds—all muscle packed in brown Dockers and a black polo shirt. A black ball cap completed his ensemble. Amber eyes set in a face the warm color of molasses surveyed them. The agent kept one hand on the Glock .22 strapped to his belt as he approached the Bronco. "You got some ID?" He looked intently at Emily and Abe, his voice sounding like the early rumblings of an approaching thunderstorm.

Emily pulled out her badge and handed it to the hovering agent. "Officer Emily Etcitty, Navajo Tribal Police. I called half an hour ago. My partner on this case is Undercover Agent Abe Freeman. And you must be Special Agent Robert Bowman."

The big Fed continued to scrutinize Emily's identification badge as she tried to hurry things along. She stretched out her hand to shake his. "Glad to meet you, Agent Bowman. Always a pleasure to work with the FBI. I guess the DiMarco woman's inside. She's expecting us, right?"

Bowman handed back Emily's ID without comment and fixed his attention on Abe. "ID."

"Never carry it when I'm working undercover. You can get yourself killed that way. Look, I've been on this case with Officer Etcitty since they found Easy Jackson's body at Clayton Lake State Park. She can vouch for that." He hoped the sweat beads forming on his forehead didn't show, and thought he saw a smirk on Bowman's face.

"Let's get moving," Emily said. "We were sent here to interview this witness and assist you. Call Captain Benally at the Huerfano substation if you need verification."

"That'll do." The big lawman stepped back from the vehicle. He hadn't shown much of a warm welcome to the visitors, but at least he wasn't asking more questions. "I've already had a couple of conversations with your captain. In fact, I'm the one who requested a woman be sent here to help with Marilu DiMarco's supervision, and the Bureau knows you're familiar with her boyfriend's murder case. You were supposed to be here when I arrived. What the hell took you so long?"

"I had personal business to take care of. I'm here now. Where's Marilu?" Emily took her ID from Bowman and returned it to her pocket.

Abe stepped out of the Bronco, keeping up the cool facade as best he could. He had made the leap from number-one suspect to investigating officer, at least in theory, and he was pretty sure of this much: Marilu DiMarco's boyfriend, Easy Jackson, had been murdered by Rico Corazón. Hadn't the Mexican Mafia leader as much as admitted it when he said Jackson got what was coming to him? Furthermore, Abe had spotted him near the scene of the crime.

The Hulk, as Abe mentally nicknamed the big cop, led the way down a rocky path overgrown with thistle. The man dwarfed Emily and stood a head taller than Abe, who considered himself a normal-size guy. "We've had our eye on you two for quite a while now. How is it you manage to show up wherever there's trouble?"

"What's that supposed to mean?" said Emily.

"For instance, what were you doing in Bisbee, Arizona?"

"Personal business. I took leave and went to see my brother."

The threesome stopped a few feet from the door while Bowman continued. "Who happened to be the victim of a mysterious explosion, but was rescued by your so-called undercover friend here. Next, there is this incident at Dick's Hot Licks in downtown Bisbee where DiMarco and his bodyguard are found bound and gagged. No witnesses, just a tape implicating those two in a murder, and possibly Rico Corazón in the Easy Jackson case. A member of the Mexican Mafia is shot in a cave near Bisbee. Need I go on?"

Emily faced Bowman, a slight smile beginning at the corners of her mouth. "Sounds like a busy place."

"Oh shit." Although relieved to hear the law was looking at Corazón as the probable killer of Easy Jackson, Abe was tired of this charade. "And I suppose you also heard that someone looking a lot like me took Emily's brother out of the hospital and brought him home. Okay, I'm no cop, but I haven't committed a crime either."

Robert Bowman chuckled. "Some would say impersonating an officer is a crime, but don't worry, I'm not going to arrest you. An extra body might come in handy, and I need a female officer to help keep an eye on the little Miss DiMarco. Looks like you got the job Pocahontas," he said, looking at Emily.

"Don't give me any more bullshit," said Emily. "I didn't know I was being interviewed for this job. Why didn't you just ask for my assistance? My boss gave me this assignment. That's why we're here."

"I did request your assistance, lady, did it on the sly, seeming as how you like to work that way. I told your Captain Benally I needed a female officer, someone who was familiar with the case. He right away said, 'I've got just the person for you.' But I don't recall him making any mention of an undercover agent."

Abe frowned and shook his head. He didn't want to be here in the first place.

"Don't take it personally. I can use both of you, so let's come to an agreement," said Bowman. We gotta do a round-the-clock suicide watch with this broad until she comes down from her drug trip and is ready to tell all on Daddy. Can you work with me?"

Emily shrugged. "That's what I was sent here to do."

"What choice do I have?" Abe said.

"None. So let's get to it." Hulk rapped on the door. "Open up, Marilu. You got company."

33

From behind the door came an angry, high-pitched voice. "Leave me alone!" She sure didn't sound like a Midwesterner, or like anyone west of anywhere. The nasal tone was East Coast, more like his home state, New Jersey.

"Unlock the door, Marilu." Bowman rattled the knob. "Crazy broad thinks I'm going to mess with her. I'd rather wrestle a nest of alligators in a Louisiana swamp." Bowman pounded on the door again. "Open up, DiMarco. You're not doing yourself any favors." He turned to Abe and Emily. "Damn woman locked me out when I went to the car for supplies."

"Go screw yourself," said the woman on the other side.

"Let me try talking to her." Emily rapped lightly on the wooden door. "Marilu, I'm Officer Emily Etcitty with the Navajo Police. We want to ask you a few questions. No one is going to hurt you. Can we come in?"

"How do I know who you are? Get outta here. Leave me alone."

"I'm tired of messin' with this broad." Bowman gave the door one mighty kick and it flew open.

Abe stepped into the room and caught a glimpse of a small dark-haired woman before she darted around a corner. A scan of the place revealed a sofa and two chairs grouped around a potbellied stove. A crude pine-slab coffee table stood on a braided rug in front of the sofa. At the back of the room he spotted a wooden table and four chairs. To the left, a closed door led to what he thought must be a bedroom, and on the right, a small bathroom. When he saw Marilu again, she was standing in the doorway of the kitchen with a butcher knife in one hand.

"Stay away from me. You want to take me back, don't you? Lock me up. Well, I won't let you."

The woman was thin to the point of emaciation. Dark eyes, sunk in a sallow-skinned face, were nearly obscured by strands of lank, brown hair. Marilu DiMarco looked like a woman coming off a long, hard drug trip. Her hands shook as she brandished the knife in front of her.

"Meth," said the big agent as if reading Abe's mind. "She's a big user, going through withdrawal—hasn't slept for three days. She's paranoid, delusional, and violent—ought to be locked in rehab instead of out here in the goddamn wilderness."

Meth, speed, ice, crystal, crank—whatever you want to call it, Abe had seen more than his share in the clubs and on the streets of Jersey.

"Marilu." Emily's voice was calm. "Put the knife down. We're here to help you."

"I know who you are and I know what you're after. When you get what you want, you'll kill me, like you killed Easy." Holding the knife above her head, she made a sudden lunge at Emily.

Abe reacted on instinct. He hurled himself at the woman, knocking her off her feet, but not before the blade sliced through Emily's shirtsleeve, leaving her right arm bleeding above the elbow. Marilu DiMarco lay sprawled on the kitchen floor. Agent Bowman kicked the knife out of her hand and pulled out his cuffs, while Abe examined Emily's arm.

"It's nothing," Emily protested. "Just a scratch."

"I'll get a towel," said Abe. "You'll have to take off your shirt, so I can see the damage."

Marilu wailed as her body twitched and jerked on the floor. "No," she screamed. "I won't tell you anything, assholes."

Bowman pulled the protesting woman to her feet, then settled her into a heavy oak chair, cuffing her wrist to the wooden arm. "Sit down and shut up."

Amazingly, she complied, and reduced her howls to whimpers. Then she closed her eyes and ignored everyone. Agent Bowman glanced at Abe with an unexpected grin and a wink. "That was a quick move you made, Freeman, for a wannabe cop. Keep an eye on her while I go out back and get the first aid kit from my vehicle."

Emily had a superficial but bloody cut. After Abe cleaned and bandaged it, she donned her shirt and joined the men, who sat huddled in conversation at the table. Marilu was slumped in the chair and appeared to be sleeping. A stream of saliva spilled from her open mouth. Bowman stood, uncuffed her, and carried her to the sofa. He covered her with a blanket before rejoining Abe and Emily.

"How'd you get her up here in the condition she's in?" Abe asked Bowman.

"Handcuffed and screaming the whole way. Ever since we put her in protective custody, she's been yowling like a cat in heat. Her old man's thugs kept her on a regular supply of meth to keep her happy and try to make her talk. Evidently she resisted the talking part."

Abe wondered what Marilu didn't want to talk about, but didn't pursue it. Changing the subject, he said, "How'd you know I'm not a cop, Bowman?"

"Easy, man. You're too skinny for one thing. You don't have that look, and no gun, no ID. You're dressed all wrong, and you don't smell right." He removed his cap exposing a billiard-ball head.

"Look, I knew you were no cop before I even saw you. This lady's boss and I have been in touch." He tossed a look at Emily, then back at Abe. "Don't know what your game is, Freeman, but I think you're harmless. I do know your so-called partner is for real."

Abe started thinking this agent might be okay when Bowman added, "But"—and his look turned menacing—"if you prove me wrong, I will have your ass, man. Don't think for one minute I'd show you any mercy."

They let Marilu sleep while Emily and Bowman filled each other in on details of the case.

Bowman rubbed his bald head. "So you think Easy Jackson was murdered and Marilu held prisoner because of a key, but you don't know what that key opens or who it belonged to?"

"DiMarco seemed to know, but he didn't say anything except that it was important to his business. Maybe Easy Jackson knew, and that's what got him killed. Corazón was interested in getting his hands on that key. That's why he came to Bisbee. If he killed Jackson for it, then he might have known its significance as well. But Rico Corazón is dead so he's not talking," Emily said. "For whatever reason, there appears to be a lot of interest in that key. What has Marilu said?"

"She's been scared shitless, won't say a word. What's your connection?" Bowman asked Abe. "You got the hots for this lady cop?"

Abe bristled. "I have the key. It fell out of Easy Jackson's pocket when he visited my campsite. I didn't realize I had it, or know it had any significance, until later. There was a showdown in Bisbee, Arizona, between DiMarco and the Mexican Mafia—both sides were ready to kill for that key."

Bowman whistled softly. "I know that gang—a rough bunch. Heard their leader had a train wreck."

Before Abe could respond they heard rustling sounds from the sofa. Marilu blinked and groaned. She stared at them through cavernous eyes. Marilu DiMarco might have been pretty once, with her chestnut-brown hair and petite build, but now her look could only be described as wasted. She lifted a skeletal hand to her mouth and groaned.

Emily scrambled to her feet. "Let's get something in her. Do you have any tea or soup, anything she can eat?"

Upon hearing these words, Marilu leaned her head over the side of the sofa and vomited a pool of yellow phlegm. Emily led the woman into the bathroom to finish the job while Abe cleaned up the mess.

After they returned, the Mafia boss's daughter sat on the sofa, shivering and clutching a cup of chicken noodle soup while taking tiny sips of hot broth. All of her anger seemed to have dissipated into a deep melancholy.

"I heard you talking. That key was our ticket outta here. Me and Easy were gonna get away." Marilu hunched over her cup and drew the blanket closer. "When I saw 'em coming, I gave Easy the key, told him to slip out the back. That's the last I ever saw him." Marilu scratched at the scabs on her arm and shuddered. "Anybody got a cigarette?"

Abe handed her a Camel from his pack and held a match to the bobbing cigarette dangling from Marilu's cracked lips, then took one for himself. He would quit again soon, he figured, but right now he wanted a smoke. Abe still felt unnerved by the incident with the knife.

Emily had retrieved her tape recorder and set it up. She perched on the edge of the old, worn sofa beside Marilu while Abe sat opposite them in the heavy oak chair. The recorder on the pine-slab coffee table slowly whirred, ready to document whatever Marilu had to say. Robert Bowman leaned against the door frame, watching everyone. Inhaling deeply, Marilu leaned her head back against the sofa cushion and closed her eyes. She continued to puff away, exhaling streams of gray smoke and saying nothing.

Emily sighed, impatience showing in her face as she looked first at Abe, then at Marilu. "*What* was your ticket out of here?"

Marilu twisted her head to stare blankly at the person questioning her, as if she only now realized there were others in the room. The soup seemed to have settled her stomach, but her skin maintained a yellow-gray pall; her dull eyes showed no life. Bowman made coffee and offered her a cup, but she shook her head and pushed it away. She held on to the butt of the cigarette, burned now to ash, while the others waited. "The tapes . . ." she said, right before her head dropped onto her chest.

Emily turned off the recorder and took the smoldering stub from the sleeping woman's hand. "Marilu," she said, gently shaking the girl's shoulder. "Come on, Marilu. We need to talk."

Bowman exhaled a long, slow breath. "Might as well let her sleep. She hasn't slept for a long time, and you're not getting anything out of her till she does. You know anything about those tapes she mentioned?"

Both Abe and Emily shook their heads. "First I ever heard of them," said Abe. It had been a long day for him, and looked like it was going to be a longer night. He wished he had his truck so he could leave the key with Emily and take off. *They don't need me*, he thought. "I'm letting Patch out, taking a walk," he said to no one in particular, leaving the stuffy cabin for the crisp, piney air.

34

Darkness descended on the mountains, carrying with it a sudden influx of cold. Abe shivered and cursed himself for having left his jacket in the Bronco. But the cool air provided clarity to his thoughts as he puzzled over the significance of the key. Abe's dog ran ahead, sniffing at new, intoxicating smells. Without realizing it, he and Patch had walked far from the hunter's cabin. Deer had recently used the trail, cluttering it with their brown-bead droppings. Now, however, nothing moved in the forest. Even the small gray juncos had given up scratching the ground for seed. They perched in silent groups on pine branches, as if anticipating some unknown danger.

Maybe Marilu had woken up and they'd finished the interview, Abe wished. He pondered the woman's words—"the tapes." What did it mean? He thought it had to be either audio or VHS recording tapes she had managed to get her hands on—something obviously very important to her father. The key had to be tied to the tapes. It was all coming together. He picked up the pace as he turned back toward the dim glow emanating from the cabin. The light bounced off millions of luminescent particles floating in the air, kissing his face. A steady snow began to fall. *Freakish weather*, Abe thought.

Way too early for snow. By the time he reached the cabin door, the path lay covered in a white blanket.

Abe brushed the flakes from his arms and warmed himself at the stove. "Can you believe this? It's practically a blizzard out there," he said.

Bowman looked out the window. "Shit. This might complicate things."

"You can't predict the weather here in New Mexico," Emily said. "It's unusual, but it happens. Some arctic air from Canada blew down and it will all be gone in a day or two. It shouldn't be a problem."

Abe rubbed his hands together and turned toward Emily and Bowman. "I had an idea while walking outside."

"Save it till after we eat." Bowman carried plates of hot dogs and baked beans to the table. "Sit down and dig in. One thing we have is plenty of food. I made sure of that."

They ate their meal off paper plates with plastic forks, and made small talk concerning the changing weather until Bowman finished his last bite of hot dog and pushed his plate away.

"This is the way it's going down. We're each pulling an eight-hour shift." He dabbed at his face with a paper napkin, wiping mustard from his chin. "Emily takes first watch and stays in the room with Marilu from ten tonight till six in the morning." Then, looking at Abe, he added, "You, undercover man, you get the six-to-two shift. I'll cover the two-to-ten. DiMarco can't be left alone. I brought a couple of sleeping bags so whoever's not on duty can crash in here and keep the fire going. If Marilu wakes up and starts talking, whoever's on duty immediately calls the others. Understand?"

Emily and Bowman must have already discussed this, Abe thought. "Okay."

Bowman retrieved a toothpick from his pocket and rolled it around his mouth. Rocking back in his chair, hands locked behind the back of his shiny head, he said, "So what's this idea you came up with, partner?"

Abe finished his hot dog and beans, washing it down with a slug of hot coffee, wishing he had a beer instead. Emily ate quietly, chewing slowly, looking pensive and a little peeved. Abe figured she was annoyed with the way this macho Fed took over, but then she probably had to deal with guys like this all the time. "It's Marilu's key."

Emily cleaned her plate, swallowed, and looked at Abe. "Yeah, well, we thought at the time she had stolen it from her old man, then gave it to Jackson."

"No. It's always been hers. But there's more. She said the key was their way out. The key and the tapes are tied together. If she already had the tapes, she wouldn't need to steal a key to get them. So the key must belong to her, and DiMarco needs her and the key if he wants to get to whatever it unlocks."

Robert Bowman stopped rolling the toothpick. "A locker at an airport or bus station. Maybe a safe-deposit box."

"It has to be a safe-deposit box, and Marilu DiMarco is the only one who can sign for it. They have her signature on file. It takes two keys to open the box—one from the bank and the other from the person who signed the contract. So her father needs the key and Marilu." Abe stood, poured more coffee. "That is, unless she's dead. If that were the case, the next of kin could view the contents, but they would need a court order, and I doubt DiMarco wants to deal with the courts." Turning to look at Bowman, he asked, "Where's the mother?"

"Died when Marilu was a kid," Bowman said. "She's been shipped off to East Coast boarding schools ever since. Ran away when she turned fifteen, lived on the streets for a while, and had a few arrests for soliciting and drugs. When her father tracked her down, she was living with Easy Jackson. After Jackson was busted for dealing and sent up, she stuck around to wait for him."

Abe peeked at Marilu. Her rhythmic breathing told him she was sleeping soundly. He rejoined the others and asked, "Where did you say DiMarco found her?"

Emily stood up, excitement showing on her face, and paced around the room before returning to where the two men sat. Looking too wired to sit down, she placed both hands on the table and remained standing. "Dumas, Texas. Not far from the prison where Easy Jackson was transferred, then released. Her house had been ransacked and her car set on fire around the same time she disappeared. It looked like arson, but no one knew what happened to Marilu."

Robert Bowman scratched a stubbly gray growth of chin hairs. "Her father's men must have grabbed her and took her back to Kansas City. Somehow she managed to escape, and a KC cop picked her up and ID'd her. She sounded pretty incoherent, high on meth, kept going on about her father killing her boyfriend. Said she had information on him that could put him away for life. That's when they locked her in protective custody. They called the FBI because she had been abducted across state lines, and that's where I came in."

Abe's fingers drummed the tabletop while he considered the significance of what might be in a safe-deposit box. "Whatever she took from DiMarco and stashed away is damn important. Corazón wanted that key as well. What do you think might be on those tapes, Bowman?"

The federal agent looked out the window, then walked to the woodstove, opened the little door, and threw a log on the glowing embers. "Something the FBI would like to get their hands on, I'm betting." He picked up a metal poker and stirred the coals, then looked at Abe. "We're gonna find out. In the meantime, we need more wood."

Abe bristled again. He didn't like being bossed around. "What am I, your gofer? What's wrong with you?" Abe snapped at the FBI agent. Bowman growled back at him that he might as well make himself useful since he had tagged along on this gig, and although true, Bowman's attitude rubbed him the wrong way. Just the same, he grabbed a flashlight, put on a coat and gloves, and stepped out into snowfall.

The first snowstorm of the year had turned into a whiteout. The wind buffeted drifts of snow, making it hard to find anything, but his flashlight singled out a couple of large mounds. The one near the back of the building turned out to be Bowman's vehicle. A smaller hill of snow stood near the south side of the cabin. Further investigation revealed a stack of dry logs cut into stove-length chunks buried under a tarp.

He carried in two bundles and dropped them near the potbelly. It was nearly ten, and he could hear Emily making washing-up noises in the bathroom. He hadn't had a chance to talk to her all day and wondered what she made of the situation. When he finished stacking the wood, he put some chunks in the stove and banked them for the night.

Bowman sat in the oak chair, a gloomy look on his face. He had thrown one sleeping bag on the sofa and pulled the coffee table to the side of the room to make space for the other bedroll on the rug. "You take the sofa. I'll crash on the floor."

"Makes no difference to me," said Abe.

Bowman sighed. "Look, man. Sometimes I get caught up in being this big, important FBI agent. I guess I have a bit of a chip on my shoulder, too. I had to work hard and put up with a lot of crap to get where I am. Not too many black guys in the Bureau, and they're still giving me shit duty, like babysitting this crazy woman. I've been taking things out on you."

Abe reflected on the truth of that for a while, and started smiling.

"What the hell are you grinning about?"

"Look at us. A Jew, a black man, a Native American woman, and an Italian Mafia princess trapped together in a snowstorm. How many minorities can you cram into one small cabin without war breaking out?" He erupted in laughter, and Bowman joined in.

"Don't forget Patch, the three-legged dog," Bowman roared.

Patch had already claimed his place on a throw rug close to the stove. When he heard his name, he repositioned himself, made two circles, and curled into a ball.

Emily emerged from the bathroom and saw the two men doubled over. "What am I missing that's so funny?" Since they couldn't stop laughing long enough to answer, she poured herself a mug of coffee and took up her post in Marilu's room.

Abe and Bowman talked well into the night, comparing stories about how it felt to be on the outside, always thinking you wanted in.

35

Except for tossing, turning, and mumbling, Marilu slept through the night. She still hadn't awoken when Emily crept out of the bedroom, her hand over her mouth, covering a yawn. "Mmm, smells like bacon in here."

"How do you like your eggs?" Abe stood over a small propane stove removing strips of bacon from a cast-iron skillet. On a second burner, an old aluminum percolator burped fresh coffee. Robert Bowman came through the door, carrying firewood. The storm had moved on, leaving behind pristine whiteness and blue skies, as well as a precipitous drop in temperature.

Emily headed for the bathroom. "Any way you want," she said before closing the door.

Bowman dropped his load of wood, and as if on cue, Marilu emerged from the bedroom, wild-eyed and raving. "What is there to eat around this dump? I'm starving."

She sat at the table once breakfast was served, and ate like she hadn't in a month. It didn't seem possible anyone as small as Marilu DiMarco could put away that much food. Abe had cooked a pound of bacon and scrambled a dozen eggs, supplemented with toast, coffee, and orange juice, and she devoured half of it, leaving Bowman looking grumpy and wiping his plate clean with a slice of bread. When nothing remained but the coffee dregs, they sat back in their chairs and looked at her, as if waiting for another explosion of profanities.

"I need to pee."

"I'll have to go with you," said Emily.

"Whatever gets you off," Marilu shot back. "They got a shower here?"

A half hour later the two women emerged from the bathroom, Marilu wrapped in a skimpy towel, and Emily looking bored.

"What are you starin' at, freaks? What's'a matter? Haven't you ever seen a real woman before? Here, I'll give you a good look, perverts." When Marilu pulled the towel open, the two men looked at each other and shook their heads.

Emily gave Marilu a gentle shove toward the bedroom. "Shut up and get dressed." Rolling her eyes at Abe and Bowman she added, "You two are a lot of help."

"Hey, I did the dishes," Bowman chuckled.

"And I cooked breakfast," Abe countered.

Once fully dressed, Emily steered the surly-looking woman toward the sofa. "Sit down and make yourself comfortable, Marilu. We have a few questions for you." She carried her recorder and set it up once again.

Marilu, though still gaunt and pale, looked a hell of a lot better with her damp hair tied back in a loose ponytail, and wearing clean slacks and a sweater. She plopped down on the sofa, glaring first at Bowman and then at Abe. "Well, this is one swingin' party." Her foot tapped the floor as she rubbed her arms in an agitated manner. "Give me a cigarette."

Bowman parked himself in the big oak chair, and Abe grabbed a wooden straight-back from the table, straddling it backward. He pulled the pack of Camels from his pocket, shook one loose, and lit up, exhaling a cloud of smoke toward Marilu. He knew to leave the interrogation to the experts, and that he should keep his mouth shut, content to play the role of passive observer, but couldn't resist. "You give us something first."

Marilu shot back, "I don't know what the hell you're talking about." She rubbed her mouth and scratched her arms, opening scabs. "You want to screw me or somethin'? You gettin' horny and your girlfriend won't put out?"

Emily sat on the other end of the ratty plaid sofa, keeping a cool distance between herself and the other woman. "You're the one who's screwing us, lady. You asked for protective custody. Said you had the goods on Daddy, didn't you? So let's cut the crap and start talking. Tell us what's in the safe-deposit box."

Bowman emptied his coffee cup and set it down. "You don't like it here, I can take you back to Kansas City. Say the word and you're free to go home to Daddy. Is that what you want?"

Marilu answered his question with a scowl, then several minutes of silence while she stared at the floor. "The tapes are in my safe-deposit box. Look, I need a smoke, and something to drink. Don't you have anything stronger around here than coffee?"

"Afraid not." Abe shook a cigarette loose from his pack of Camels and handed it to her along with his lighter.

Marilu lit up and took a few puffs before beginning. "The last time they kicked me out of one of those shitty private schools, my old man didn't have anyplace left to send me, so he had to take me home. Imagine, Vicente DiMarco, big-time gangster, playing daddy. I hate him for the way he treated my mother, and he can barely stand the sight of me." She shuddered, as if the thought was too repulsive to contemplate, and began drumming her fingers on her knee.

Emily turned on the tape recorder and ran through the necessary preliminaries before proceeding. "Take your time, Miss DiMarco. It's Sunday and we aren't going anywhere today."

Sitting must have increased her agitation because Marilu jumped to her feet and walked to the stove, holding her hands over the heat, rubbing her arms as if chilled. She continued moving around the room, circling like a cat on the prowl, puffing away on her cigarette.

"I didn't care at first because I could get into his private stash of liquor and pretty much do whatever I wanted. He threw parties all the time—lots of big shots and plenty of booze, coke, beautiful women—anything his guests wanted."

The FBI agent looked up with interest. "Who're we talking about here? What big shots? You mean Mafia types?"

"Hell, no." Her sneer displayed the level of contempt she must have felt. "I'm talking city commissioners, building inspectors, Chamber of fucking Commerce, and more. Oh yeah, let's not forget the big honcho himself, Mayor Pete Sanderson. Seemed like they all wanted to come to one of DiMarco's catered parties—strictly men, invitation only, except for the hookers, of course." A humorless laugh passed through her lips. "Everyone knew my old man was crooked, but nobody could pin anything on him. They were all in his pocket one way or another." Marilu stared out the window at a blanket of untarnished snow. "Yeah, everybody havin' a good time—for a while."

Emily looked up. "What happened?"

"What do you think? They're all drunk and high. My generous old dad made sure whatever they desired was available. And if someone wanted to fuck a girl or, say, another guy, that could be easily arranged. They were given a private room, but no one told them the rooms were bugged and cameras were rolling." Marilu stopped talking and laughed, a sound like broken glass.

"So, he took video tapes of important public figures and big shots in some compromising positions," said Bowman.

"Yeah." Marilu nodded. "Snort'n, fuck'n, pass'n money for whatever they could get. Something they don't want the little lady and kiddies at home, not to mention the general public, to find out while they're at a so-called 'business meeting,' that's for damn sure."

"And then he blackmailed them, threatened to make the tapes public if they didn't pay up," Emily said.

Marilu found her way back to the sofa and collapsed. She closed her eyes and leaned back, holding her head with both hands as if in pain. "You catch on pretty fast. He made duplicates of the tapes so they'd know what he had, and sent a copy to each unsuspecting asshole. I stole his copies of the tapes and stashed them in a safe-deposit box in Dumas."

"What bank?" Bowman asked.

"Citizens something or other . . ." Then Marilu drew up her knees, lay down, and curled into a fetal position, tucking in her chin and covering her head with both arms, signaling she had had enough.

Bowman and Emily exchanged a look. "You should get some rest, too," the agent said.

Emily switched off the recorder, but before she headed for the bedroom she covered the girl's body with a quilt that lay folded on the back of the sofa.

Abe watched in silence, more than willing to leave police work to the law. Marilu had presented a story of corruption and greed, one that had been played out at different levels throughout time. Maybe his reasoning was off center, but he sympathized with this damaged child-woman, wanting to disappear with her boyfriend, perhaps to some tropical island to live their dream—a life of luxury while their money grew interest in an offshore bank somewhere—a dream that sadly never measures up to expectations. Abe learned firsthand about greed after his father's death. He had watched his mother fight with family members over the will and walked away in disgust, wanting nothing more than to have his father back. This girl, this tough-talking, sad little girl, had lost her mother at an early age and never had the love of a caring father. A pathetic, broken young woman lay crumpled on the sofa.

Abe called Patch, put on a coat, and walked out into the immaculate snow. Sunlight bouncing off untainted drifts struck his eyes, momentarily blinding him. Though the cold air stung his face, azure skies promised a quick melt. Bowman's low-slung Chevy Impala would not make it out today, but they would be able to leave tomorrow or the next day. He leaned against the south-facing wall and lifted his face to the sun, engulfed in its soothing warmth.

"It's your shift, man," said the deep voice from the open door, breaking his trance. "Should be easy. She's out like a light."

"Right." Abe called Patch and reentered the cabin. Marilu had not moved. Her body made a small rounded lump under the quilt. He glanced at Bowman before settling into the big oak chair. "What will happen to her now?"

"We're taking her to Dumas, Texas, Citizens Bank, to retrieve the tapes. Then into protective custody and an unknown rehab center. When she's up to it, she'll testify against her father."

"Are you sure she'll do it?"

"You heard her. She hates him. He never showed her an ounce of human compassion. That bastard would sell his only child's body to those scumbags if he thought he could get a few more bucks out of it. And who knows, maybe he did." Bowman shook his oversize bald head. "Shit."

Stretching his legs so he could rest his feet on the coffee table, Abe asked, "How are you working this in Dumas?"

Bowman rubbed his back against the door frame, scratching an itch he couldn't reach, then stood, hands in his pockets. "Looks like we might need your help after all. I need a woman in the vehicle when I transport Marilu to Dumas, so Emily's riding with me. I'd like you to follow in the Bronco."

"No problem. I can manage that." He could pick up Emily afterward, head for her place, and get his truck. The next morning he and Patch would be back on the road bound for the West Coast.

"There is a slight problem," Bowman said. "My sources inform me that DiMarco is out on bail, and best guess as to where he's headed."

Abe's eyebrows raised, forming question marks, but it didn't take more than a second to figure things out. "Dumas, Texas."

"You got it. He'll be watching the bank, waiting for Marilu, and he won't be alone."

"Jesus, won't you have backup when you get there? Why don't you arrest them when they show up?"

"The Bureau is sending a couple of agents, and we'll notify local law enforcement in Dumas, but we want them to keep a low profile so we don't scare anyone off." He screwed his mouth into a frown. "We can't arrest anyone unless they try something first. Look, Freeman, Emily and I talked this over and decided maybe you should escort Marilu into the bank, look like a young couple. You're not nearly as conspicuous as I would be in Texas, a big black dude hanging on to that little white girl's hand."

"Forget that. I'm done. I'm not a cop or a babysitter." *I only came along on this trip as a favor to Emily's mother and Will*, Abe thought. *And all right, damn it, I wanted some more time with Emily, but I didn't figure on getting involved in an FBI sting operation. Let them handle it.* "You're the professional, Bowman—it's your problem now." Abe opened the door to step outside. "I'm going out for some fresh air. I'll be back in a minute."

"And Emily's problem. You want her to walk in with Marilu?"

The agent's words stopped him. Abe spun around. "What's wrong with that? Emily can take care of herself." But as soon as he said it, Bertha Etcitty's words came back . . . *I would like for you to make this trip with my girl. She is an excellent police officer, very competent, but headstrong and foolish at times. She needs someone to look after her.*

"I need Emily with me to cover you and Marilu when you come out of that bank. There'll be a couple of agents watching the street, but the Bureau has no idea what a loose cannon Marilu is and they only sent me two Feds for backup. Said that's all they could spare. Emily and I decided they should both stay on guard outside, because we don't have any idea how many snakes are going to be crawling in there. Okay, we're a little shorthanded, but we'll have your ass protected at all times. In an emergency, we can always call the locals for assistance, but I'd rather not involve them in the setup. Sometimes too many yahoos just get in the way." Bowman put his hands on his hips and glared at Abe. "It won't be the first time you and Emily got involved in a rogue operation, and to tell the truth, I don't have a problem with that. It's gonna be easy this time. Walk in, walk out—should go down as smooth as Tennessee whiskey." Bowman walked over to Abe and tapped on his chest. "Nobody's forcing you to do this. You can sit in the car and wait till it's all over if you want." The two looked each other in the eye for a long moment before Bowman threw up his hands and turned away. "Go on outside, but before you step out that door I want to remind you, it's your watch, so don't spend too much time feeling sorry for yourself. You came along on this trip." He walked into the kitchen to an old rotary-dial telephone connected to the wall and picked up the receiver.

36

For as long as he could remember, Abe had felt alienated, a disembodied specter peering down from his perch on high at the poor slob who occupied his body. He stumbled through life, never in control of his destiny. Abe would shake his head and mutter, *You idiot, what are you getting into now?* That old feeling returned as he tailed Bowman's Chevy away from Datil, New Mexico, northeastward toward Dumas, Texas.

He followed the FBI agent's car down I-25 to Albuquerque, where they caught I-40 East at an intersection called the "Big I"— the only place in New Mexico he had encountered anything resembling traffic congestion.

Trucks dominated the scene on Interstate 40. The big eighteen-wheelers roared through the sparsely populated eastern plains, leaving a trail of noise and noxious diesel fumes. Tumbleweeds skittered across the highway, settling in huge piles along fence lines.

They had left Datil before dawn because the trip to Dumas would take over six hours, and they needed to get to the bank before closing time. Emily and a subdued Marilu, dressed entirely in black and wearing dark shades and a head scarf, rode with Bowman in the lead car. Abe followed, with Patch at his side riding shotgun. He turned and looked at the little dog, who sat alertly staring out the window. "You and I are two of a kind, Patch. We get into trouble and don't know how to get out, so we tag along no matter what the odds are against us." Patch gave him a wag and a grunt that sounded like he concurred. He rubbed the dog's head. "Don't worry, boy. It'll be over soon."

Bowman had filled Abe in. "We need someone to stay with her until she goes into the vault, then walk her out to the car when she's finished. In her condition she'd never make it on her own. Agents Wilson and Peters will be there ahead of us posted outside on each side of the bank. They've been advised to keep an eye out for DiMarco and his bodyguard. Evidently those two left the Bisbee courthouse in a black Buick with Kansas plates. He must have a fleet of them since one registered in his name was recently found in a motel parking lot outside of LA."

Abe and Emily had exchanged knowing glances as he recalled the blond floozy in Bisbee. He hoped she hadn't been arrested for car theft.

"Emily and I will post ourselves inside so that we can see you and whoever comes into the bank at all times," Bowman continued. He made it sound simple, walk in and walk out.

Abe mulled this over as he tried not to lose sight of Bowman's vehicle. The long drive provided plenty of time to think, and he came to the conclusion nothing much mattered anymore, so he might as well do this and move on. He'd lost Sharon and, after dismissing all hope of finding someone else, he had found and lost Emily as well. He had his dog, and that was enough. He made Emily promise that if anything happened to him, she would give Patch a home. Her grandfather's sheep ranch would be the perfect place. With that settled, he no longer feared dying, and accompanying Marilu into the bank seemed superfluous.

But Abe had always been inquisitive by nature—too smart for his own good, his mother was fond of saying. There were puzzles to unravel and he wanted answers. How did the Aryan Brotherhood fit in? What were they doing in Bisbee? He knew Easy Jackson had been a member of that gang, but what was their connection, if any, to this case? He decided to ask Bowman when this crazy episode ended—that is, if he got the chance.

They crossed into Texas a little before one p.m. Even though they had made a quick stop outside of Albuquerque for gas, a pee, and some premade breakfast burritos and coffee to go, Abe's stomach growled—more from nerves than hunger, he reasoned.

At Amarillo, Bowman steered them north on Highway 287. The road shot through level prairie, varied in places by the meandering Canadian River and irrigated croplands. On the outskirts of Dumas he saw a sign that read "Welcome to the seat of Moore County, population 13, 529." Below the sign was a round logo of a comical cowboy clicking his spurs, accompanied by the words "I'm a Ding Dong Daddy from Dumas, Texas" printed around the edge. Bowman pulled off the road where it widened into a rest area, and Abe sidled up to the Chevy.

Everyone got out to stretch and use the bathroom. Patch found an accommodating bush and relieved himself; then they stood in a circle and rehashed the plan.

"Marilu switches to your car now, Abe. Wait here till Emily and I give the all clear."

"Bowman and I will do a drive-through, looking for anything suspicious, vehicles with out-of-state plates, people who don't seem to fit in the town, things like that. If there isn't a problem, we'll radio you and you can proceed to the bank. The local law is aware of our operation, but we've asked them to keep out of sight unless we need them." Emily started walking in the direction of Bowman's Chevy, then turned around. "You know how to operate the radio, right?"

Emily carried a two-way radio in her Bronco, and she had shown Abe how to use it the night before. "Yeah, I understand, Em, channel twenty-one. Press the PTT button if I have something to say, otherwise listen for you." It was kid stuff. He had used a walkie-talkie as a youngster. He pushed the power button to turn on the device, then squelched the static.

Emily and Bowman returned to the Chevy Impala and drove off, leaving Abe and Marilu shuffling uncomfortably in their departure dust. "Want to get in the car?" said Abe. Marilu shrugged, but walked toward the passenger door, her pale face drained of emotion, as if she, too, didn't care what happened.

Back in the Bronco Abe took the pack of Camels from his pocket and shook a cigarette out, offering it to Marilu sitting beside him in the front seat. "Smoke?"

She accepted the cigarette, and he held his lighter while she closed her eyes and inhaled, then blew out a gray cloud, filling the vehicle. Abe rolled down the window and lit one for himself. Several minutes passed as the two smoked in silence. When she spoke, her voice sounded distant and detached. "So, this is it. I'm glad it's finally going to end, one way or another."

Abe turned to look at Marilu DiMarco. Her face was aged beyond her years. The furrowed brow, pinched mouth, and dark pouches under her sunglasses revealed the stress she felt. Wearily rubbing his head, he responded, "So am I." Abe reached for his pack in the backseat and fumbled in the pocket until his fingers found the key. "You're going to need this," he said, handing it to her. "And this to put the video tapes in," he added, indicating a black briefcase on the floor. Then, slumped in his seat, waiting, he started drumming his fingers on the window ledge.

Marilu shot him a look and he stopped. She dropped the key into her purse, placed the briefcase on the seat between her and

Patch, and stared out the window. After several minutes of gloomy reticence he glanced at her again. "I don't get it."

"What?" Her voice contained an edge of irritation, or maybe defensiveness.

"Why'd you ever hook up with a guy like Easy Jackson—petty criminal, convict, drug dealer, and whatever else he was mixed up in."

"You didn't know him." The cigarette smoldered down to her fingertips and she tossed it out the window, immediately asking for another. After a few minutes, she said through a haze of smoke, "He was different from the others."

"The others, meaning the Aryan Brotherhood? Those racist assholes? Then why did he join them?"

A derisive chortle escaped through her parted lips. "You have no idea what it's like in prison, do you? Easy was sent up on some petty charge when he was a country kid barely out of his teens. The Mexican Mafia jumped all over him, and the Brotherhood came to his rescue. They didn't do it out of the goodness of their hearts, though. Those bastards have no hearts. They gave him a knife someone honed out of a spoon and told him he had to kill a certain Mexican gang member if he wanted to survive prison. That was his initiation into the Aryan Brotherhood. He got off on a self-defense charge, and had some extra time added to his sentence. But the Aryans owned him—from then on he did whatever they asked." She grimaced and stubbed her cigarette in the ashtray. "Blood in, blood out. That's their way."

Abe squirmed, knowing he was the last person to see Jackson alive. Looking straight ahead, he said, "I talked to him, you know—that night before someone killed him. He came down to my campsite at Clayton Lake."

She twisted in the seat to stare at him. "You talked to Easy? What did he say?"

"He wanted to hitch a ride with me, to Bisbee." Abe avoided looking at her face. With his chin resting in his palm, he gazed out the window at the Ding Dong Daddy sign, remembering his own brush with the law at an early age on a minor drug charge, and wondered if he and Jackson were really so different after all. "I'm a loner, I didn't want him along, so I left early." He didn't know why he felt guilty, as if he were responsible for Easy Jackson's death. "He didn't look like a skinhead or an Aryan. His head wasn't shaved, clothes weren't right. He kind of looked like a drifter or hippie, except for the tattoos."

"Easy wanted out, and so did his friend in Bisbee. They were going to hide out near Bisbee and wait for me—then we were going to slip into Mexico and start a new life." Marilu's voice broke. "We could have done it, too, if my old man and his goons hadn't shown up."

"Do you think your father or one of his henchmen killed Easy? Rico Corazón as much as confessed to it." Abe could hear the Mexican Mafia boss's words once again. *Jackson got what he had coming.*

A chilling silence followed his question. When Abe turned to look at Marilu, her mouth had set in a hard line and tears streamed down her face. "I don't know who killed Easy. The Mafia, they don't use knives—that's not their way—but my father caused his death one way or another." She sniffled and wiped tear-stained cheeks, then began to absentmindedly pet Patch while the dog rested his head in her lap.

Marilu's words settled over him like a shroud as he recalled the night of his meeting with Easy Jackson. After Jackson left and before Abe drifted off to sleep, he had clearly heard a motorcycle, maybe more than one. Rico Corazón could have killed Jackson, revenge being a strong motive, and Corazón had arrived in Clayton the day Jackson was murdered. But then, so had DiMarco. And now . . . His thoughts were interrupted by the squawk of the two-way radio.

"Abe, can you read me?"

Holding the talk button down, he responded, "Yeah. Go ahead, Em."

"No sign of anything out of the ordinary in town. Not much traffic but we're holding a parking spot for you directly in front of the bank. Pull in beside Bowman in the empty slot. Do you read?"

"Roger. Then what?" He threw a quick glance at Marilu, who gnawed her thumbnail while he talked to Emily. She had taken off her glasses to wipe the tears, and her wide eyes resembled those of a panicked deer caught in the headlights of an approaching car.

"Wait for further instructions. Bowman and I . . ." A loud crackling sound interrupted the transmission, drowning out Emily's voice.

"What's that? Repeat. What did you say, Emily?"

Static preceded her voice. "I say again. After you park, wait for further instructions. Do you read me?"

"Yeah, okay. One question. Where the hell is the bank?" Sweat beads formed on Abe's forehead, even though an early-fall breeze chilled the air.

He waited for another rash of static to clear before he heard Emily's voice again. "Stay on 87. It becomes First Street. Citizens Bank is on the right, corner of First and Maddox, near midtown. Do you read?"

"Okay. We're on our way."

"We'll have you covered and Agent Wilson will be positioned outside."

Abe held his breath, biting his lip during the silence that followed, until Emily said, "Abe, are you sure you want to go through with this?"

He swallowed hard, and tried to sound composed, in spite of his nervousness and the sudden realization that, more than anything, he wanted to live. "Absolutely, Em. Roger and out."

37

The Citizens Bank of Texas, a two-story brick structure, was easy to spot—being the only two-story building on First Street and occupying a prominent corner. Abe slowed, then pulled into the empty slot beside Bowman's black Chevy, parked near the front entrance. As soon as Abe parked the Bronco, Bowman got out of his vehicle and went inside the bank, presumably to join Emily. Abe looked up and down the nearly deserted street. He and Marilu had not spoken since Emily's call, but the tension in the air buzzed like a jar of wasps.

"Waiting time again," Abe said.

She responded with an audible sigh, but followed it up with a show of bravado. "I can't wait much longer to get the bastard."

A short time later, Emily's voice broke the silence. "We're inside. It's all clear. Do you read?"

"Roger." Looking toward Marilu, Abe saw the determined set to her jaw as she put on her dark glasses. "We're ready. Over."

"Walk into the bank side by side. Don't forget the briefcase. Be casual. Go to the bank president's office. His name is Elmore Grimm; he's expecting you. Make sure Marilu has possession of the key. She is the only one who can go into the vault. Wait for her near the vault entrance. Copy?"

"Yep. Let's get it done, Emily."

"Wait a minute. When Marilu comes out of the vault, take the briefcase from her and walk beside her to the Bronco. We'll be right behind you. Then drive back to the rest stop outside town and wait for us. Do you copy?"

"Copy—over and out."

The hush that followed the silenced radio settled over Abe like the stillness of a cemetery. He stole a glance at Marilu and saw her gulping air through her mouth as if she couldn't catch her breath. He reached across the seat and gave her hand a quick squeeze, then opened the door and stepped onto the sidewalk. Abe scanned both directions of First Street. A few pickup trucks and utility vehicles dotted the main street, but nothing suspicious. There appeared to be no sign of out-of-state plates or ominous-looking Buicks. Abe came around and opened the door for Marilu, telling Patch to stay put, then picked up the briefcase. He grasped Marilu's elbow, helping her out of the seat, and carefully guided her through the bank's main entrance.

Emily stood at a small table in the center of the lobby filling out forms as if she were going to make a deposit or withdrawal. She glanced up and locked on Abe's eyes before returning to her paperwork. Robert Bowman stood behind a teller's window. When Abe looked his way, Bowman tilted his chin toward a desk in a small glassed-in office with the sign "Elmore Grimm, President."

A chubby, pink-faced man, sweating profusely, sat behind an ornate cherrywood desk. When Abe and Marilu walked into his office, the man retrieved a handkerchief from the inside pocket of his black gabardine suit jacket and wiped his forehead.

Ignoring Marilu, the banker extended a pudgy, well-manicured hand to Abe. Grimm's grip was flaccid and fleeting.

"Elmore Grimm, glad to meet y'all. I unnerstand y'all need to get into yer safe-deposit box?" He flashed a butt-crack smile and fixed his pale, beady eyes on Abe.

Marilu stood with her arms crossed in a protective gesture over her chest, not uttering a word, so Abe spoke up. "It's Miss DiMarco who needs to do that. I'll wait for her. Where is the vault located?"

The banker squinted and looked at Marilu as if he just noticed her presence. "It's back through this here door behind my office. Course you have the key, young lady?" he asked Marilu. "Can't get in without your key and my key. It's teamwork, Miss, uh . . ."

"DiMarco," Abe said. "She has the key. Is there any other way in or out of that vault, Mr. Grimm?"

"No siree. One way in, one way out. Ever'body's gotta go through me. Now we need to fill out a little paperwork here and take care of this so you folks can be on your way." The white handkerchief reappeared and Elmore Grimm mopped his pink head.

"I'll be right outside this door," Abe said to Marilu. He couldn't see her eyes, but he felt her fear.

"You can wait here in the office, Mr. . . . uh, DiMarco. Jis take a seat and after I get the little lady's John Hancock she and I'll go on back to open that vault."

Abe sat down in one of the swivel chairs while Marilu remained standing. He didn't bother correcting the banker on his name. Marilu showed her ID and signed the signature card, then handed her key to Grimm. He verified the signature, and she picked up the briefcase, following him through a wooden door and down a short hallway. A quick look confirmed there were no other doors in that part of the bank except for the one leading to the vault. *We'll be out of here in a few minutes*, he thought.

While he waited, he swiveled around to face the front window and caught sight of a long, black sedan crawling past the bank. *It could be anyone*, Abe told himself, but a sudden chill ran through his body, setting his nerves on edge. Emily and Bowman noticed it, too. The Buick turned the corner, momentarily out of sight, but Abe's adrenaline had kicked in. He stood up, his heart thudding in his chest. Emily threw him a look and signaled with her hand to sit down. Sitting back in the chair and turning around, Abe's always restless fingers began drumming the desktop as he looked down the hall for any sign of Marilu. Although she had been gone only a few minutes, it seemed an eternity. Traffic noise was barely audible from the confines of the bank, but his overactive mind registered what could be the sound of motorcycles. He stood up again and turned to scrutinize the street, looking for anything, then glanced back to check the hallway for Marilu.

The part of him that watched from a distance tried to tell him none of this was happening—a bad dream, that's all. That was how he felt when Sharon begged him to end her suffering. He went through the motions, zombie-like, trying to detach himself from the reality of the situation. It hadn't worked then—it didn't work now, yet he still played along.

Grimm appeared, and after three or four long minutes, Marilu strode in, clutching the briefcase to her chest. "Here, let me carry that," Abe said. She seemed reluctant to give it up, but did.

"Well, now, anything else I can do for you folks . . . open a new checking or savings account?" Grimm began, but Abe cut him off.

"No thanks." He took Marilu's arm and turned toward the door, hoping the ominous-looking black car was some rich Texas rancher come to town to spend money. Elmore Grimm appeared relieved to see them go.

Bowman jabbered into his radio, trying to reach Agent Wilson, who had positioned herself on a side street. After several minutes he placed the radio back in its holster and pulled out his gun instead. He turned his attention to Abe and Marilu. "The Buick's gone. Wilson said she couldn't see who was inside because the windows were dark, but it appeared to have left town. Then I lost contact with her, probably some local interference." Bowman's furrowed brow and clenched jaw gave Abe the feeling the FBI agent knew it was not local interference. "We're going to play this close and careful, so stay behind me. A little change of plan—we'll escort Marilu to my vehicle, settle her in the backseat. You put the briefcase on the floor in the front."

"I'm riding with Bowman until we locate the other Fed," Emily said. "Follow us in the Bronco, Abe." It sounded like an order.

When they reached the door, Bowman stepped out first, telling the others to wait while he checked the street. As soon as he gave the all-clear signal, Abe and Marilu followed, with Emily flanking them from behind, her Glock ready. But without Agent Wilson's input they had no way of knowing who or what waited around the corner.

The motorcycles were on them so fast no one had a chance to respond. First one, then another, followed by a third. They roared onto the sidewalk, the leader plowing directly into Bowman before he could get a shot off. The FBI agent went down, cursing in pain and losing the grip on his weapon in the process. The biker rolled over him and kept going. Bowman lay in a pool of blood and appeared to be unconscious, or dead.

The second rider concentrated on Abe and Marilu. He came in close, trying to run them down as well. Marilu screamed and Abe jerked her back, flush with the wall of the bank. The bike went into a skid, tires screeching, and landed on its side, pinning the rider underneath. Abe figured the Aryans were after the briefcase. He held it tightly behind him with one hand. With the other he tried to restrain Marilu, who in a panic attempted to flee. "Stay back. If you run, they will get you," he yelled, pulling her toward the bank entrance, where Emily remained.

Then he heard a gunshot and hoped like hell it came from Emily. She crouched down on one knee in the alcove of the doorway, steadying her Glock with both hands. When the downed biker pulled out a gun, Emily fired off a round, hitting him in the shoulder. He dropped his weapon and screeched in pain. The third bike circled around and returned to the side street without making contact.

Emily tried to push the bank door open, but it didn't give. Abe heard her mutter, "That asshole locked us out." She darted out to Bowman and took his pulse, then rummaged through his pockets before scurrying back. "He's still alive. Take Marilu and the brief-case and make a run for Bowman's car. It's faster than the Bronco," she said, tossing the keys to Abe. "Get out of here before the other two come back. I'm calling for assistance."

Quickly letting go of Marilu's arm, he caught the keys, then hesitated.

"Go on, Abe. Get the hell out of here. Bowman's still breath-ing, but he needs an ambulance." She had her radio in her free hand and began shouting into it. "Officer down, officer down. Do you read?"

Go where? Abe wondered. But he knew he and Marilu were sit-ting ducks—they couldn't remain there, pasted against the wall like a pair of butterflies pinned to a mat. They had no way to defend themselves and Marilu had become hysterical. As for Abe, in this new life-threatening situation he assumed his zombie-like persona, going through the motions again, no matter how crazy, while some-body, the real Abe, watched in horrified fascination.

It had only been a couple of minutes since they stepped out of the bank and Bowman went down. *Where in hell was the FBI backup?* Abe's mind raced. Someone must have heard Emily's gun-shot and called the police, and she had radioed for help. The local cops and an ambulance would arrive soon. But he knew the other two gangsters would make another run for the briefcase, and Emily could be hurt or killed in the process if both bikers came at her. He couldn't let that happen, so he made a decision to draw them away. He knew Patch would be safe in the Bronco.

Abe took Marilu's arm and ran for Bowman's vehicle. Opening the back door, he yelled, "Get in and lock the door. Lie on the floor, and don't get up, no matter what." She stood frozen in place, but he gave her a shove and slammed the door. "On the floor, damn it." He jumped in the driver's side, and after making sure all doors were locked, placed the briefcase on the seat beside him, started the engine, cracked his window, and listened for the sound of motorcycles. He didn't have to wait long.

38

As soon as he heard the motorcycles, Abe shifted into reverse and screeched to the side street, blocking the bikers' exit. When they spotted him, he held the briefcase up to the passenger-side window, changed gears, and sped off, burning rubber in his departure. Marilu lifted her head and let out a shriek when she saw the bikes.

"Get down now, and stay down." He didn't know where he was going, or what to do when he got there. His only objective at the moment—draw the bikers away from Emily.

The motorcycles had better maneuverability, but Abe thought he could circle around and get back to the bank before they caught up with him, giving the local cops time to respond to Emily's call. Riding his horn, he ran a red light, then took a reckless corner. For once he wanted to see flashing lights and hear a siren. Then he saw them in his rearview mirror—two Dumas Police cars followed by an ambulance and red fire department paramedic vehicle crossed the intersection behind him. They turned on their sirens and sped by, intent on reaching their destination and oblivious to Abe and the bikers. *Good*, he thought. *They're responding to Emily's call.*

The motorcycles were forced to stop while the emergency vehicles passed. Abe took advantage of the opportunity and tried to shake them by turning around a corner and pulling into an alley. He thought he could ditch the bikers and return to the bank. Instead, he found himself on a dead end.

"What's happening?" Marilu said from the floor. "Why are we stopped?"

"Quiet, Marilu, stay down." The bikes hadn't discovered the alley yet, but he wanted to figure out how far away they were. Dumas was a small town, and it would be only a matter of time before they found him. He heard the rev of engines and knew they were close, maybe two blocks. A single siren droned in the distance. *It's the ambulance taking Bowman to the hospital,* Abe thought. He put the car in reverse and started to back out. He knew he had to hurry off the dead-end street before the bikers found him.

When he checked the rearview mirror his heart started pounding. A long, black sedan had pulled up perpendicular to the alley, blocking his exit. Two motorcycles flanked the Buick. Abe began to sweat despite the goose bumps on the back of his neck. He scanned the alleyway, looking for an opening between the buildings, but saw nothing. He wiped sweaty palms on his pant legs and, inhaling deeply, trying to steady his voice, told Marilu, "Stay put. Don't get up. Don't talk."

"What is it?" she hissed, raising her head enough to look around. When she saw her father's car, she let out a whimper and crumpled to the floor, covering her head with her arms.

Abe pulled forward, stalling for time, trying to think. The bikers rode down the alley in his direction, not hurrying now, knowing he was trapped. He saw the radio, grabbed the receiver, and pressed the talk button. "Emily, Emily, this is Abe. Do you read? Over." A burst of static came back in response. With his other hand he reached under the seat, looking for a weapon, finding nothing, then in the glove compartment—still no gun. Abe remembered the call number Emily told him to use on the radio, and switched the channel to twenty-one.

Marilu screamed, "You bastard. You brought me to him. They're going to kill us."

Ignoring her, he tried the radio again. "Emily. This is Abe. Do you read? I repeat. Do you read?"

The static continued, followed by silence, then finally a response. He sighed in relief when he heard her voice.

"Abe. This is Emily. Where are you?"

"Dead-end alley. Not far, somewhere behind the bank. Can't get out. DiMarco and the two bikers have me pinned in." Even in that tense moment, he wanted reassurance she was safe. "Are you okay?"

"I'm all right, Abe. No time for small talk. Give me a street name, something. I'll find you."

"Sorry. It's an alley behind the bank." When Abe glanced up, two Harleys had stopped beside the car. Abe took a deep breath. "They're here and they're armed, Em. Gotta go." The skinheads had dismounted and stood beside the door. He put the radio receiver down and met the glare of two muscle-bound brutes.

A straggly beard reached the chest of the tall one. Shoulder-length, dirty-blond hair fringed a bald head; steely gray eyes smoldered. The tattoo of a swastika centered on his forehead added emphasis to his scowl. He carried a tire iron and, with a single swing, smashed Abe's side window.

Marilu shrieked.

The second biker, shorter and stockier, with tattoos encircling his throat like a turtleneck sweater, pointed a semiautomatic assault weapon at Abe.

Behind the bikers, Abe caught a glimpse of DiMarco and his bodyguard walking toward them. Benavutti had one arm in a sling, a reminder of his last encounter with Abe and Emily. He carried a .22 pistol in his free hand and a malicious grin on his face.

"Get out of the car, asshole," said the biker with the gun. There didn't seem to be a choice. The Aryan stretched his neck to look inside, saw the briefcase, saw Marilu cowering on the floor, and smirked. "Well, well, well. Look what we found here. Daddy's little girl." He pointed the gun at Marilu. "You, too, bitch. Your old man's been looking for you." At the same time, DiMarco and Benavutti sauntered onto the scene.

Abe opened the back door, looked at Marilu. "Better do what he says."

Marilu stumbled out of the backseat. Keeping her head diverted away from the men, she stood behind Abe and didn't bother to look up when she heard her father's voice.

"Get your ass over here, Marilu." He had dressed in a gray pin-stripe suit, a blue shirt open at the neck, and Italian loafers. No cowboy hat covered the thick mane of gray hair this time. The goon with the tire iron took the briefcase off the seat and handed it to DiMarco. Marilu continued to look away from her father. "I said, come here. You're going with me," he repeated, then walked up to her and grabbed her arm.

She slapped him soundly across the face. "Go to hell. I'd rather be dead."

It was the distraction Abe needed, as everyone's attention switched to DiMarco. Abe brought his knee up into the groin of the biker holding the gun, then followed it with a hard fist to the gut. When he doubled over clutching his crotch, Abe grabbed the AK-47. He pulled Marilu behind him and pointed the gun at DiMarco. Benavutti had his pistol centered on Abe, but looked at his boss and didn't shoot. The other biker still held the tire iron over his head, ready to crush Abe's skull, when the piercing sound of police sirens filled the air. In an instant the biker dropped the weapon and made a run for his motorcycle. His buddy lay on the ground, clutching his testicles and gasping for breath.

Two Dumas City Police cars and a pair of gold-and-white Moore County Sheriff vehicles surrounded the Buick and cut off any means of escape. The officers, wearing bulletproof vests, their guns drawn, knelt behind their vehicles. With the assault rifle still fixed on DiMarco, Abe glanced at the new arrivals, quickly scanning their faces until his eyes settled on Emily, her body partially hidden behind a Sheriff's SUV.

She picked up a megaphone and he heard her voice, strong and clear. "Put your weapons down and your hands behind your head."

The biker on the ground struggled to his feet and tried to run, but stopped when he saw Abe with the gun.

Benavutti, his eyes darting wildly, and with his gun pointed at Abe, said, "I can kill both of them before he gets a shot off, boss."

"Put it down, you fucking idiot," DiMarco said. With eyes narrowed into slits, and a scowl, he looked at his daughter. "I can't believe you did this to me, Marilu. After everything I gave you when that whore of a mother of yours left. You're probably not even my kid, anyway, the way that cunt played around. But you'll pay for this. You'll see."

Upon hearing these words, she looked directly into her father's eyes. "My mother didn't leave me, she died—OD'd on depression drugs. You know it, and you know why. I've been paying all my life. It's your turn."

Abe picked up the weapon Benavutti had dropped and slipped it into his pocket. Marilu, her head held high, turned her back on her father, and walked toward the police cars. With his eyes still fastened on the Mafia boss, Abe grabbed the briefcase with his free hand and waited for Emily. DiMarco looked stubborn and defiant. Maybe he thought his lawyers and connections would get him off again. Abe didn't think so. Not this time.

A familiar voice, calm, melodic, got his attention and he looked into the grinning face of Officer Emily Etcitty of the Navajo Nation Tribal Police.

"You can put the gun away, cowboy. The Indian is taking over now."

Abe's mouth cracked into a wide smile. Under any other circumstances he would have taken her in his arms. Now he just laughed and handed the two guns to one of the local lawmen.

Vicente DiMarco, Vito Benavutti, and the biker, still holding his gut and breathing heavily, were cuffed and led away.

Abe draped his arm around Emily's shoulder, then, realizing it would appear unprofessional to the other officers, chuckled and dropped it. "Where's the ape who made a run for it?"

"He didn't get far. He's already in custody."

Abe still had a lot of questions, but only one that couldn't wait. "Bowman—is he going to make it?"

"He was alive and alert when the ambulance picked him up. I don't know the extent of his injuries, but he's tough. They found Agent Wilson knocked unconscious behind a Dumpster on the side street and transported her to the hospital, too."

"Bowman's a good cop, has a big heart, too. I'm willing to bet he'll pull through, but his days with the FBI might be over."

They reached the car, brushed broken glass off the seat, and got in, with Abe behind the wheel.

"Would you have used that gun, Abe?"

Abe turned on the ignition and paused before answering. "I don't know, Em. Who knows what anyone is capable of doing until the situation arises?" He blew out a long stream of air. "I guess so."

39

Emily wanted to stick around until the doctors declared Bowman
out of danger, so the three of them, counting one happy dog,
shared a room at the Hampton Inn in Dumas. And that was fine
with Abe—hot showers, steak dinners, and a soft bed. To make it
even nicer, Emily slept in the same room, and the Navajo Nation
picked up the tab. After they checked in, Abe took advantage of the
opportunity to clean up and rest while Emily met with authorities
at the Dumas Police Station and filed her report.

That first night alone with her, Abe felt hesitant and unsure.
Though he wanted more than anything to crawl into Emily's bed,
hold her in his arms, and make love, he didn't pursue it—afraid of
rejection. They dressed and undressed in the bathroom, slipped into
their separate beds, and pulled the covers up, then talked half the
night. He learned that the other FBI agent, Peters, had been discovered unconscious near his post. He had, evidently, been ambushed
by the bikers, and was recovering in the hospital with minor injuries.

"Damn. No wonder he never showed. What else did you find
out, Em?"

Emily explained the connection between Vicente DiMarco and the Aryan Brotherhood as Bowman had described it to her on the long ride to Dumas.

"Bo got filled in on this bit of information just before we left Datil. The Feds had been keeping tabs on DiMarco and his involvement in the drug trade for quite a while, trying to gather enough evidence to form a solid case. The Aryans had partnered up with the Kansas City Mafia. The skinheads manufactured meth and sold it to DiMarco. He distributed it through his connections in the Midwest, and when he needed some strong-arm or dirty work done, he called on the Aryans."

"So, who killed Easy Jackson?" Abe asked.

"The Aryans. They had more than one reason. Jackson wanted to break ties with the gang, but getting out of the brotherhood alive wasn't an option, and DiMarco wanted him eliminated because of what he knew about the tapes. So they were getting paid for a job they planned on doing anyway."

"How do they know DiMarco's hit man didn't kill Jackson?"

"It wasn't Benavutti's style. He would have put a bullet in the back of Jackson's head instead of slitting his throat."

"But where's the proof the Aryans killed Jackson?"

"When rats are trapped, they start to squeal. Those three we picked up started pointing fingers at one another. One of them finally confessed to killing Jackson, but said it was DiMarco's idea. I don't know what kind of deal was made. According to the skinheads, DiMarco arranged the killing, but he didn't want to get his hands dirty." Emily went to the mini-refrigerator, pulled out a couple of cans of Miller, and handed one to Abe. "That motorcycle you heard at the campsite probably belonged to the skinhead that killed Jackson. The DA will get more from those goons we picked up because they will no doubt go for a plea bargain," she said as she pulled the tab and settled back on her bed.

The cold beer tasted good. He gave her an appreciative look. "Thanks." Abe repositioned his pillow and leaned against the head-board, letting everything she told him sink in. He realized he was no longer a murder suspect and let out a whoop of joy. "Goddamn. That means my name is cleared, Emily. I am a free man."

She laughed at his reference. "Yes, you are, Abe Freeman, free to do whatever you want.'"

"Let's drink to that," said Abe, reaching across so they could click cans. He closed his eyes, feeling as if a huge weight had been lifted, relishing the moment.

Abe finished his beer, set it on the bedside table, and faced Emily. "It's all beginning to make some sense," he said. "Except this—what did Corazón and the Mexican Mafia have to do with anything?"

"This is something Bowman and I didn't get a chance to discuss, though I'm curious as well. Maybe he can fill in the gaps when we talk to him. If we get the chance . . ."

"We will. He's going to be all right," said Abe. It was more hope than certainty. "I wonder what's going to happen to Marilu."

"She's still pretty shaken. The authorities have taken her to a private drug rehab establishment up north. She will probably require long-term psychological counseling as well."

"Did you talk to her before she left?" Abe said.

"For a short time." Emily smiled. "Marilu was crying when I last saw her. No more tough, bitchy attitude—just a sad young woman. She told me she was sorry she came after me with the knife, sorry she gave us so much trouble, and she thanked us, especially you, Abe."

"The kid had a hard life," Abe said. "I hope she can turn it around."

After several minutes of quiet, Emily whispered, "Are you lonesome over there?"

"Yeah. Want to join me?" Abe scooted over and watched in the semidarkness as Emily stood up and pulled the oversize T-shirt over her head. He could barely make out the outline of her naked body, but when she crawled in beside him, he felt the taut smoothness of her breasts and the warmth of her strong legs as she snuggled next to him. He ran his hand over those breasts, traced the curve of her hip, her flat stomach, felt the wetness between her thighs. Emily crawled on top of him and he entered her. Lost in their lovemaking, they didn't care what the occupants in the adjoining rooms heard.

The following morning, they visited the hospital. Robert Bowman had undergone surgery and remained in critical condition in the ICU with a ruptured spleen, several broken ribs, and a smashed vertebra. He wasn't allowed visitors, so the two returned to the motel room. After Emily wrote her report, they spent the remainder of the day relaxing and getting reacquainted. In the afternoon they played tourists, walking hand in hand through the town and visiting the Window on the Plains Museum and Art Center. In the evening they feasted on barbecue at the Alley Café and, after stuffing themselves, returned to the motel to sprawl on the bed and watch reruns of classic movies, followed by a night of lovemaking.

On the third day the doctors deemed Bowman out of danger and moved him to a room of his own. When they arrived, the attending physician, a perfunctory-appearing Asian man with a name tag reading "Dr. Lee," informed them the FBI agent was awake, and allowed a brief visit.

"You can talk to him, but make it short. He's heavily medicated and in a lot of pain. He needs rest."

Bowman's large frame, bulked up by layers of bandaging, filled the narrow hospital bed. His brown-sugar head, propped on pillows, offered the only splash of color in a sea of white. Despite the monitors registering every heartbeat, and tubes delivering oxygen through his nose and liquids through his arm, Bowman managed a grin when Abe and Emily entered the room.

"You look great in white," Abe said, smiling down at the prone body.

"Thanks. It's my new fashion statement. You two are looking pretty good." He gave Abe a knowing wink. "I see you survived without any battle scars. Ever think of applying for a position with the FBI, Freeman?"

Abe laughed at the offhand remark. "I'm not pushing my luck. Glad you can still give me shit, though."

"What's the damage, Bo?" Emily said.

Robert Bowman reached for a glass of water and grimaced, so Emily held the glass close to his lips as he sipped from the straw. Afterward he lay back. "Ah, nothing that can't be fixed over time. But don't think I'll push my luck. Time for a job change." He took another sip, and Emily replaced the glass.

"How're Agents Wilson and Peters?" said Emily.

"The doc said Wilson has a cut on the head and a concussion, but she's okay, in another room, and will probably be dropping by for a visit with me in a couple days. Peters is in worse shape, but he came out of the coma this morning. They'll both pull through. They're tough like me. What about Marilu?"

"Marilu's safe and sound, off to a quiet rehab center at some undisclosed location. She's in the Bureau's hands now, but she wanted me to tell you she would testify." Emily smiled down at Bowman's expectant face. "She said thanks, too. We got the bad guys, Bo—DiMarco, his ape, the skinheads, and the tapes. But there's a couple of things I haven't figured out. Do you feel up to talking?"

Dr. Lee poked his head in the door and gave the visitors an impatient look. "Five minutes," he said before leaving.

"What's not clear?"

"Corazón," Abe cut in. "What did he have to do with any of this?"

Abe thought Bowman had fallen asleep. His eyes closed and he didn't respond right away. After a few minutes, Abe looked at Emily and she shrugged. They started to leave.

"My boss dropped by to see me a short time ago. The FBI had been questioning some former members of the Mexican Mafia and picked up a few details we didn't have before."

Abe and Emily turned and waited for Bowman to take a sip of water before he continued.

"Seems Easy Jackson couldn't keep his mouth shut and Corazón was an eager opportunist," said Bowman.

"That's it?" Abe said.

"Jackson bragged to anyone who would listen. Said as soon as he got out he and Marilu were going to cash in on a key that would make him a rich man. No telling how much he blabbed, but friends of Corazón got wind of it and put him onto Jackson. Corazón was on Jackson's tail when you saw him in Clayton, Abe." The agent's voice sounded tired when he added, "The Aryans reached him before the Mexicans, but no one knew what happened to the key."

"And you didn't know this ahead of time?" said Emily.

"No. I was in the dark as much as you till a short time ago." Bowman closed his eyes again and Dr. Lee beckoned at the door that it was time to leave.

Emily planted a kiss on his forehead. "We'll keep in touch, Bo. It's been a pleasure working with you."

"Take it easy." Abe squeezed the other man's shoulder. He hoped Bowman would find his niche, just as he longed to find his own.

Abe and Emily spent a final night at the Hampton Inn. Their love-making was tender and desperate, as if both knew it might be the last time. Neither spoke of the future, and long after Emily's breathing had taken on the rhythmic cadence of slumber, Abe remained awake. Early the next morning they loaded their few belongings into the Bronco and, arm in arm, strolled with Patch through the quiet predawn streets of Dumas, Texas.

After walking several blocks in silence, Emily stopped and faced Abe, taking both his hands in hers. "You can stay, you know. Will and Grandfather would welcome you. Will wants to become a *hataali*, a traditional healer, and Grandfather has agreed to teach him when his strength returns. You could find a job around Farmington—the gas rigs are booming now. The money is good and you can bunk at the sheep camp with Will and Grandfather until you get your own place."

"Emily, I wouldn't be happy doing that kind of work. I'm a musician, not a gas or oil rigger. My love is music . . . I hope I can get back to my music. It's been a long time since I wanted to, but I think I'm ready. I miss my piano. But the truth is I'm not ready to settle down. I still have some things to work out in my head."

"You don't want to take a chance on me again, do you?"

"It's not you, Emily." Abe's mind flashed back to the scene in the bedroom just before he placed the pillow over Sharon's face, so drawn and full of pain, her eyes begging him to end her suffering. He blinked back tears, and when he spoke again, his voice was barely above a whisper. "There's something I have to tell you, Emily—it's about Sharon."

"That you still love her and you always will? I know that. I'm not asking you to give that up, Abe. You know what I have been struggling with, and I need time to heal as well."

Patch had run out of ammunition after peeing on every wall and hydrant within reach. The little dog stood looking at his master as if asking, *What's next?* "Let's head back," Abe said. "You don't know my story, Em, not all of it."

They turned around and retraced their steps to the motel. "So, tell me your story, Abe."

He took a deep breath. With his face turned away, and voice husky, breaking at times, he said, "Sharon was dying, and I helped her. I held the pillow over her face until her breathing stopped." He had never said the words aloud before and held his breath, wondering if Emily would hate him now, as he often hated himself, but feeling at the same time less burdened, as if the load of guilt he carried had become a little lighter.

She said nothing at first, but took his hand and walked with him to the Bronco. Before they got in she stopped and took both his hands in hers. "In our culture death is nothing more than a change of worlds, not to be feared, and when it is inevitable, assistance is welcome as long as it is swift and painless. Your Sharon understood this."

"I don't know, Emily. In my culture it would be murder."

"Not murder, Abe Freeman. There is a poem, in Navajo," Emily said. "I will try to translate it for you: 'When the time comes, when the last breath leaves me, I choose to die in peace to meet *Shi'dyin'*— the creator.' My people value the right to choose, as Will did. He did not want to die in a strange hospital far from the Dinétah. Your loved one also valued this choice. If you wish, Grandfather could help you unburden your mind by performing a purification ceremony."

Abe wrapped his arms around her, holding her close, unabashedly letting his tears fall.

They drove back over the flat plains and low mesas and canyons, then on through the Duke City, as Albuquerque is often called, and, leaving the city, turned toward the west through the checkerboard BIA land into the dramatic and beautiful landscape of the Diné.

Abe spent the following day in the sweat house, while the ancient medicine man chanted healing prayers and Emily poured water over hot stones. When he stepped out into the cool night air, his mind felt clear, his body cleansed. Emily poured ladles of cold water over him, rinsing away not only sweat, but the weight of his burdens.

At dawn the next morning, as the breaking light extinguished the stars, Emily walked with Abe to his truck. He had packed the night before, and was ready to leave. Patch, still sleepy, curled in his usual place, riding shotgun.

"Will you be back?"

Before he climbed into the truck, Abe looked into her eyes, dark pools of mystery. "I don't know. I plan on stopping to spend a few days with Sally. She deserves to know what happened. Then, I have an ocean to see, and then . . ." He took her face in his hands and kissed her softly. "I don't know."

As he drove away, a fiery sunrise erupted, forming a halo around *Dzil Ná oodili*, the sacred mountain where Changing Woman gave birth to her warrior twins. He looked back and saw Emily, standing tall, regal as a mythic warrior in the golden light.

Abe swallowed the lump in his throat and scratched Patch between the ears. "I'm going to miss this place, boy." He knew in his heart that was not all he would miss. He stepped on the accelerator, stirring up a tail of dust, obliterating the image of Emily, fighting the urge to turn around, and set his sights on California.

ACKNOWLEDGMENTS

I would like to give thanks to those friends and acquaintances who have assisted me in making this book a reality. Thanks to Steven Havill, for being the impetus that started me on this journey. Your writing workshops, tutorials, and nagging insistence that one must write every day were invaluable. And thank you to Pat Walsh, Steve Anderson, and John Johnson for always being there with your edits, critiques, encouragement, and friendship. I couldn't have done this without you. Finally, I would like to thank my wonderful family for their continued love and support.

ABOUT THE AUTHOR

Sandra Bolton lives in Raton, New Mexico, with her dog, Sam, and cat, Fidel. When not writing, she can be found hiking and looking for inspiration for her next story in the rugged Southwestern landscape. *Key Witness* is her second novel. Her first, *A Cipher in the Sand*, was published in 2011. She is currently working on a sequel to *Key Witness*.